Dear Reader,

As I wrote *Theft and Thanksgiving*, I thought about how much the people in the Blue Hill community care about each other. Although the book is a cozy mystery dealing with identity theft, the story is about so much more than that. It's about a community filled with people who make you laugh, make you cry, and maybe even make you worry a little.

I've known many people like those in our series. Anne is the quintessential mother who will do anything for her children, Liddie and Ben. Mildred, Alex, Wendy, and other folks in Blue Hill round out the cast of characters you are likely to find in a small town. They have active lives that are intertwined, and they are willing to go the extra mile for their neighbors.

In today's world of rapidly changing technology and people chasing careers, I find it refreshing to be immersed in such a delightful community with characters I have fallen in love with. I'm sure I speak for all the authors of the Secrets of the Blue Hill Library series when I say our common goal is to create stories that entertain and add an element of pleasure to the lives of our readers. Most of all, we want you to feel at home in Blue Hill.

Grab a cup of tea, find a comfortable chair, and go on this journey with me. I hope you enjoy reading this story as much as I liked writing it.

Many blessings to you,
Debby Mayne
writing as Emily Thomas

Theft *and* Thanksgiving

Secrets of the
BLUE HILL LIBRARY

EMILY THOMAS

Guideposts

New York

Secrets of the Blue Hill Library is a trademark of Guideposts.

Published by Guideposts
16 East 34th Street
New York, New York 10016
Guideposts.org

Cover and interior design by Müllerhaus
Cover illustration by Rob Fiore, represented by Artworks Illustration
Typeset by Aptara, Inc.

Printed and bound in the United States of America
10 9 8 7 6 5 4 3 2 1

CHAPTER ONE

"Mommy, I don't wanna wear my coat today." Liddie Gibson scrunched her face as she looked up at her mother with eyes that never failed to melt Anne's heart. "It's too heavy, and it's hard to play."

Anne sighed. "Okay, but it's nippy out, so you'll need to wear layers." She turned to her son and smiled. "Ben, would you mind going upstairs with Liddie, in case she needs help?"

He glanced down at his feet as he shuffled them. "I don't…"

She leveled him with one of her mom looks that she rarely used. "I really need your help, Ben."

"Sure, Mom." Ben started toward the stairs. "C'mon, Liddie. I don't want to be late for school."

Liddie shrugged out of her heavy coat and skipped along after her brother, dragging the coat behind her. Anne watched them until they disappeared from sight.

The library door opened with a *whoosh*, letting in a blast of cold air. In walked Alex Ochs, wearing a slight grin on his face. "Sorry I'm a little early, but I thought if Ben and Liddie were ready we could be at the head of the drop-off line."

She smiled. "They'll be down in a few minutes. Liddie is putting on some layers."

"Good idea. It's starting to get cold out." He leaned against the counter. "Do you have some time later this morning to go over plans for the new display case I'm building for the library? With Thanksgiving three weeks away, I need to get started soon."

Anne gave him an apologetic look and slowly shook her head. "I'm sorry I can't today. We're having our first Tea and Book Club meeting."

"Sounds interesting." He lifted an eyebrow. "What kind of tea?"

She chuckled. "Variety. As of now, it's an all-women's group, but you're welcome to join us if you like."

"All women, huh?" He folded his arms and pretended to ponder before shaking his head. "Nah, I think I'll pass on this one. But thanks."

When the children returned, Liddie glanced up at Alex and then to her mom. "Ben helped me find layers, see?" She took a half step back and opened her arms to show off her pink cardigan that clashed with her bright orange long-sleeved T-shirt that didn't quite cover the yellow undershirt beneath it. "Is this okay?"

"You can take off your sweater when you get to school." Anne nodded toward Alex, who was obviously having a difficult time keeping a smile off his lips.

He cleared his throat. "Time to go to school."

Liddie ran over to Anne and wrapped her arms around her mother's legs. "I love you, Mommy."

Anne kissed Liddie on the cheek and brushed a lock of hair from her face. "I love you too, sweetie. That sweater is fine for today, but when it gets colder, I'm afraid you'll have to wear your heavy coat."

Liddie scrunched her face again but nodded. Alex grinned as he reached for her hand. "C'mon, Liddie. We don't want to be late." He looked at Anne, winked, and focused back on Liddie. "I bought you a new booster seat so we don't have to keep moving yours back and forth between your mother's car and my truck."

"What color is it?" Before Alex had a chance to answer, Liddie asked, "Is it pink?"

"Of course it's pink." Alex smiled down at her. "What other color is there?"

Anne opened her arms and pulled Ben in for a hug. He leaned into her momentarily, but then he stiffened. When Anne let go and saw how red his face was, she felt a tightening in her chest.

Alex reached for Liddie's hand. "We can talk later about the display case, but one thing I wanted to tell you now is —"

The library phone rang, interrupting him. Anne cast an apologetic look his way as she answered.

It was Mildred Farley, one of Aunt Edie's closest friends and a dedicated library patron. She sounded frantic.

"What happened?" Anne asked.

"My friend Claire Daniels went shopping yesterday, and when she went to use her credit card, the man at the store told her it was denied."

"I'm sure there's probably just a glitch in the system," Anne said. "That kind of thing happens all the time."

"That's what I told her. But when we got back to her place, she called the credit card company and found out someone has been using it for the past couple of weeks. They've charged that thing all the way to the max."

"Do you think maybe Claire charged some things she might have forgotten about?"

"Nope. She's been home taking care of her sick husband for the past two weeks. That's why we went out. She needed a little retail therapy."

Alex held up a finger and mouthed that he'd see her later. Anne nodded and focused on her conversation with Mildred as he left the library with Liddie and Ben.

"What did the credit card representative say?"

Mildred sighed. "They're investigating. Poor thing. Claire has been up to her elbows in taking care of other people, and the moment she tries to do something for herself, something always seems to happen to ruin it. I sure wish there were something I could do to help."

"You're being a good friend simply by listening to her."

"I know, I know. That's what Claire told me, but I also know that she has her hands full, and this will only make things worse."

"What happened to her is terrible, but I'm sure the credit card company will make things right."

"That's what the man on the phone said." Mildred let out an audible sigh. "Poor Claire."

"Are you still planning to come to the Tea and Book Club meeting today, or do you—?"

"You know I wouldn't miss it for the world."

"Good. I bought a variety of teas so everyone will have what they like."

"I love tea, but I have to stay away from the chamomile," Mildred said. "That stuff makes me sleepy, and it would be downright rude for me to start yawning right in the middle of your meeting."

Anne laughed. "Then you can have the peppermint tea. That should keep you awake."

"I'm sure it will. Well, I'd better run. Claire is probably up by now, so I need to call and check on her before she gets too involved in her busy day. Once her husband gets up, she runs nonstop making sure he gets what he needs."

"Do you think she can pull herself away for an hour or so to come for tea?"

"I doubt it, but I can ask her." Mildred sighed. "I'm sure she'll want to be home if the guy from the credit card company calls. I better go so I can get everything done. See you later."

After Anne hung up, she rocked back on her heels and thought about her many blessings—including the fact that her aunt Edie had taken care of Anne's little family in her will and how quickly Anne, Ben, and Liddie had been accepted in Blue Hill.

A couple of calls came in inquiring about the Thanksgiving programs for children she'd advertised. She got another call from her friend Wendy Pyle, part-time volunteer library assistant, mother of seven, and one of the most voracious readers in town.

"I might be a little bit late today. It was rough getting the kids out of bed this morning."

"That's okay," Anne said. "We've been slow."

"Thanks! The twins are finished with breakfast now, so I need to take them to preschool. I'll be there right after I drop them off."

"Take your time." Anne couldn't imagine how difficult it had to be with so many children all going in different directions.

After Anne got off the phone with Wendy, she started toward the kitchen to set up for the tea when the phone rang again. This time it was her mother-in-law, Marlene. "Anne, dear. How is life in Blue Hill?"

"It's great. The kids and I have really settled in."

"Well then, your great-aunt obviously knew what she was doing when she left you that house."

"Yes, I agree. Are you excited about Thanksgiving? It's only three weeks away."

Eric's mother sighed. "Yes, and that leads me to why I called. You know how much I love seeing the children during the holidays."

A strange sense of foreboding washed over Anne. "Yes, and we love being with you and Byron too."

Anne heard her mother-in-law draw a deep breath. "Now I feel terrible about what I'm going to ask. Some of our friends from church purchased a cruise, but now they need to back out because their daughter was in a terrible accident. The cruise line refuses to refund their money at this late date, so we were thinking...Well, we thought it might be nice to buy the cruise from them. Byron and I haven't had a vacation, just the two of us, in a while, and it would really help...that is, if it wouldn't be too upsetting to the children. I mean, if you need us, you know we'll be there for you."

Anne knew how much the children looked forward to seeing their grandparents, but she understood. "A cruise sounds wonderful, and I want you to go! I'm sure the kids will be disappointed, but they'll understand. They know how much you and Byron love them."

"Thanks for understanding, dear. We'll send postcards during the cruise."

"Have fun and don't worry about us," Anne said. "The kids will love getting postcards."

After Anne got off the phone, she stared at the wall for a moment to regroup. For the first time in her children's lives, they wouldn't be with at least one set of grandparents for Thanksgiving. No matter how bad she felt, she was determined not to let Ben and Liddie know how disappointed she was.

She'd had her share of disappointments. Not long after Eric passed away, she'd lost her job at the New York Public Library due to cutbacks. That had been the job of her dreams, and it upset her terribly to lose it. If Aunt Edie hadn't left the house for Anne to convert to a library and a home, she didn't know what she would have done. Thank God for family!

Anne went back into the kitchen to finish setting up for the tea. Since she didn't expect a large group, she thought it would be easiest to have it in the old library kitchen. She'd barely filled the pots with water when she heard the sound of someone behind her. She turned and grinned.

"Hi there. Looks like you've been busy," said Mildred.

"Hi. Have a seat. I'll bring the tea over when it's ready."

"I'm here to help." Mildred rolled up her sleeves up as she approached the cabinet. "How many teacups do I need to set out?"

"We're expecting about half a dozen women."

Mildred nodded. "I'll rinse out a couple extras, just in case we have more."

Wendy joined them a few minutes later, carrying a platter of pastries she'd baked. "What's a tea party without goodies?"

Before anyone could answer, she added, "Have you decided on a book?"

Anne nodded toward the stack of books on the table. "I have several possibilities. The group can decide."

"Good thinking." Wendy winked at Mildred. "That way if someone doesn't like the selection, you won't be the bad guy."

Mildred rinsed the teapots with hot water from the faucet to temper them before Anne poured the boiling water from the kettle. They put tea balls filled with loose tea in a couple of them and tea bags in the others. Wendy cut up some lemons and placed them in a bowl in the middle of the table, while Mildred filled tiny cream pitchers and sugar bowls. By the time they had everything done, all the women who had signed up to come were there.

"Help yourself to the tea and pastries," Anne said. "I'll give you a short synopsis of the books so we can decide which one we want to read first. All of these can be ordered for purchase, or if you don't want to buy one, we'll have a couple extras to check out. Before we continue, let's decide how often we should meet."

"Weekly," Wendy said.

"Too frequent." Mildred shook her head. "I think we should meet monthly."

Wendy made a face, so Anne intervened. "How about twice a month?"

Mildred turned to Wendy, who nodded. "Okay, that's fine, but since we're just getting started, why don't we meet again next week?"

Everyone looked around and nodded.

"Good, then it's settled." When people started talking, Mildred held up a finger to get everyone's attention. "If you can spare the money, it's always a good idea to buy the books to help out the library. Every little bit helps, you know." She stopped suddenly and smiled toward the doorway, where someone must have entered. "Are you here for the Tea and Book Club meeting?"

"Y–yes ma'am." The soft voice at the door didn't sound familiar.

Anne glanced over her shoulder and spotted a woman who appeared to be around thirty, wearing faded jeans, a bank giveaway T-shirt, athletic shoes, and a baseball cap pulled down low over her forehead. Her hair sticking out of the back of it appeared mousy brown. The woman was unkempt, unlike the rest of the people in the room.

"Have a seat," Anne said. "We're trying to decide which book we want to read."

The woman slid into the chair closest to the door. She didn't look Anne in the eye. Anne tried hard not to stare at the new woman, who kept looking at Mildred but turning away when Mildred looked back. How odd!

Mildred picked up one of the books, turned it over, and read the back jacket. "I vote for this one."

"That looks good," Wendy agreed as she picked up another book and studied the blurb. "Or maybe we can read two. This one also looks good."

Two other women simultaneously said, "No, just one."

A look of amusement played on Mildred's lips. "With seven young ones to look after, I don't see how you have time to read a magazine article, let alone books."

Wendy grinned and playfully wiggled her eyebrows. "I don't sleep."

"This tea is delicious," Mildred said. "The peppermint is refreshing but not too strong."

Wendy lifted her cup. "As long as I have plenty of cream and sugar, I don't care what kind of tea I drink." She downed her tea and poured more from the closest teapot.

"Would you like some tea?" Mildred asked the new woman.

The young woman squirmed in her seat. "I'm not much of a tea drinker."

"Then what do you think about the books?"

The woman picked up the book in front of her, glanced at the cover, and opened it. Anne wasn't sure, but it appeared that she was only pretending to read. "I don't know..."

"That's okay, dear. But I think we should vote," Mildred said.

With the exception of the new woman, the vote was unanimous for the first book Anne had mentioned, one of the Father Tim novels by Jan Karon. Wendy jotted down each person's name but stopped when she came to the mystery woman. "I'm sorry, but I didn't catch your name. I'll need your phone number too."

The woman shook her head. "I won't be buying one."

Wendy lifted an eyebrow and looked over at Anne. The sound of someone coming in the front door of the library echoed throughout the downstairs, so Anne stood. "I'd better go see if I'm needed. I'll be right back."

Anne helped the patron find the book she was looking for and hurried back toward the kitchen. She'd barely made it to the door when she overheard Mildred talking.

"I'm sorry, dear, but I didn't hear what you just said. You've got to speak up."

Anne leaned around and saw Mildred facing the mystery woman, so she stepped back. She didn't want to interrupt.

The young woman cleared her throat and spoke slowly. "How long have you lived in Blue Hill?"

"All my life," Mildred replied. "What brings you here?"

"I'm just visiting. Is — is your family from here?"

"Yes. Why do you ask?"

"Just curious. What's your mother's maiden name?"

"Why?"

"I might…well, I might know some of your relatives."

"You should have said that in the beginning. My mother's maiden name was—"

Anne stepped into the kitchen to save Mildred. "I'm so glad you were able to join us."

The woman gave her a self-conscious smile. "Thank you."

"I'm so sorry, but I never caught your name."

The mystery woman glanced nervously back and forth between Anne and Mildred before she lowered her head. "It's…Joan. Joan…Smith."

"Joan Smith?" Mildred cast a doubtful glance in Anne's direction but didn't say anything else.

Anne tried to keep the conversation going. "Why don't you fill out a library card application, and I can put you in our system."

The woman stood abruptly, shook her head, lowered her cap farther down on her forehead, and slipped out of the room.

CHAPTER TWO

Mildred turned to Anne with a puzzled expression. "Such an odd reaction. I wonder what that was all about."

Anne went to the window and pulled back the curtain. The woman had gotten to her car very quickly and was already pulling away from the curb. Anne made a mental note of the color, make, and model of the car. She let the curtain fall back into place as she turned back around to face Mildred. "I sure wish I knew."

"Such a peculiar person," Mildred said.

"I agree," Anne said. "Do you have any idea why she was asking you so many personal questions?"

Mildred shook her head. "No idea whatsoever."

"I hope you didn't give her too much information." While Anne didn't want to alarm Mildred, she wanted to protect her.

Mildred let out a snort of laughter. "I wasn't born yesterday. I know better than to tell a complete stranger more than she needs to know."

"Hi, Mildred," Wendy said as she approached. "I heard about what happened to Claire. Do you think the credit card company will ever find out who did it?"

Mildred shook her head. "I have no idea. When Claire pulled up her statement online…" She turned to Anne. "Your great-aunt Edie taught her how to do that, you know."

"What were you saying about her statement?" Wendy leaned toward the older woman.

Mildred looked back at Wendy. "Whoever did this sure does love to shop online."

Wendy chuckled. "In my world, that's the only way to shop."

"What is Claire going to do to protect her other accounts?" Anne asked.

Mildred sighed. "She contacted the bank to let them know about it. I don't think there's much else she can do."

As Mildred talked about Claire's situation, Anne realized how helpless someone would probably feel after experiencing identity theft. "There has to be something people can do to protect themselves."

The phone rang, so Wendy offered to answer it and dashed off. After she left, Mildred placed her hand on Anne's arm. "With so many health issues in Claire's family, she has been through much worse than having her identity stolen, but she said this is the first time she has felt violated."

"I can only imagine how she must feel."

Mildred started to say something, but Wendy breezed past them, pulling on her jacket as she went. "Gotta run. Someone from the school called and said that Justin got sick and I need to pick him up. If you need me later, I can probably come back."

Anne shook her head. "Don't worry about it. I'll be fine."

"Thanks!" She stopped when she got to the door. "Call if you need me." With that, she was gone.

Mildred snorted. "That girl's batteries never run low." She glanced up at the clock. "I need to get going too. Call me later...or maybe I'll call you."

After everyone left the library, Anne went into the kitchen to finish cleaning up. The women who attended the meeting had washed most of the dishes, but there were a few stray napkins and other items that needed to be picked up.

She began stacking the books on the table, but when she spotted the one in the place where the mystery woman sat, she noticed a slip of paper sticking out of it. She pulled out the paper and saw that it was a to-do list with names of businesses and an address. The woman must have stuck it in the book when she started talking to Mildred.

Anne stuffed the paper into her pocket and finished cleaning up the kitchen. As she wiped down the table, her thoughts wandered to the identity theft and what she could do to help with the investigation. She'd been in Blue Hill long enough to know many of the people in town, and she couldn't imagine any of them being the thief. It had to be someone she didn't know. Maybe it was someone from out of town.

As she turned to rinse the rag, the paper crinkled in her pocket and a thought shot through her mind. She didn't know that woman who had slipped into the meeting, and the questions she asked Mildred seemed odd. Hmm. With the identity theft fresh on her mind, she couldn't help but be suspicious. She normally wouldn't read something that might be personal, but considering what was happening in Blue Hill, she skimmed it. The name of a rental car company at the top of the list had been checked off.

Anne decided to make a copy of the list, just in case. It was probably nothing significant, so she stuck the copy in a folder in the back of the file cabinet and the original note back in her purse in case the woman returned. A pang of guilt seized Anne. She wondered if she might be infringing on the woman's rights to privacy by making a copy of her list. And yet, if she could be helpful in stopping criminal activity…

While Anne was rationalizing her actions and thinking about the woman, she decided to look on the Internet for the address of the rental car company she'd noticed on the bumper sticker of Joan's car. The closest office was in a town about thirty minutes from Blue Hill. She pulled out her cell phone, punched in the number, and asked the representative for the name of the person renting the car she described.

The man made a low grumbling sound. "I'm sorry, but we can't disclose personal information about any of our customers."

She pulled the paper from her pocket and looked at it. "But I have something she might need."

"If it's urgent, we can contact the customer for you. What do you have?"

Anne described the to-do list. "She left it in the library, and I thought it might be important."

The rental car representative snickered. "I hardly think a to-do list is all that urgent, but I can let the manager know about it, in case the customer calls."

"Okay, thanks." Anne hung up and sighed. She shouldn't have expected anything different. After all, if someone had called her looking for a library patron, she wouldn't have divulged information either.

When she turned around, she saw that Grace Hawkins, editor of the *Blue Hill Gazette*, had entered the library. She tilted her head in concern. "What's wrong?"

Anne slowly shook her head. "Nothing's really wrong."

"So have you heard the buzz about the spate of identity theft that's hit the town lately? I think I'll run a short piece in the paper about how to avoid it and what to do if it happens to you."

"That's a great idea. It seems to be all people are talking about lately." Anne paused. "In fact, one of the women in our new book club mentioned it this morning."

"That's why I'm here," Grace said. "I have a little spot on page two, and I thought I'd see if you'd like to talk about your programs."

"Yes, as a matter of fact, I would love for you to mention the meetings. It's a combination of a social tea and book club discussion."

"Wonderful!" Grace started jotting notes. "You talk, and I'll write. Tell me all about the book you're reading now, and maybe that will get a few new folks interested."

After Anne finished, Grace thanked her and left.

The remainder of the day was filled with answering the phone, filing, shelving books, and helping patrons look for information. One of the visitors to the library asked to use the computer to look up identity theft.

Anne blinked as she tried not to show surprise. "Of course. But why?"

"Someone managed to take money right out of my mother's bank account, and when she told the other women in her Bible study, she found out that Donna had the same thing happen to her."

"Are you talking about Donna Slade from the Library Guild?"

"Yes."

"That's terrible. It's hard to believe something like this is happening in Blue Hill."

The woman nodded. "I know, but it just goes to show that crimes can happen anywhere."

"Grace said the newspaper is going to run a story about it soon. But let's see what we can find for now."

Anne showed the woman how to access the Internet and helped her do a search. As she pulled up the sites, she realized how common this type of crime was, and her concern grew even more intense.

Anne did as much as she could to help the young woman find information on identity theft, until she heard the rumbling of Alex's truck as he brought the children home from school. "Sounds like my children are here."

"I'll be fine," the patron said. "Go take care of your kids."

As soon as the front door opened, Liddie streaked across the floor with Alex and Ben following right behind her. "Mommy, look what I made in school!" She held up a picture colored with yellows, oranges, reds, and browns. "We traced our hands and colored them to make them look like turkeys."

"Very pretty." Anne took the picture from Liddie and studied it. "This is the perfect Thanksgiving decoration to put on the refrigerator."

Liddie beamed. "I even put my name on it."

"Yes, I see that." Anne turned to Ben who stood a few feet away, his hands in his pockets, looking uncomfortable. "What did you do in school today?"

He shrugged. "Nothing."

Alex leaned over and whispered to her, "That's boy talk for 'I'll tell you later when we don't have an audience.'"

"Thanks. I didn't realize I'd ever need an interpreter to understand my own son."

"It happens." Alex's smile faded. "Can you spare a few minutes to discuss the display case I'm building?"

"Sure, but first I need to get snacks for the kids. Where's Ryan? If he's anything like Ben, I bet he's starving."

"Of course he is." Alex went to the door. "He's still in the truck. I'll go get him."

Anne set out plates of sliced apples and peanut butter cookies for the kids, and then she poured some milk. The boys devoured the cookies and asked for more. "Eat your apples first," Anne said. "Then you may each have one more cookie." She focused on Ben. "As soon as you're done, you need to take Hershey for a walk. I've taken him out on the leash in the backyard a couple of times, but he needs some exercise."

"Okay."

Liddie had already eaten her apple slices, and now she was nibbling on a cookie. With stuffed cheeks, she looked up at Anne. "I don't want another cookie. I'm full."

"Why don't you go to the Children's Room and play for a little while?"

Liddie hopped down from her chair and did as her mother suggested. Alex told the boys to join Liddie as soon as they had finished their cookies and walked Hershey.

Once the children had been taken care of, Alex sat down at one of the tables in the Nonfiction Room facing the checkout desk. Anne joined him. "So what did you have in mind?"

"Here's what I was thinking about for the display case." He sketched on a piece of paper as he explained how he wanted to make it easily accessible so she could change it with the seasons.

Anne studied his drawing and nodded. "I like that."

"Another idea I had is to make it portable so you can move it around. I can even put wheels on it."

"Which do you think is better?" She had a difficult time concentrating on the display case with the identity theft so fresh in her mind.

He leaned back and folded his arms. "Both have advantages, but for the most effective use, I think a portable case with wheels might be better."

"Then let's do that."

Alex grinned as he shook his head. "I have a feeling I could have said, 'Let's put it on the roof and add fluorescent lights with a disco ball on top,' and you would have agreed to it. Your mind isn't on this, is it?"

She shrugged apologetically. "I'm sorry, Alex, but I'm concerned about this identity thief who is going after the residents of Blue Hill."

"I understand, but you really shouldn't worry so much."

"I'd like to do something to help," she said. "So many of our citizens are older, and they might not understand how things have changed. I'd hate to see anyone in town lose everything they've worked so hard for."

"Why don't you go to the bank and talk to the branch manager about this? No doubt she's aware of the scam, and she might be able to shed some light on what they're doing for their customers."

"Excellent idea."

Alex offered a slight smile. "I agree, if I do say so myself."

"You are so funny." Anne stood and scooted the chair back beneath the table. "When do you think you'll be finished with the display case?"

"It won't take long. It's basically a big box with a window."

"And wheels, right?" she wanted to double check since she knew her mind had been wandering.

He got up from the table. "Right, if that's what you want. I have all the materials, so I can go ahead and start working on it right away."

Alex started walking toward the stairs but stopped and turned to Anne. "What color would you like me to paint or stain the display case?"

"Since we'll be using it for all seasons, why don't you try to match the wood on the baseboards?"

"Sounds good. I need to get Ryan so we can get started on homework. I've noticed an increase in the amount this school year."

"So have I." Anne was actually happy when Ben came home with his backpack filled with assignments. It gave her an opportunity to spend more time with him without coming across as hovering, something he seemed to resist lately. "But I think it's good to keep their minds busy."

Alex made a face. "It keeps my mind pretty busy too. I don't remember how to do most of what he's studying now, so when he asks questions, I have to look everything up."

"Thank goodness for the Internet."

They'd reached the Children's Room. Alex stopped and pointed toward the corner where Anne had placed a cluster of child-sized beanbag chairs. Liddie lay curled up in one of them, the whisper-soft breathing sound of a sleeping child whistling through the air.

"She looks like an angel," Alex said.

"I know." Anne nodded. Liddie looked so much like Eric with her sun-kissed honey-brown hair, Anne could almost imagine his presence at times like this.

"Want me to carry her up to her room?" Alex asked. "It would be such a shame for something to disturb her slumber."

Anne smiled her acceptance. "Ben, would you and Ryan mind picking up everything and stacking it neatly on the shelf? I'll put the books away tomorrow."

She led the way to the elevator, and when they got to Liddie's room, she turned down the covers on the twin bed. After Alex gently put Liddie down, Anne removed her shoes and pulled the blanket up to her chin. Fortunately, Liddie hadn't started getting homework yet, so when she woke up later, all Anne would have to do is fix her something to eat, let her play for a while, and put her back to bed.

After Alex and Ryan left and she locked the library, Anne and Ben went back upstairs for dinner and homework. Ben sat at the kitchen table while Anne prepared leftover vegetable soup and grilled cheese sandwiches — one of the children's favorite meals.

"Mom, what is identity theft?" Ben blurted as he opened one of his books.

Anne froze for a few seconds before slowly turning around to face him. "Why?"

"Some of the kids at school were talking about it, but I don't understand."

Anne didn't want Ben to worry, so she decided to keep her explanation simple and brief. "It's when someone steals personal information from another."

"Why would someone want to do that?" He tilted his head in a questioning gaze.

"There are dishonest people who don't care about others, and their greed makes them do bad things. You don't have anything to worry about though, Ben. I'll protect you."

He looked at her for a few seconds before nodding. "And we all have Hershey here to protect us." The chocolate Lab looked up at Ben when he heard his name. "I guess I better read this chapter so I don't look like such a dweeb when Mr. Layton calls on me."

Anne grinned back at her son, grateful for having such a wonderful kid. "We definitely wouldn't want that."

CHAPTER THREE

The alarm clock startled Anne early the next morning. She groaned as she slid out from beneath the covers and into her robe. Liddie had awakened hungry a couple of hours after she went to bed, so Anne had made her a sandwich, played with her for a while, and rocked her afterward until she fell back to sleep. Liddie had always been her little cuddle bunny, something both she and Eric relished.

Ben was sitting at the kitchen table waiting for her when she arrived. "I left the cereal out for you," he said.

"Thanks, sweetie. I was up and down with Liddie last night. She had a restless night after falling asleep so soon after school."

He glanced up from the magazine he'd been reading. "I know. I heard her." He reached down and scratched behind Hershey's ears. "She woke Hershey up too."

Anne smiled at her son. "Sorry, but I'm not too worried about Hershey. He gets to nap all day if he wants."

Ben shrugged as he shuffled his feet and looked back down at his magazine. Anne leaned over and saw that it was from the vintage collection Eric used to have.

"I miss your dad," Anne said.

"Yeah, me too." Ben didn't look up as he turned a page.

"He would be very proud of you, Ben. You're doing so well in school, and..." She couldn't finish her sentence.

"Mom-meee!" The sound of Liddie hollering echoed down from the third floor of the house. "I can't find my shoes!"

Anne gave Ben an apologetic look as she walked toward the hallway. "Finish your breakfast, sweetie. I'll be back with Liddie in a few minutes."

As Anne went to help Liddie, she said a brief prayer that Ben didn't feel slighted. He was so good and tried his best to be self-sufficient, and she had to remind herself he was still a little boy.

"Here's one," Liddie said as she held it up when Anne appeared at her bedroom door. "I don't know where the other one is."

"Try looking under the bed," Anne said. "I might have accidentally kicked it under there when I put you back to bed last night."

Liddie leaned over and held up the bed skirt. "There it is." She pulled it out and turned around to face Anne. "I got dressed all by myself. See?"

"Yes." Anne smiled at the color combination. Liddie's purple sweatshirt over her green pants was shocking, but she didn't want to hurt her daughter's feelings. Instead, she said, "Very nice, sweetie, but it's going to warm up a little bit this afternoon, so why don't you wear that turtle T-shirt you like so much? It's perfect with those pants."

Liddie grinned. "I didn't think you'd want me wearing that."

"You'll still need a sweater until it warms up."

"Will it be warm or cold on Thanksgiving?" Liddie asked.

"I'm not sure." Anne looked through Liddie's closet, pulled out a white sweater, and helped Liddie into it.

"It doesn't matter." Liddie pulled the front of the sweater together as she grinned up at her mother. "Grandma and Grandpa Gibson will be here, and we'll have fun no matter what."

Anne knelt down in front of Liddie. "There's something I need to tell you, sweetie. Something has come up, and Grandma and Grandpa Gibson won't be coming for Thanksgiving."

Liddie's jaw dropped, but she didn't say a word. She just turned and headed for the stairs to the kitchen, with Anne following close behind.

Ben had just gotten up from the table and was putting his cereal bowl in the sink when Liddie plopped down in her chair. "Ben, did Mommy tell you Grandma and Grandpa Gibson can't come for Thanksgiving?"

"No." Ben's eyes widened as he looked at his mother. "So what are we gonna do for Thanksgiving?"

Anne cleared her throat, but before she had a chance to say a word, Liddie piped up, "I bet there's a whole bunch of people who don't have anywhere to go for Thanksgiving. Why don't they come over here and eat with us?"

"You know what, Liddie?" Anne smiled down at her very kind and gracious little girl. "That sounds like an excellent idea. Let's make a list of people when you get home from school, okay?"

"We can make a sign and put it up at church so everyone will know they can come here," Liddie said. "That way, we won't leave anyone out."

Ben rolled his eyes. "We don't have room for that many people."

Anne shrugged. "Maybe not, but we could ask Reverend Tom if he knows of anyone who doesn't have a place to go."

Liddie beamed. "I want everyone to have a place to go for Thanksgiving."

Anne marveled at how quickly Liddie had recovered from her disappointment. She turned to Ben. "Please go feed Hershey now while I fix Liddie something to eat."

Ben did as he was told while Liddie ate her breakfast. Anne moved around the kitchen, putting things away and rinsing breakfast dishes as she pondered who might be interested in joining them for Thanksgiving. If more people than she had room for in their living area wanted to come, they could overflow into the library.

They were finished with their morning routine on time, so when Alex stopped by to pick up Ben and Liddie, he didn't have to wait. "Did you get all your homework done, champ?" Alex asked Ben as they strode toward the door.

Ben nodded. "It took a while."

Alex cast a glance in Anne's direction when he reached the door. "I hope we don't have that much homework too often."

Anne laughed. She didn't miss the fact that he used the word *we*.

Once they were gone, she prepared the Children's Room for the story time and then went into the kitchen to assemble snack bags. A couple of her volunteers would arrive soon to help hand them out, but she liked having everything ready to go.

When Anne got back to the Children's Room, she spotted Mildred sitting in one of the child-sized chairs, flipping through the books she'd pulled out. "Hey. I thought I'd stop by early and see if you need any help before the little ones arrive."

"Do you know where the sock puppets are?" Anne asked.

"I will as soon as you tell me."

Anne pointed to the cabinet near the door. "There's a box of them on the bottom shelf. I thought we could act out some of the stories."

"Good idea. I'll get them."

Mildred didn't waste a second before putting down the book and pitching in. Anne appreciated the woman's can-do nature.

"Oh, I was wondering if you've heard anything from Claire," Anne said. "Did she ever find out what happened with her credit card?"

Mildred shook her head. "No, not yet. It's the craziest thing how fast someone managed to charge up a whole bunch of stuff without anyone realizing what happened until it was too late."

"From what I understand, it doesn't take long for a thief to hack someone's account."

"*Hack?*" Mildred gave her a questioning look. "What do you mean by that?"

"Oh, that's a technical term for breaking into someone's account."

"Yes, you definitely take after your great-aunt Edie. She understood all that technical stuff."

Anne grinned. "That's about the extent of what I know."

"So apparently, Claire's account has been *hacked*."

Anne arranged some books on the table. "Poor Claire."

"I know. Bless her heart. She has been through so much. I'd like to do something for her, with Thanksgiving coming up soon."

That reminded Anne of her plan. "Why don't you, Claire, and her husband join the kids and me for Thanksgiving dinner?"

Mildred took a step back, looked at the box of puppets for a moment, and then turned back to face Anne. "Oh, I wouldn't want to intrude on your family. I'm sure your in-laws will want you to themselves."

"That won't be a problem since they won't be here. Some of their friends weren't able to take a cruise they'd purchased, and they needed the money, so—"

"In that case, I'd love to join you," Mildred said. "I can't speak for Claire, but I can talk to her...unless you want to."

"We both can," Anne said. "If you want, you can tell her I'll be sending her an invitation in the mail."

"Oh, so it's going to be a formal event?"

"No," Anne said. "This was actually Liddie's idea, and she likes making things, so I thought that decorating invitations would be a fun craft."

Mildred grinned. "I agree."

Another volunteer arrived from the Library Guild. "Hello, Donna." Mildred pointed to the box of sock puppets. "Want to help sort through these so we can hand them out to the kids?"

"Sure," said Donna as she waved to Anne. "Sorry I'm a little late. I had to stop off at the bank to check on my account. Seems there's been some activity that I didn't know about."

Anne nodded. "I heard about that. Did you get everything squared away?"

Donna sighed and shrugged. "I'm still not sure, but Rita, the bank manager, said she'd look into it and get back with me. In the meantime, the bank has put the money back in, and they issued me a new debit card."

Mildred cast a questioning glance at Anne, and Anne nodded. "You better keep an eye on that account," Mildred said. "Seems someone's been getting information from quite a few of the folks in Blue Hill, and they're stealing our identities."

Donna frowned. "I don't know how this could happen. I'm not missing any checks, and I keep my debit card in my wallet at all times."

"That doesn't matter," Mildred said. "Claire hasn't left her house much, except when I take her shopping, and someone started charging up her card all over the place."

Donna still looked perplexed. "Why on earth would someone want to steal my identity? I'm not famous or rich or anything."

"It doesn't matter. People who do that don't care about the person they're stealing from. All they want is to access your information as quickly as possible and then move on before they get caught." When Anne realized both women were staring at her, waiting for more, she shrugged. "I've done a bunch of research on the Internet."

Mildred planted a fist on her hip, winked at Donna, and turned back to Anne. "I'll have you know your aunt Edie would have done the exact same thing. She was the first of all my friends to sign up for e-mail, and she taught the rest of us how to do it."

The children started arriving for the program, so Anne, Mildred, and Donna turned all their attention to reading and helping with the puppets. Wendy poked her head in every now and then and gave a thumbs-up for encouragement. Anne used to have Wendy lead Story Time, but she thought it would be a nice change of pace for her to work with adults since she had so many of her own children to take care of when she got home.

Anne tried to keep everything on schedule, including snack time, but the threat of identity theft looming so heavily over Blue Hill and hitting her friends shook her up. With that nosy mystery woman showing up at the same time, she couldn't help but wonder if there was some sort of connection.

"What's wrong?" Donna asked as they stood off to the side while the children ate their crackers. "Are you feeling okay?"

"I'm concerned about what happened to you and Claire."

"Don't worry," Donna said. "We're watching our account, and if it happens again, we'll just close it and open a new one."

"You shouldn't have to do that." Anne held her gaze. "It's terrible that someone has intruded on your personal life. Are you afraid?"

"Not afraid, but I am concerned." Donna placed her hand on Anne's shoulder. "There are a lot of things that can rattle me if I let them, but this is one of those times I choose to do what I can and leave the rest up to the Lord."

"That's really all any of us can do." Anne pointed to the children. "Looks like they're finished with their snack and ready for the next story."

Mildred grabbed one of the extra puppets and started showing the children what to do. Anne watched as Mildred taught the children how to make their puppets work. The kids giggled as they manipulated the socks with wiggly eyes and pom-pom noses.

After Anne read the first story with the puppets, the children begged for another one. Donna stepped up and read the next story. When she finished, she closed the book, gestured toward the parents standing by the door waiting to pick up their little ones, and leaned toward the children. "It's time to say good-bye for now. We'll see you next week."

Even though Anne thoroughly enjoyed the weekly story time, she was always exhausted when it was over. Wendy had their lunch ready in the library's kitchen after she finished cleaning up the Children's Room. "I thought you might be hungry."

"You didn't have to do this, but I really appreciate it." Anne lifted her spoon and scooped up some of the vegetables in the homemade soup Wendy had brought from home.

Wendy joined her at the table. "So what's this I hear about Donna having her identity stolen too?"

Anne put down her spoon. "This is turning out to be worse than I thought."

"It looks like the thief knows exactly what he's doing."

"Or she," Anne said. "It could be a woman."

"True." Wendy lifted her hands. "Whatever the gender, this is a whole new thing for Blue Hill."

"One thing I've noticed is that most of the people being targeted are senior citizens."

Wendy frowned. "Yeah, it does seem that way."

"But that doesn't mean the thief will stop there," Anne said. "Everyone in town needs to know what's happening. I'm sure Grace will run a story about identity theft and prevention, but I want to do something too. I was thinking we could call in some experts and offer seminars here at the library."

"Not a bad idea."

Silence fell between them as they both thought about it. Finally Wendy stood up. "Let me know if I can help in any way. In the meantime, I need to get home and do some laundry. With seven kids, it sure does pile up fast. And then I have to start supper and get the assembly line going for bath time."

The afternoon was slow, with only a few patrons coming to check out books. Anne was delighted to see Ben and Liddie when they walked in the door. She gave each of them a kiss on the forehead. "Would you like your snack now?"

Liddie sat down in the chair at the small table Anne had placed beside the checkout area. "I want to color first."

Ben went around behind the counter and dropped his backpack in the middle of the floor. "What's that guy doing outside the library?"

"What guy?" Anne asked as she lifted the backpack and put it in the corner, out of the way.

"Some guy's messing with the electric meter." Ben plopped down in the chair. "It's not the regular guy who comes around every month to check it."

"Wait right here, Ben. I'll go see what he's doing." Liddie got up and started to follow her, but she pointed to Ben. "Stay here with your brother. I won't be long."

Ben nodded. "Let's go upstairs and get Hershey."

Anne closed the front door quietly behind her and walked around to where the meters were fastened on the sidewall of the building. A man wearing a khaki uniform and a hat bearing the name of the utility company stood a few feet from the meter, peering into one of the outside garbage cans. The lid lay on the ground.

As soon as the man spotted her, he lifted the lid and placed it on the can. "Wind must have blown it off."

"Is there anything I can help you with?"

The man pulled out a screwdriver and tapped the side of the meter shield. "I'm doing an energy audit to see if we can save you some money."

"I didn't ask for anyone to come out."

"You didn't have to." He pulled a sheet of paper from his back pocket. "It's a free service provided by the power company." He studied his paper. "So Alex Ochs recently did some remodeling on your property? He does nice work. I've surveyed a number of places where he's done remodels and the like."

"Yes. Yes, he does good work." Anne watched as a car pulled in front of the library and three young children piled out of the backseat, their mother chasing after them toward the front door. "Well, okay. I'll let you get back to your work. I should really get back inside. If you need me, I'll be at the checkout desk."

He lifted his screwdriver and gave her a mock salute. She started to go inside but turned around once more to see what the man was doing. The meter cover was still in place, and he'd stepped back a few feet.

As soon as she stepped inside the library, she pulled out her cell phone and called Alex. "Do you know anything about some guy from the power company doing an energy audit?"

"No. I have no idea what you're talking about."

CHAPTER FOUR

"Do you want me to come over and check things out?" Alex asked. Hershey let out a short bark.

Anne glanced out the window and saw the man getting into his truck. "Too late for that. He's leaving now."

"Can you get a license plate number?"

She squinted, but he'd already pulled away from the curb, and it was impossible to see the letters and numbers. "No, he's too far away. But I can tell you that he drives a white pickup truck with some lettering on the side."

"I don't suppose you can see what the lettering says."

Anne wanted to kick herself for missing that. "From this angle, it's too hard to see. I should have paid closer attention. The letters are royal blue."

"Well, he's probably legit. But if you see him again, you might want to ask to see some official documentation."

"He wasn't breaking in or anything," Anne said. "But you're right. I'll ask more questions if he comes back around."

"I doubt you have anything to worry about. Whoever has stolen people's identities has probably moved on to a bigger target than Blue Hill."

"We still need to inform people."

"Sorry, but I forgot to ask how your Tea and Book Club meeting went yesterday."

"That's okay. We had a really nice time. Everyone who said they were coming showed up, and we even had a new person I've never met before."

"That's always a good thing." Alex paused. "I need to run and help Ryan with his history lesson. Looks like the boys got slammed with more homework again."

"I think it's mostly just a reading assignment and a few questions in the back of the chapter."

"Just a reading assignment," Alex said. "Spoken like a true librarian. My nephew would rather be tortured than have someone else tell him what to read."

Anne laughed. "He likes to read when he comes here."

"That's because he can pick whatever book he wants."

"Uncle Alex, I need your help."

The sound of Ryan's voice in the background ended the phone call. Anne hung up and went back to check on her children, who were deep in conversation about Thanksgiving.

"Mommy, can we have tomato soup and grilled cheese sandwiches for Thanksgiving?" Liddie looked up at her with big brown eyes.

"No, sweetie. I'm cooking a turkey, and I'm sure everyone else will bring their favorite Thanksgiving dishes."

Ben looked at Liddie. "See? I told you we couldn't have soup and sandwiches."

"But why?" Liddie looked at Ben first and then at Anne. "Is it against the law or something?"

"No," Ben said before Anne had a chance to respond. "It's just a Thanksgiving rule. Like pumpkin pie. You have to have turkey and pumpkin pie." He looked up at Anne. "Right, Mom?"

"Something like that." Anne led them to the kitchen. "Liddie, why don't you help me start dinner while Ben does his homework?"

Liddie's eyebrows shot up. "You want me to make dinner?"

Anne smiled. "You can pour the sauce over the casserole."

Liddie jumped around in place and clapped her hands. "I love to cook." Without missing a beat, she added, "Can we make cookies soon?"

"Sure. Here." She handed Liddie a spoon and placed a bowl on the table. "Why don't you stir the sauce, while I brown the meat?"

As the three of them worked in the kitchen, Anne reflected on how far they had come since they'd been in Blue Hill. Eric's death rocked their world, but the town of Blue Hill had provided warmth, security, and loving friends who never let them down. Every so often, she saw a melancholy look on Ben's face, but when he caught her staring, he always broke into one of his charming grins.

* * *

The next morning, the children were ready and waiting for Alex when he arrived. "Do you mind if we stop off for a soda after school?" Alex asked. "I promised Ryan I'd do that for him if he finished reading his chapter and answered all the questions by eight last night."

Anne tilted her head and looked at her children. "Would you like to do that?"

Ben nodded, and Liddie grinned. "I love soda!"

"Then by all means, yes." Anne gave each child a kiss on the cheek.

Ben didn't wait around for extra affection, but Liddie hugged her and said, "I'll be really good. I promise."

"I know you will, sweetie. Have fun!" Anne stood at the door and watched as they got into Alex's truck and pulled away.

"That is one good man," Wendy said from behind Anne. "His nephew is very fortunate to have him."

Anne nodded her agreement. "I'm glad you're here early. I need to run the deposit to the bank, and I didn't want to go until you got here."

Wendy stepped back as Anne brushed past her. "We had a good morning at the Pyle house. It was one of those miracle times when no one lollygagged and everyone was ready on time. Even the twins." She puffed her cheeks and blew a breath as she raked her fingers through her chin-length bobbed hair. "And that's rare."

"I can imagine." Anne slung her bag over her shoulder, pulled out her keys, and headed for the door. Need anything while I'm out?"

"I'm fine. Take your time."

As Anne drove through town, she glanced around at all the places her aunt used to frequent. Anne remembered going with her when she was younger, and everything appeared the same. Blue Hill was one of those places where time seemed to stand—still—something that never failed to give her a sense of peace.

She'd pulled up to the light beside the Blue Hill Inn, when a car pulling out of the parking lot on the adjacent road caught her attention. It was the rental car she'd seen the mystery woman driving, and the driver was pulling out, going in the opposite direction.

Anne decided to stop off at the inn on the way back from the library and drop off the note that the mystery woman had left at the library. If it weren't for the cash deposit she had with her, she might have turned around and tried to follow the mystery woman.

The bank parking lot was packed, so she had to drive around in circles until a car eventually pulled out. This was odd. Normally, weekday midmornings were steady but not crowded to this degree.

She walked in and had to wait in a teller line to make her deposit. The teller smiled, handed her the deposit slip, and said, "Is there anything else I may help you with, Ms. Gibson?"

"I'd like to see the branch manager. Is she in?"

The teller gestured toward the offices across the lobby. "I think there may be someone in with her, but she shouldn't be long."

"Thanks." Anne walked over to the waiting area and picked up a magazine before sitting down.

A few minutes later, the office door opened, a man came out, and the thirty-something-year-old manager smiled at Anne. "What can I do for you?"

Anne got up and dropped the magazine back down on the table as she followed the manager into her pristine office with a nameplate on the desk that read *Rita Sloan*. "I hate to bother you, Ms. Sloan, but I wondered if you knew anything about the identity theft problems some of the folks in Blue Hill have had."

A quick flash of acknowledgment darted across Ms. Sloan's face. "Call me Rita." She smiled as she gestured toward the chair. "Please have a seat."

Rita's reaction confused Anne. This was no smiling matter.

The bank manager sat down, folded her hands on her desk, and leaned forward. "Are you concerned about your bank account?"

Anne shook her head. "Not so much mine, but..."

Rita opened her arms. "Then what seems to be the problem?"

"I've been hearing stories about how people's identities have been stolen. Credit cards are charged, and bank accounts are getting cleaned out."

Rita sucked in a breath as though she preferred to talk about anything but this. "I can assure you that we do everything in our power to keep our clients' accounts safe. As for identity, it's up to you to—"

It was painfully obvious that the woman was only giving her lip service to placate her, so Anne stood. "I just wanted to discuss this matter with you to see if...well, maybe I can help...not that I know much about it." She gave Rita what she knew was a look of frustration. "I better get back to the library."

"Thank you for stopping by to chat with me, Ms. Gibson. If you have any problems with your account or the library's account, please don't hesitate to let me know."

Anne cleared her throat. "I can't help but worry about some of the elderly people who don't understand how something like this can happen."

Once again Rita smiled. "I wouldn't worry too much about this. I suspect whoever is doing this knows the victims. You probably have plenty of other things to do with your time."

Rita's blasé attitude frustrated Anne, but there was nothing she could do about it. "Thank you, Ms. Sloan."

On Anne's way to the bank exit, she overheard a customer talking with one of the tellers. "My account can't possibly be overdrawn. My husband deposited a thousand dollars two days ago."

The desperation in the woman's voice touched Anne deeply. She slowed down and hovered close enough to eavesdrop.

"I'm sorry, ma'am. I still can't cash that check for you."

"I promise there is money in my account."

"Why don't I walk you to our manager's office? She might be able to help you more than I can." The teller came out from behind her window and escorted the woman in the direction of Rita's office.

Chills ran down Anne's spine as she thought of the number of people she knew about who were dealing with identity theft. There were probably more. She glanced in the direction of the manager's office and saw that same expression of dismissal on Rita's face as she spoke with the customer.

Anne couldn't take it anymore, so she went out to the parking lot and got into her car. As she drove, her discussion with Rita and then the conversation between the teller and the customer played over and over in Anne's mind. Something didn't seem right about the way Rita reacted.

A thought flashed through her mind that perhaps Rita wasn't who everyone thought she was, but Anne shook it off. Surely the bank executives would have checked out the person they'd put in charge of the Blue Hill branch.

Anne remembered the mystery woman's to-do list stuffed in her handbag, so she pulled into the inn parking lot. There were only two other cars there, and the rental car wasn't one of them. The inn had changed hands since Anne had been in town, and she didn't know the new owners very well.

Charlotte, the owner of the inn, greeted her. "What can I do for you?"

"Someone left something at the library, and I think she's staying here." Anne pulled the note out from the side pocket of her purse and laid it on the counter.

Charlotte picked it up and studied it. "Whose list is this?"

Anne shrugged. "I don't know her name, but I saw her rental car pulling out of your parking lot about forty-five minutes ago." Anne described the mystery woman and her car. She could tell when Charlotte realized who she was talking about. "Can you please tell me her name?"

"I'm sorry," Charlotte said, shaking her head. "I'm not allowed to discuss any of our guests without their permission."

Frustration welled inside Anne's chest. Now more than ever, she wanted to know who the woman was. "Can you have her call me?"

Charlotte hesitated for a few seconds before nodding. "Yes, I can do that. Would you like for me to give her this list?"

"So someone by that description is staying here?" Anne focused her gaze on Charlotte.

The inn owner's face quickly reddened as she glanced down. "I didn't say that." Her shoulders rose and fell as she took a deep breath. "What I meant to say is if someone by that description happens to come in, would you like for me to give her this?"

Anne had the copy in her file cabinet, so she nodded. "Yes, that would be fine. And would you mind asking her to either call or stop by and see me?"

Charlotte's lips tightened as she offered a clipped nod. Anne knew she'd made the woman uncomfortable, so she backed toward the door.

"Thank you, Charlotte. Have a nice day."

On her way to the library, images of all the different people she'd encountered over the past few days played in her mind. First, there was the mystery woman who asked Mildred those personal questions. Then there was the guy tinkering with the electric meter. Rita Sloan didn't act as concerned about identity theft as Anne would think a bank manager should. And now Charlotte appeared somewhat cagey. Anne had met Charlotte and her husband Henry at church, but the new inn owners were not regulars, so she hadn't gotten to know them very well. Anne shook her head, second-guessing herself. Was her mind just playing tricks on her, making her suspicious of everyone, or could one or more of these people really be involved in identity theft?

CHAPTER FIVE

Anne spotted Alex's truck in the library parking lot as she pulled in. She wondered if he might have the display case ready. At least that would be a diversion from her otherwise frustrating day. When she opened the door, Alex grinned at her from behind the checkout desk.

"Hey there," he said. "Did you get all your banking squared away?"

She paused and nodded. "Where's Wendy?"

"She went to the kitchen to put on another pot of coffee." He came from around the desk. "She asked me to look after things, and I thought it might be fun to play librarian."

Anne laughed. "So was it everything you thought it would be?"

His eyes widened as he made a goofy face. "And then some." As he narrowed his eyes and took a good look at her, concern replaced his teasing expression. "So what's wrong? Did something happen at the bank?"

She didn't want to express her feelings about Rita, so she changed the subject. "I've been thinking about that guy who was fiddling with the electric meter."

Alex nodded. "Well, he's probably on the up-and-up, but if you see him hanging around here again, you give me a call and I'll be here in a flash." He grinned and held his hands up. "I know, I know, you can handle everything on your own without my help…but sometimes just the appearance of a rough-and-tough guy like me will scare off a creep."

Anne laughed. "Well, he looked official. But let's hope he doesn't come back, and then we won't have to worry about either one of us scaring him off."

Alex tightened his lips and stared at Anne. "Okay, so what else is bothering you?"

Anne sighed. "If you must know, I'm still worried about all the innocent people in town who are having their identities stolen. You don't think the culprit is anyone we know, do you?"

Alex looked thoughtfully at Anne before slowly shaking his head. "I doubt it's someone we know…at least not anyone we know well. It might be an acquaintance."

Most of the people in Blue Hill were still acquaintances to Anne. The only ones she'd gotten to know well were regular library patrons and people in her adult Bible study at church.

"Make sure you keep your cell phone with you at all times and call the police if you see anything suspicious." Alex smiled. "And now, how would you like to see what I've done with the display case?"

Anne perked up. "You've finished it?"

"Most of it," he said. "I still need to add the finishing touches, but it won't take long."

"Where is it?" Anne glanced over her shoulder and looked around. "Is it in your truck?"

Wendy came out from the back carrying two mugs, one that she extended to Alex. "Here ya go. Two spoons of sugar added and nothing else."

"Thanks. I was just telling Anne about the display case."

"Have you seen it yet?" Wendy asked, her eyebrows lifted as she sipped her coffee.

"Not yet, but I'm dying to."

Wendy laughed. "Then by all means, you better go look at it. We don't want you to die yet. Why don't you take her and show it to her? I've got the front desk covered now."

Alex gestured ahead of him as he talked about the finishing touches of the project. "There are still a few rough edges along the side and back. I'll have to sand them down and stain them to match the rest of it, but I thought I might as well bring it on over so you can start using it."

The instant Anne spotted the case, she knew it was perfect. "That's ten thousand times better than anything I could have imagined." She walked up to it, touched the glass front, and tugged at one of the handles. The front of it opened on hinges installed at the sides, and it didn't make any creaky or squeaky sounds.

"Ten thousand times, huh?" Alex folded his arms, rocked back on his heels, and gave her a closed-mouth smile. "You must not have expected much."

"That's not what I meant. It's just that—" She contorted her mouth. "I better stop now. Let me just say that it will work perfectly." She took a step back to see the bottom that appeared to hover about an inch and a half above the floor. "I thought you were putting it on wheels."

"I decided that casters looked better. They're tucked back so you can't see them." He pointed to the floor. "If you want to get down on your hands and knees and look under it with a flashlight, you'll see what I did."

"No, thanks," Anne replied. "I'll just have to take your word for it."

He opened the case and pointed to the corner. "I taped the two keys here so we don't lose them. You might want to keep one in your apartment upstairs and the other on the library's key ring."

"Thank you so much for this, Alex."

"You are mighty welcome." He glanced at his watch. I'd better get back to my crew. They're probably wondering if I dropped off the face of the earth." He took a couple steps toward the door and stopped. "I'll see you later on with the kids. Don't forget we'll be a little late since I'm taking them out for a soda."

After he left, Anne walked back to the checkout area, where Wendy gestured toward another mug of coffee. "You look like you can use a cup. What happened?"

Anne took the mug, sipped it, and sighed. "I must be super easy to read. The bank visit…and then the drive back were both disconcerting."

Wendy lifted her eyebrows. "Oh yeah? How so?"

As Anne explained her experience with the bank manager, what the bank customer said to the teller, the bank manager's reaction to that customer, and then her experience at the inn, Wendy nodded.

"Suddenly, it seems we are surrounded by strangeness," Anne said, shaking her head.

"Do you think you might be overreacting just a touch?" Wendy asked.

"Maybe, but you have to admit that having so many identity thefts happening to the people of Blue Hill is just cause for suspicion."

"True." Wendy nodded. "But for now, let's not worry about it. We have a library to run. By the way, I got the e-mail from the school with their recommended reading list order. We have most of the books, but there are a few we need to get...that is, when we have the budget for it." She pointed to the desk. "It's right there. I highlighted the books we don't have in yellow."

Anne glanced over at the list. "Thanks. That really helps."

"Before I forget to tell you, I heard Hershey barking and whining, so I went up to your apartment and got him. When I took him out, he seemed awfully interested in something on the street, but I couldn't for the life of me figure out what it was."

"He's done that a few times lately," Anne said. "He just stands at the edge of the yard and stares at something, lets out a few barks, and eventually turns back around."

"Yes, that's exactly what he did this morning." Wendy momentarily appeared contemplative, but her eyes eventually crinkled as she broke into a smile. "How awesome is that display case! It's big enough to have a nice showing but small enough to put it in any room."

"Why don't we start working on a Thanksgiving display tomorrow?"

Wendy reached beneath the counter and pulled out a gourd filled with papier-mache vegetables. "I've already started. When

Emily came home from school with one of these, I got the brilliant idea to use it as a centerpiece, so on Saturday my whole family started making more. I thought it would be a good starting point for the library."

"Perfect. Why don't we get the children who come here to do all the decorations?"

Wendy winked. "Sounds good to me. They'll love it."

A patron arrived, so Anne went about the business of helping her find the books on her list. Wendy checked her out while Anne helped the next patron do a genealogy search on the Internet. Anne couldn't think of a place she'd rather be than Blue Hill. When she worked at the library in New York, she had a more specific job description. Everyone there specialized in something, so she often found herself doing the same thing every single day. She loved specializing and having the depth of understanding about her job. However, here in Blue Hill, she got to do a little bit of everything, making her days fly by because she enjoyed it so much.

It seemed as though the day had just gotten started when Alex arrived with Ben and Liddie. Ryan was right behind them.

"I hope you don't mind a little racket for a few minutes," Alex said as he lifted his toolbox. "I thought I'd finish the display case so you can go ahead and start using it."

"Of course I don't mind," Anne replied. "Remi is here, so she can watch the front while I take the children to the kitchen for a snack."

Liddie patted her tummy. "I don't need a snack. I had too much soda."

Anne glanced at the boys, who had eager looks on their faces. "I don't suppose you had too much soda."

"I'm starving," Ben said. "Got any cookies?"

"Yes, but you can have a piece of fruit first, and then I'll give you each one cookie. I don't want to ruin your dinner."

"Mommy, can I go watch Mr. Ochs do his work?" Liddie asked.

Anne glanced at Alex who gave her a thumbs-up. "Sure, but don't get in his way."

"C'mon, Liddie," Alex said as he reached for her hand. "I'll give you a job to do."

"I like jobs." Liddie and Alex disappeared around the corner. "Mommy says I'm a good little worker."

The boys scarfed down their snack in a couple of minutes. Anne had no doubt they would have eaten twice as much as she gave them, but she also knew Ben wouldn't eat his dinner later. "That's enough for now. Why don't we go see how the case looks?"

They walked out of the kitchen in time to see the case coming their way. Someone was obviously behind it, pushing, but it appeared to be moving on its own.

"Cool!" Ben said. "Is it remote control?"

Liddie peeked her head from around the back of it and giggled. "No, silly, Mr. Ochs and I are pushing it."

"Where would you like it?" Alex asked.

Anne pointed to the small section of wall beside the front door. "Right there will be fine for now."

Once it was flush with the wall, everyone stood back and admired it, including Remi who had joined them. "Looks great. I like the fact that we can show off some of our cool projects."

"Mommy says the kids can decorate it for Thanksgiving." Liddie pointed to the cornucopia Wendy had left on the desk. "We can use all those colors."

Remi leaned over and looked Liddie in the eye. "That will be so pretty!"

Alex placed his hand on Ryan's shoulder and gently nudged him toward the door. "We need to get on home now. Let me know if you need anything," he said to Anne.

Everyone said good-bye. After the guys left, Ben excused himself to do his homework. Liddie followed Remi back to the desk, chattering away about all the decorations she planned to put in the case. The sound of a car pulling up caught Anne's attention, so she glanced out the front window. It was the rental car she'd seen Joan driving.

Chapter Six

The car stopped, but no one got out, so Anne opened the front door and took a step outside. She was sure it was the woman who had identified herself as Joan. The young woman had been looking in her direction, but as soon as she saw Anne, she turned away. She didn't budge from behind the wheel. This raised Anne's curiosity even higher.

The moment Anne started down the porch steps to investigate, the mysterious woman started her car and took off, leaving Anne staring after her until she turned the corner.

Anne pondered what to do next. What the woman had done was strange, but she hadn't committed a crime. There was nothing to report to the police. She didn't want to call Alex because...well, he couldn't very well do anything, so there was no point.

Anne thought about what the woman's actions could possibly have meant as she slowly walked back inside. When she opened the door, she found herself face-to-face with Remi.

"Where did you go?" Remi asked. "I heard the door close, and then I heard a car take off."

"I saw someone pull up, and I thought I knew who it was." Anne glanced away. "Obviously, I was mistaken."

"I've noticed some strange things around here myself lately," Remi said. "But I didn't want to say anything."

"Strange?" Anne looked Remi in the eye. "Like what?"

"Well, for one, there's this guy who has been going up and down the street, looking at everyone's electric meters. I spotted him over near my house too. My mom says he's with the power company, but I'm not so sure."

Anne nodded. "Yes, I've seen him too. Did you notice anything else strange?"

Remi nodded. "Yes, there's some woman who keeps pulling up in front and watching the library."

"Is she in a white car?" Anne paused. "A sedan?"

"You've seen her too?"

Anne pursed her lips. "I think she's the woman who came to the Tea and Book Club meeting. She said her name is Joan Smith."

"I wonder what she's looking for."

"I've wondered the same thing," Anne replied. "I'd also like to know who she is and where she's from."

Remi shook her head. "There's no telling. Maybe she's planning on moving here, and she's checking us out to see if she thinks she'd like it. I hate to admit this, but I sort of hope we don't see a lot of new folks moving into Blue Hill. I like our town exactly as it is. Too many more people, and I think we'll lose some of our charm." She gave Anne an apologetic look. "I'm sorry. I know you're from New York and all, but I—"

Anne held up her hands. "Oh, don't feel as though you have to apologize. I understand what you're saying. Blue Hill is such a quaint and cozy little town. I don't want it to change either."

"I'm pretty old fashioned sometimes, especially when it comes to my hometown." She laughed. "But I do realize that change is inevitable." Remi went behind the counter and got her backpack. "My shift is over, so I better be going." She slung the pack over her shoulder and started for the door, then paused. "Don't you worry, though, Mrs. Gibson. My dad always says that worry indicates a lack of faith. 'Worry less, trust God more,' he tells us." Remi paused at the front door just long enough to give Anne a little wave, and then she was gone.

Anne pondered the wisdom of the words young Remi had so casually tossed her way. She was fortunate to be surrounded by people—of all ages—who didn't hesitate to remind her of what was truly important.

* * *

The next morning, after the children went to school and Wendy arrived, Anne decided to take a drive through town. She never ceased to be amazed by the charm of all the locally owned businesses that catered to the needs of the community.

Anne drove past the inn, continued on past the bank, and headed toward the church she and the children had been attending since she'd moved to town. That was when it dawned on her to talk to the pastor. He could probably share some insight.

Anne entered the church and went straight to Reverend Tom's office. His receptionist smiled.

"He's in with someone at the moment, but he won't be long. Do you want me to have him call you, or would you like to wait?"

"I'll wait." Anne took a seat in one of the chairs across from the reception desk.

"Coffee?" The receptionist stood. "I just brewed a fresh pot."

"Thanks, but I've already had enough coffee."

Anne could tell that Reverend Tom and the person he was meeting with had gotten close to the door by the volume of their voices sounding closer — and the woman's voice sounded very familiar.

"Sounds like they're wrapping things up," the receptionist said.

Anne started to stand when the pastor's office door opened. When she spotted the mystery woman with the same baseball cap pulled down low over her forehead, she momentarily lost her balance and sat back down.

As Joan Smith from the Tea and Book Club meeting said good-bye to Reverend Tom, Anne stood back up and approached them. The woman's eyes widened, and a panicked look dashed across her face. Out of the corner of Anne's eye she could see the pastor's look of confusion.

"Do you two know each other?"

Anne started to speak, but the mystery woman began coughing. The receptionist hopped up from her desk. "I'll go get you some water."

The woman turned to leave, but Anne stepped in front of her. "Did Charlotte give you the note you left at the library?"

The woman glanced at her, nodded, and quickly looked back down at the floor. She took the cup of water from the receptionist and lifted it to her mouth.

Anne's mind whirled with a combination of suspicion and curiosity about the person standing before her.

"We're having another Tea and Book Club meeting in a few days. I hope to see you there," Anne said.

"I—I didn't read the book."

"That's okay." Anne forced a smile. "We understand that life sometimes gets in the way. If you are interested, you can stop by the library this afternoon. I have a copy of the book behind the counter that you can borrow. Even if you don't have time to read the whole thing, you can at least skim it."

The woman's gaze lifted to meet Anne's, but she didn't hold it long. She glanced down, coughed once more, and nodded.

Anne was aware that the pastor remained standing off to the side, observing. She turned back to the woman. "Would you like for me to hold the book for you?"

"I might stop by later, but you don't have to hold it for me."

"But I want to." Anne looked over at the pastor then back at the woman.

"I'm not sure—" The woman paused, sighed, and then took off toward the door.

"I'll be back at the library in about an hour," Anne called out.

Joan didn't respond. She opened the door and darted out to the parking lot.

Anne turned to face the pastor. He gestured toward his office door. "It's nice to see you, Anne. How are Ben and Liddie?"

"They're doing great, although they are disappointed about their grandparents not being able to come for Thanksgiving." She followed him into his office and sat down in the side chair as he went around behind his desk and took a seat. "We'd hoped my in-laws could come for a visit over Thanksgiving, but they are helping some friends by purchasing cruise tickets they weren't able to use."

Reverend Tom chuckled as he shook his head. "A cruise, huh? Such a sacrifice."

Anne grinned. "I'm sure they'll have a good time, but my in-laws love Ben and Liddie so much that I really do think this is a sacrifice for them."

"Yes, Lord willing." He leaned back and folded his hands in his lap.

"Liddie came up with an idea to invite some people who don't have family to share Thanksgiving dinner with us."

"That's very sweet," he said. "But knowing what I do about Liddie, it's not surprising."

"She has always had a soft place in her heart for others."

"That is truly a special gift. Would you like some names, or do you already know who you want to invite?"

"We've already got a few names, but we can always add more."

The pastor jotted something down before leaning back again. "I'll get back with you later on that. So how's Ben?"

Anne laughed. "Ben is doing great, but I'm sure he'd love it if his teacher didn't assign so much homework."

"Homework for a boy his age is torture. I'm sure he'd much rather be outside riding his bike."

"Or reading or working on his computer," Anne added. "Ben has always been the quiet, studious one."

After a few more minutes of small talk, Reverend Tom leaned back and smiled. "So is there anything else I can do for you?"

Anne wanted to ask about Joan, but she wasn't sure how to start, so she just blurted, "That woman who was in here before me...Joan?"

He nodded. "Yes, what about her?"

"Can you tell me anything about her? I mean, like where she's from or what she's doing here? She came to our first Tea and Book Club meeting, but she didn't say much. And then, she—"

"I'm sorry, but I'm not at liberty to discuss this," he said, interrupting her with an apologetic grin.

"I understand." She paused as she thought of a different approach. "Have you heard about the identity theft that's been happening in Blue Hill?"

A look of consternation crossed his face. "Yes, I have. In fact, some of our members here at Blue Hill Community Church have experienced it."

"Some of the older members?" Anne asked.

"Why yes, how did you know?"

"Senior citizens seem to be the target. I've been worried about them."

"I can certainly understand your concern."

"I'm thinking about offering a program to help the victims. Of course, I'll bring in an expert to conduct it. Maybe we can start with the victims so it won't happen to them again. Would you mind giving me the names of the ones you know about first?"

The pastor pursed his lips then smiled. "I'll have to get their permission first, but I'm sure that won't be a problem. Why don't I call you later?"

"Okay." She stood and walked toward the door.

"I'll also call you later with the names of some people who might enjoy some Thanksgiving fellowship."

Anne started toward the door but stopped when Reverend Tom softly said her name. She turned to face him with a questioning look.

"Please proceed with caution, Anne."

She tilted her head. "I beg your pardon?"

"I couldn't help but notice that you were only half listening to me throughout our entire conversation. Your mind was elsewhere, and I suspect you were thinking of ways to help with the investigation."

"Sorry."

"No worries." He gave her a look of understanding. "As a friend, I want to recommend leaving this to the authorities."

"Of course." Anne had no intention of putting herself in harm's way, but she did want to do something. "I just want to serve as a resource person."

"That's probably a good idea, but make sure you have the proper resources to refer people to and don't try to do everything yourself." He smiled as he paused. "You can still be proactive and help the citizens of Blue Hill, but you need to be very cautious and not do anything that may put you in jeopardy."

"Okay." She pulled the door open and turned back to the pastor. "Thank you for taking the time to chat with me."

"Of course. It was my pleasure."

CHAPTER SEVEN

A nne drove straight back to the library thinking about her conversation with Reverend Tom. She understood why he'd advised her to leave everything to the authorities, but she also knew that she wasn't the type to ignore signs.

When she turned the last corner, she spotted the rental car parked at the curb, and as she got closer, she saw that there was no one behind the wheel.

Anne pulled into the parking lot beside the library, hopped out, and scurried into the building. She fully expected to see Joan at the checkout desk, but Wendy said she'd left — without the book.

"Where did she go?" Anne asked.

Wendy shrugged. "I have no idea. Another patron came in looking for a children's book. After I helped her, I came back to the desk, and she was gone."

"Did she get a library card and check out the book for the book club?"

Wendy shook her head. "No, she just asked for you. As soon as I told her you weren't back yet, the other person came in."

Anne went over to the window and glanced outside. The rental car was still there. Something was definitely not right. She dropped her purse off at the desk, asked Wendy to keep a very close eye on the door, and then headed upstairs to get Hershey.

To be on the safe side, she ran through all the rooms on the second floor, and when she didn't see anyone, she went to the third-floor bedrooms. After she was assured that there was no sign of anyone having been there, she grabbed Hershey's leash, put it on him, and they went back down to the first floor.

"Did she come back?" Anne asked.

"No. I haven't seen her since she first came in." Wendy leaned against the wall. "What's going on?"

Anne explained how she'd run into Joan at the church and how she'd noticed the rental car still parked at the curb outside the library. "This has me so puzzled; I'm not sure what to do next."

Wendy went over to the window and grimaced. "The car is still there. Want me to call the police?"

"I don't know what they can do. After all, as far as we know, she hasn't committed any crimes."

"We are definitely in a pickle, aren't we?" Wendy drummed her fingers on the desk.

"Maybe I missed something. I'll go check some of the rooms again."

"I'll be right here. Holler if you need me."

Anne and Hershey walked into each of the rooms, where she glanced behind bookcases and opened each of the closets. She eventually found her way to the Children's Room. That was when she heard voices outside the window, and one of them sounded like Joan. Hershey let out a low growl, which was out of character for him.

"C'mon, Hersh. Let's go see what's going on." They took off for the front door. As soon as they rounded the corner of the house, she spotted Joan talking to the man she'd seen days before at the meters. The man had his back to her, gesturing, while Joan stood there listening.

"Joan!" Anne waved as Hershey pulled on the leash.

The man stopped talking and frowned at her before he mumbled something to Joan and headed for his truck. Anne patted her pocket and realized she had left her cell phone in her purse. Joan stared at her with a wide-eyed, frightened look. That was strange.

"Hey, Joan. I forgot something, and I have to run back inside and get it. Want to come with me?"

Joan shook her head. "No, I think I'll wait here."

Anne paused. She didn't like the idea of leaving Joan, given her propensity to take off, but she didn't see that she had a choice. "Okay. I'll be right back."

Anne ran into the library with Hershey, called the police to report the man she'd found lurking on the library property again, and went back outside, this time without the dog. The instant she opened the door, she spotted the back of the rental car as it pulled up to the stop sign at the end of the street. What was going on with Joan, and why was she leaving after saying she'd wait? And the biggest question was why had she been talking to that man?

Wendy came to the door holding the library's cordless phone. "For you," she said.

It was Alex. "Just checking on you to see if everything is okay."

She told him about the most recent events. "I'm sure it will all come together eventually, but I'm still perplexed."

"Please don't try to take any of this on yourself," he said. She could hear the worry in his voice. "You have no idea what you're dealing with."

"That's just it. I'm not doing anything. I'm just talking to people."

"Anne, you know what I'm saying."

"Yes, I do know." Anne glanced up and saw that Wendy was watching her. She smiled as she walked into one of the quieter rooms. "You are bringing the children home right after school, aren't you?"

"Yes, unless you need a little more time to yourself. I can take them out for sodas again. I don't think they'd mind." She could practically hear Alex smiling over the phone.

"I'm sure they would love it, and I appreciate your offer, but I'd really like them home with me. I want to start thinking about normal things again."

"I understand. Let me know if you change your mind."

When Anne went back to the front desk, Wendy gave her a questioning look. "I never thought we'd see this much excitement at the library."

"I know." Anne pulled her purse out from beneath the counter, dug through it to get her cell phone, put it in her pocket, and then turned back to Wendy. "I keep telling myself—and promising Alex—that I'll leave all the sleuthing up to the authorities, but odd things keep happening."

Wendy planted her fist on her hip and frowned. "What else besides that strange woman who showed up at the book club meeting...oh, and the identity theft?"

"I haven't told you about the guy at the meter yet, have I?"

Wendy's eyebrows shot up. "Guy at the meter?" She shook her head. "No, you haven't mentioned him."

Anne told her about the man who'd been looking at the electric meter and had mentioned Alex. "But Alex didn't know a thing about him."

Wendy frowned. "Something similar happened at the apartments down the street from where I live…you know, those duplexes?"

"Yes." Anne had actually considered moving into one of them while waiting for the renovations on Aunt Edie's house to be finished.

"My neighbor said some guy was lurking around the buildings. When one of the residents asked what he was doing, he said something about energy savings."

"That's what he told me."

Wendy clicked her tongue. "I wonder if he's for real. Why don't you call the power company?"

"Alex did, and they said they did have an employee doing surveys in this area, so it seems like he's legit." Anne shrugged her shoulders.

Wendy glanced toward the door. "Well, look who just walked in," she said with a smile. "Hey, Officer Banks."

Michael Banks smiled back and turned to Anne. "We followed up on your call, but there doesn't appear to be a problem. I talked to a man meeting your description, and he says he was talking to a woman who is considering moving to Blue Hill."

Anne turned to Wendy. "I heard him outside chatting with Joan." She glanced back at Michael. "But did he say why he was here in the first place?"

Michael shook his head. "He was in a hurry, but he showed me a badge. It checks out."

"I understand." Anne rubbed the back of her neck. "What should I do next time I see him?"

"Nothing, unless he appears to be harassing innocent people."

Anne shook her head. "I haven't seen him doing that."

"How about trespassing?" Wendy asked.

Michael opened his arms. "Unless you get the sense he is stalking you...this is a library—a public place."

"Good point." Wendy glanced over at Anne. "We just need to be careful."

"Sorry about the call, Michael—I mean Officer Banks," Anne said. She tried to remember to call her former classmate by his title while he was on duty.

"That's what I'm here for, Anne. If you have any more problems, please don't hesitate to call again." He smiled as his attention turned toward the door. "And here come a couple of my favorite children. Hey there, Ben." He squatted down. "How are you doing, Liddie? I sure did like that safety poster you made."

Liddie beamed. "I colored it all by myself."

"I know. That's what makes it so special." The police officer stood and gave a mock salute to Anne and Wendy. "It's been a pleasure, ladies. I'll leave now so you can get on with what's really important."

Wendy left right after him. She'd been able to stay later than usual because her husband was home with their children.

"Where's Alex?" Anne asked her children.

Ben shrugged. "Ryan said he needed lots of help on his homework, so they left after Alex made sure you were here."

As Liddie chatted about her school day, Anne noticed that Ben was being very pensive. She planned to ask him about that later, after Liddie went to bed.

A few more patrons came in for various things, and Anne was able to help them all without leaving the front desk. Ben started on his homework beside her, while Liddie colored on some paper.

"I'm making another poster for Officer Banks," she said. "See, Mommy?"

Anne smiled at the poster filled with pink and purple, Liddie's favorite colors. "He'll like that."

"I know." Liddie resumed coloring, while Ben and Anne exchanged a brief mother-son look.

Anne appreciated how well behaved her children were, but ever since Eric's passing, she'd noticed how Ben tried so hard to be the man in the family. Fortunately, there was enough little boy in him to keep him playful, but every now and then, a spark of adult-like understanding flashed across his face.

When closing time arrived, Anne locked all the doors to the outside and went upstairs with the children. Ben lifted his nose and sniffed the air. "Something smells good, Mom."

"I'm starving!" Liddie ran straight for the kitchen.

"I'm cooking pot roast in the slow cooker."

"*Mmm.*" Ben sat down at the table before he remembered it was his turn to set the table. Without being asked, he hopped up, went to the flatware drawer, and got each of their place settings.

Liddie hovered at Anne's side as she sliced the roast and put it on plates. "Can you give me some extra carrots?" Liddie rubbed her tummy. "I love carrots! They're yummy."

Anne filled three plates — one with extra carrots for Liddie, one with extra potatoes for Ben, and hers with a very small amount of everything. She wasn't hungry, but she liked to set an example of healthy eating for her children.

Liddie talked throughout dinner, and Ben remained mostly silent as he ate. As they neared the end of their meal, Anne noticed that Liddie's chatter had slowed down.

"Tired, sweetie?" Anne asked.

Liddie nodded without saying another word.

"Why don't we get you ready for bed." Anne glanced up at Ben. "Go ahead and finish your homework. I'll be back in here after I read Liddie her bedtime story."

Liddie was so sleepy she selected the shortest of her storybooks. After Anne read it to her, she pulled the blanket up to Liddie's chin, said a brief prayer, and leaned over to kiss her on the forehead.

"Good night, sweetie. See you in the morning."

Anne had barely walked into the hallway when she heard the soft, rhythmic sound of Liddie's breathing. Times like this reminded her of when she and Eric would exchange a smile as they thought about how they'd had another blessed day with the children God entrusted to them.

When she got to the kitchen, Ben had his book open, but he was staring at the wall. He turned and forced a smile.

"What's wrong, Ben? Did something happen at school?"

He shook his head. "Mom, why was Officer Banks here?"

"Is that what's worrying you?"

Ben shrugged. "I guess."

Anne didn't want to upset Ben, but she also had a policy of telling her children the truth. She decided to give him an abbreviated version and to keep it light.

"I called the police department to have them walk around the property. I like to make sure we stay safe."

"Why would he have to walk around the property?"

Now that she was cornered, Anne knew she had to tell him. "Remember that man who was messing with the electric meter?"

Ben nodded.

"He was back. He's probably a very nice man, but I never want to take a chance."

"Oh." Ben picked up his pencil. "Are you worried about identity theft? Some of the kids are still talking about it at school. I don't get it."

"I don't get it either, but everyone in Blue Hill cares about keeping our community safe. We're committed to making sure our children have a safe place to grow up and eventually raise your families."

"That's a long way off, Mom." Ben finally gave her the smile that never failed to warm her heart. "I only have two more questions to answer before I'm done. Do you mind if I read in bed for a while after I finish?"

"Of course not. You know I hardly ever mind if you read in bed."

Half an hour later, Anne was in her own room with a stack of books she wanted to peruse before the next book club meeting. When her cell phone rang, she glanced at the clock before answering it. No one ever called this late, so she braced herself.

"Hey, Anne," Mildred said. "I just wanted to let you know that I saw that woman from the book club meeting driving by my house again this afternoon."

"Are you sure it was her?"

"I wasn't positive until she parked her car at the curb and walked up to the front door. I was watching from the window, but by the time I opened the door, she'd turned around and left.

CHAPTER EIGHT

The next morning when Alex stopped off to pick up Ben and Liddie, he leaned over and whispered in Anne's ear. "I heard about what happened to Mildred last night."

Alarm bells sounded in Anne's head. "Something happened?"

"Well, nothing actually happened, but she spotted that woman from your book club driving by her house again."

"Yes, she already told me." A sense of relief washed over Anne. "She makes me very uncomfortable, but so far, all we know is that her name is Joan, and she's very quiet."

"And she's curious about Mildred," Alex added.

"Yes, there is that."

Alex gestured for the children to follow him. "We need to get going. Ryan has to turn in some homework he forgot at home yesterday. Good thing their teacher is letting him do that."

"He might give a lot of homework, but at least he understands kids," Anne said.

As soon as Ben and Liddie were out of earshot, he whispered, "I'll call or stop by later."

Anne went behind the desk to go over the books again so she could offer two choices to the book club the next day — maybe a classic, like Dicken's *Great Expectations* or one of Chesterton's Father Brown mysteries. She wanted them to help pick, but she also knew that if she gave them too many to select from, they might be there all day.

Wendy called to let her know she couldn't work because one of her children was sick. Fortunately, there were no morning programs at the library that day, and Donna would be in later for the genealogy group meeting.

Between patrons, she pondered the book selections. Finally, she narrowed down the options to two, so she put the others away.

Alex called around eleven. "So how is your day going so far?"

"Slow," Anne admitted, "but sometimes that's a good thing."

"I understand. Did Ben mention anything to you about some of the discussions the kids are having about the identity theft?"

"Yes," Anne replied. "He doesn't understand why anyone would do that, so I tried to assure him that we're committed to keeping Blue Hill safe."

"I suppose that's all you can say right now, but you know how kids his and Ryan's age can build things up in their minds."

"I'm sure seeing Officer Banks in the library when he got home didn't help. His imagination must have been on overdrive."

"What did Michael say?"

Anne explained how nothing could be done about the guy walking around the building since it was a public library. "I suppose if there is any downside to living above the library, that's it. Otherwise, it's perfect."

"Everything has a downside, but once the identity thief is caught and we figure out what that man is up to, any threat you feel will be gone."

"That's what I'm counting on," Anne said.

"Keep me updated on any new developments. I need to run and check on my crew at City Hall. We're updating all the employee areas, like the break room and restrooms."

"Sounds like fun," she said.

"A blast."

Anne hung up laughing at the tone of Alex's voice. He enjoyed being a contractor, but there were some jobs he liked more than others. His specialty was renovating historical buildings such as the one she was in.

* * *

Alex walked Ben and Liddie into the library after school, but he didn't stick around. He and Ryan had some errands to run before they went home.

"Mommy, we need to start decorating for Thanksgiving," Liddie said.

"The preschoolers made some things in the program," Anne said. "We can use their decorations."

Liddie nodded. "They'll like that."

"Sounds good." Anne turned to her son. "I need your help too, Ben."

Ben nodded. "I can hang stuff if you want me to."

"That is so grown up…of both of you," Anne said. "Why don't we get started right after dinner?"

Ben didn't have as much homework as he normally did. Anne suspected his teacher was backing off so they could all enjoy some pre-holiday activities. Another thing Anne had noticed was how festive the town of Blue Hill was this time of year.

Both children ate their dinner quickly, and they carried their plates to the sink without being asked. "Okay, so where do you want to start? The library or our home?"

"*Li-bary.*" Liddie frowned at her mispronunciation of the tricky word. "I mean *li-brrrrary.* I want everyone to see our decorations."

"Good! I have all kinds of things we can use." Anne led the way down the stairs and flipped lights on in each room as they went. "Let's get started with the display case Mr. Ochs built."

Anne arranged the papier-mache cornucopia and vegetables on the middle shelf, while Liddie placed the pilgrims and Native American figurines around in a circle on the bottom. Anne handed Ben some garlands of leaves to stream around in different places.

They taped and pinned pictures that the children had made during the craft programs to the wall at the entrance and on the bulletin board. Anne had designed a *Happy Thanksgiving* sign, and she handed it to Ben to hang across the top. She watched his face as he carefully climbed the step stool, centered the sign, got down, stood back, and then climbed back up to adjust it some more. Pride swelled in her chest at the very thought of how responsible and careful he was.

"Mommy, we made the library really pretty, didn't we?"

"Yes, sweetie, it's very pretty."

Liddie frowned. "Where is the picture of my hand turkey? I thought you were gonna hang it up."

Anne squatted down beside her daughter. "Of course, I'm going to hang it up, but not down here. That's so special I want to keep it up on our refrigerator."

"But I want everyone to see it." Liddie's bottom lip stuck out as it always did when she was disappointed.

"Well, it is very special, and I don't want anything to happen to it, but I suppose we can put it someplace where no one can touch it."

Liddie folded her arms over her chest, lifted her hand to her face, and tapped her index finger against her chin as she glanced around the main section of the library. Her eyes lit up, and she pointed to one of the taller bookcases.

"How about over there? We can put it up real high, and that way everyone can see it, but no one can reach it…except very tall people like Mr. Ochs."

Anne looked at Ben, and he nodded. "Want me to go get it?"

"If you don't mind," Anne replied. "And I'd like for you to hang it for me too."

Ben left and came back with the picture. "Here, Liddie, hold this while I move the stool over there."

Anne watched as her children worked in tandem, putting up the last decoration of the evening. Realization struck her that these two people she'd given birth to only a few years ago were becoming independent. The very thought of them not needing her gave her a strange feeling of sadness and happiness. She wanted them to be able to stand on their own, but she also loved being needed.

Ben got down off the step stool, took his sister's hand, and studied their work. He turned to Anne and smiled. "Cool, huh?"

Anne nodded. "Yes, very cool."

Liddie let go of Ben's hand and clapped hers together. "Everyone is gonna love it. Mommy, will you tell all the little kids that if they eat their vegetables, they can grow up and decorate for Thanksgiving too?"

Ben's gaze darted to Anne's, and they exchanged a smile of understanding. "If that's what you want me to tell them, then I certainly will."

They were about to go back upstairs when the cell phone in Anne's pocket rang. It was Alex.

"Ryan suddenly remembered that he was supposed to read a book to make up for some work he forgot. Would you mind terribly if we stop by and pick it up?"

"Of course I don't mind. In fact, the kids and I are downstairs in the library now. How fast can you get here?"

"About ten minutes."

"See you then." Anne turned to Ben and Liddie. "Mr. Ochs and Ryan are stopping by to pick up a book."

"Goodie! We can show Ryan all our decorations!" Liddie jumped up and down, clapping her hands.

Ben tried hard not to look pleased, but the half smile on his lips told Anne otherwise. She knew he was proud of himself for how he'd helped, so she tried to think of a way to tell Ryan without embarrassing him.

When they arrived, Liddie blurted, "C'mon, Ryan, I wanna show you what Ben and I did. We helped Mommy decorate the *libar – brary*. Ben had to hang all the way-up-high stuff 'cause I'm too little, and he's real big." She pulled him by the arm through the library, leaving Anne and Alex standing there watching.

"She's pretty high energy, isn't she?" Alex said.

"Yes, but she also winds down quickly. With her, it's either fast or stop, and that's only when she's sleeping."

"I've noticed." He paused as they looked at the children for a few seconds. "Do you have a few minutes? I don't want to interrupt anything, but I would like to catch up on some of the latest goings-on in Blue Hill."

"Sure. I think the kids are too wound up to go to sleep now anyway."

Alex lifted his hand and motioned for Ryan to listen. "Mrs. Gibson and I are going to chat for a while."

Ryan grinned back at his uncle. "Can we play in the reading cave?"

"As long as you don't jump around too much," Alex replied. "And remember that you have a little girl with you, so no roughhousing." He turned back to Anne. "I'm glad he listens to me, but I have to admit, I feel lost most of the time. I had no idea what was involved in child rearing."

"But if you had it to do all over again, you would, right?"

He nodded. "Of course. I love my nephew."

"It's obvious." Anne smiled. "Say, do you remember that guy you saw at your meters?"

Alex glanced at Anne then over her shoulder toward the front door.

Anne nodded. "Sure. Have you learned anything new about him?"

"No, not really. But evidently he's been spotted all over town, checking meters. From what everyone has said, it appears he is on the up-and-up. I think we must all be on edge because of this identity theft business."

Anne nodded as she pondered that possibility. "And speaking of identity theft…" He studied his steepled fingers before looking back at Anne. "Apparently, several more bank accounts have been tampered with recently." Alex shook his head. "But the manager doesn't seem too worried."

"I've noticed that about her," Anne said. "When I asked if she was aware of the identity theft, she basically just brushed me off."

"To me, that's the oddest behavior of all. You would think a bank manager would be concerned enough to act on it."

"Oh, and how well do you know Charlotte and Henry at the Blue Hill Inn?"

Alex shrugged. "Not all that well. I did some work for them when they first bought the place, but they pretty much stay to themselves, with the exception of the few times they've attended church."

"At least they go occasionally." Anne thought about how evasive Charlotte was. "But something doesn't seem right."

"They seem reserved, but otherwise, I don't see any reason to be suspicious of them. The branch manager, on the other hand…well, something isn't adding up with her. The last manager was let go, or at least that's what I heard. And then they moved someone here who had no ties to Blue Hill."

"You don't think—" Anne cut herself off before blurting her suspicion of Rita. She didn't want to speak about something she couldn't back up.

"Honestly, I don't know what to think anymore." Alex leaned back in his chair, stretched his legs, and shook his head. "I have to admit, when you first started talking about this, I thought you might be overreacting. But now I see it differently."

Anne offered him a closed-mouth smile. "Do you think we should do anything? And if so, what?"

He splayed his hands. "I don't know."

"Why don't we see if the police have access to some sort of program that could teach people how to protect their personal business?"

Alex's eyes lit up. "Sounds like a good plan."

She gestured around the room. "We could even offer to have it here."

"I like that." Alex glowed with respect, warming her heart. "You already use the Resource Room for various meetings. I'm sure you could accommodate something like this meeting there."

"With the holidays coming up, when do you think would be a good time to hold this seminar?"

"Before we make any hard plans," Alex leaned forward, "why don't we talk to the police first and find out if they're even interested. If they are, they probably have some insight on timing and what size crowd to expect."

Alex's phone rang, so he stood up, walked a few feet away, and answered it. After he clicked the Off button, he looked back at Anne with concern.

"That was my mom. My parents' bank account has been wiped out."

CHAPTER NINE

Now they didn't have a choice but to get involved. Anne stood up and walked closer to Alex, who appeared truly upset. She knew that Alex's parents had their accounts in the same bank she used because one of his dad's old pals was the branch manager until he retired.

"Have they spoken to Rita about it?"

He shook his head. "Not yet. They just discovered it late this afternoon when they went to the ATM to withdraw money to pay the kid who cleans their gutters." He met her gaze with the saddest look she'd ever seen on him. "How can anyone do something like that to a couple of elderly people who would give a complete stranger the shirt off their back?"

Anne's heart ached for Alex's parents. "This is all the more reason we need to act quickly. We don't want this happening to anyone else if we can help it."

"I need to stop by and see them on my way back home." Alex called out for Ryan. "We can talk more tomorrow. I'll be by to pick up Ben and Liddie at the regular time."

"Would you like me or Wendy to take them to school? I can call her and see if she can add our kids to her van load. If I weren't so nervous about all the unusual things going on in Blue Hill right now, I would let them walk."

"No, I have to be out early anyway." Ryan appeared, so Alex motioned toward the door. "But thanks for the offer. See you tomorrow."

* * *

The next morning, Anne had a difficult time waking Ben and Liddie. They'd stayed up much too late the night before, but she wouldn't have changed it for anything. The time they'd spent decorating was precious, and she knew it would be in all their memories in the years to come.

Fortunately, Alex didn't arrive early as he sometimes did. She'd got Ben and Liddie ready with seconds to spare.

She waved at Alex as he walked into the library. He told the children to wait by the door as he crossed the room to talk to Anne.

"I thought about something last night. You should probably change all the passwords to the library and personal computers."

Anne agreed. "Good thinking. I'm afraid I sometimes get in a rut and don't bother with some of the details."

"I changed mine last night," he said, "and I plan to go to my parents' house and change theirs after I talk to Rita at the bank." When he mentioned Rita's name, distrust flickered in his eyes.

"As soon as help arrives, I'm going to run over and talk to someone at the police department," Anne said.

"We'll catch up later. I'm sure we'll both have plenty of information to share soon." On his way to the door, he waved. "See you after school lets out."

Wendy rushed in a half hour later, appearing disheveled. "Everyone is well at my house, but it was touch and go at first. I never know if the kids are sick or if they just don't want to get out of bed on these cold mornings."

"I know what you mean." Anne smiled. "We were up late decorating the library. Add that to the cold floor, and it was really hard to get started."

"You decorated?" The tone of disappointment lacing Wendy's voice wasn't lost on Anne.

"We started on it, but I thought you and the other volunteers would want to add some things."

Wendy grinned. "I would love to do more. I have an excess of orange and yellow paper leaves that my children insist on putting all over the house this time every year. Maybe I can scatter a few around the library."

"Remember that whatever we put out now needs to be picked up in time to decorate for Christmas," Anne reminded her.

"Absolutely." Wendy let out a low, throaty laugh. "That's what the kids are for. I'll give them some incentive for coming in to clean up. They'll do anything for my Oreo truffles."

Anne agreed. "I understand that. *I'll* do anything for your Oreo truffles."

"In that case, cleanup shouldn't be a problem," Wendy said.

After a few more minutes of small talk, Anne asked Wendy if she minded being alone for a while. "I need to talk to Michael Banks and see if we can host a program on protecting against identity theft."

"I love that idea. I keep hearing about more people who have lost money from their accounts or had their cards charged up."

"I know." Anne wasn't sure if Alex wanted her to mention his parents, so she didn't. "If anyone calls about the book club meeting this afternoon, tell them it's still on."

"I'll get everything ready."

"You don't have to do anything. I won't be gone long."

"Take your time. I'll make sandwiches that we can eat when you get back."

As Anne walked out to her car, she couldn't help but smile at Wendy's mothering nature flowing over onto her. She had to admit it was rather nice to have another person care enough to make the extra effort.

She drove to the police department, only slowing down slightly as she passed the inn. There were several vehicles in the parking lot, one of them Joan's rental car and several spaces down was the truck she'd seen the meter man driving. That piqued her curiosity. The lettering on the side of the truck read *Save Money with an Energy Audit*. She wondered what he was doing at the inn but resisted the urge to stop and find out.

The police station was only a few blocks away. The woman at the desk greeted her with a smile. "Hi, Anne. How can I help you?"

"I'd like to talk to someone about having a seminar at the library on how to protect against identity theft."

"Great idea." The receptionist hopped up from her desk and backed toward the door behind her. "Let me go see if Officer Banks is available. He's the one handling that." She gestured toward the row of chairs across the room. "Have a seat."

Anne did as she was told, but she'd barely warmed the chair when the receptionist arrived with Officer Banks. "I hear you're interested in hosting an identity theft seminar," he said as he sat in the chair next to her. "This is very timely."

"I know," Anne admitted. "Several of the library patrons and other friends are victims, and I'm sure they're only a fraction of people it's happening to."

He nodded. "We've been working with other agencies to get to the heart of this, and I'm sure one of them probably has a program I can use. When would you like to have this?"

Anne shrugged. "Whenever you can do it." She paused. "As soon as possible."

"Okay, good. I'll get back to you about dates and times." He stood up and walked Anne to the door. "Identity thieves target people who have their guard down, and we need to make sure everyone is alert and knows what to look for."

"Too bad we have to do this."

Officer Banks opened the door for her. "It isn't necessarily a bad thing. We need to be prepared for anything. Once we catch whoever is doing this and get justice, others will think twice before messing with the great town of Blue Hill."

Anne laughed. "That's right. I'll look forward to your call."

On her way back to the library, Anne saw that the meter man's truck was gone, but the rental car remained in the parking lot at the inn. Wendy met her at the door of the library. "You won't believe what just happened."

Anne's insides lurched. "I can only imagine."

"Mary Zumfelde stopped by and wanted to know why she wasn't invited to the book club."

"Did you tell her everyone is invited?" Anne relaxed. She thought Wendy had more shattering news.

"I most certainly did," Wendy replied indignantly. "But she seems to think she should have a special invitation, perhaps lined with gold?" She made a face. "I don't know why she thinks her loaded bank account makes her so special."

"So will she be here?"

Wendy shook her head as she moved back behind the counter. "She refuses to go where she's not invited."

Anne grinned and winked at Wendy. "Then let's make sure she's invited properly."

"She probably gets more invitations in a month than I do in a year. I think that's one of the perks of being in her social circle." She motioned for Anne to follow her toward the library's kitchen. "C'mon, let's grab a bite before we finish setting up for the tea. I made egg salad just the way you like it…with extra sweet pickle relish and a dab of mustard."

"Yum." Anne's stomach growled as she entered the kitchen. "You are the best cook."

"I admit I'm a good short-order cook, but don't ask for anything fancy, or I'd disappoint you."

"Okay, it's a deal," Anne said with a quick nod. "Short order is perfect as busy as we are around here."

Wendy nodded toward the breadbox by the stove. "Grab the loaf in there, and I'll get the bowl of egg salad. We can make our sandwiches at the table."

As they sat across the table from each other, Anne enjoyed the camaraderie between them. She'd only known Wendy since she and the children had moved to Blue Hill, but she felt as though they'd been friends for life.

"So what did they say at the police station?" Wendy asked as she sawed her sandwich in half with the butter knife.

Anne told her about her conversation with Officer Banks, while Wendy listened attentively. "He's supposed to call so we can work out the time and date."

"From what I've seen, we might need more than one seminar. There may be a lot of interest in something like this."

"It certainly seems that way," Anne agreed. "When I suggested having it at the high school gym, he said it would be more comfortable for everyone to have it here at the library. I don't mind putting this on the schedule several times. Besides, we'll need to make it available at the convenience of anyone who wants to attend."

A knock on the kitchen doorframe caught their attention. Anne glanced up and saw Mildred smiling at them.

"Is this a private meeting, or may I come in?" Without waiting for an answer, Mildred crossed the room, slung her handbag over the back of a chair, and sat down. "So what are you two discussing?"

"The identity theft program we're planning to have," Wendy replied.

"I thought so. Seems everyone in town is talking about... Wait a minute. Did you say program?" Mildred's forehead crinkled as she turned to Anne.

"Yes." Anne once again explained her conversation with Officer Banks.

"Having it here would be good," Mildred said. "And maybe we can get Rita to open up a bit and have her talk about protecting our bank accounts."

"Good luck with that," Wendy said. She clamped her mouth shut when Anne shot her a warning look.

"I think I'll make some tea if you don't mind," Mildred said as she stood up. "All this talk about identity theft sure does make a girl thirsty."

Wendy pointed to the kettle on the stove. "The water might still be warm. It won't take long to heat it up."

Mildred prepared her tea and took it back to the table. "How many do you expect at the meeting today?"

"The regulars," Anne replied. "I'm not sure if Joan plans to be here, but we have enough if she and Mary Zumfelde decide to join us."

"Mary might come?" Mildred put her teacup back on the saucer and leaned back. "Are you kidding me?"

"I doubt she'll be here," Wendy said before Anne had a chance to speak. "But it's possible."

"That woman..." Mildred's voice trailed off. "Oh, never mind. I'm sure she'll enjoy our group if she decides to come. So how did you two like the Jan Karon book we chose?"

"I enjoyed it," Anne said. "But I'd already read it."

"I liked it too," said Mildred. "The only problem I had was — "

"I rather enjoyed it." The sound of a different voice by the kitchen door caught the attention of all three women. Mary Zumfelde made her way toward them and lowered herself into a chair. "Don't let me interrupt you ladies. I just came early to see if I could help liven things up at your little book club meeting."

CHAPTER TEN

"So let me get this straight," Mary said as she sat down at the table with the rest of the Tea and Book Club attendees. She tilted her head toward Anne. "You pick a couple of books and let everyone vote on the selection?"

Anne nodded. "Yes, that's right."

"I see." Mary picked up the book in front of her, turned it over, and glanced back at Anne with a smile. "That seems like a fair enough way to select a book. Too many choices could be confusing and cause this meeting to last much longer than necessary. I've always thought efficiency is a good thing." She looked up, scanned the group, and smiled. "When do we start?"

Anne glanced at Wendy who winked.

Mildred spoke up. "We generally like to enjoy our tea and a little conversation first. This is as much a social get-together as a book club meeting."

"Oh." Mary's shoulders relaxed. "Then I suppose I should sit back and observe."

"That's an excellent idea." Mildred turned to Wendy. "I heard a couple of your children made the honor roll."

This was old news, something Anne was sure Mildred brought up to show Mary what she was talking about. Anne listened as Wendy bragged about how smart her children were. "But as you all know, they're certainly not perfect. Just this morning, we had a little skirmish over a turtleneck sweater."

Mildred laughed. "I remember mornings like that. Some days you just have to get through on prayer."

"Isn't that the truth!" Wendy said as she lifted a stack of discussion questions she'd prepared for their last book. "Take one and pass it around." She handed it to Mildred, who passed it to the next woman. "What do you think was the theme of this story?"

"I think the heroine struggled with trust," Mildred said.

Wendy nodded. "That is certainly understandable, considering all she went through as a child."

"But at some point," Mildred added, "you have to let go of the past and look at where you are now."

They went through each question on the list, some debatable and others with unanimous agreement. Anne reveled in the fact that everyone in the group seemed engaged.

Wendy's gaze darted toward the door, and then she smiled. "Hi there, Joan. I'm so glad you could make it." Wendy motioned toward one of the empty chairs as she hopped up from hers. "Have a seat. I'll get you a cup and saucer."

"You don't have to," Joan replied as she sat down.

"Oh, but I want to." Wendy took a couple steps toward the kitchen cabinets but stopped and turned to face the group. "However, we always welcome anyone who wants to arrive early to help set up. We have some of our best conversations then."

Anne watched and listened as Wendy did what she did best—make others feel at ease. She never ceased to be in awe of how relaxed Wendy was around everyone.

Mildred's jaw tightened for a moment, but she quickly got over whatever was bothering her. "Our current selection options are on the table," she said, looking directly at Joan. "We still haven't decided on our next book yet."

Joan nodded but didn't even glance at the books. She only seemed interested in Mildred, who flashed a quick look in Anne's direction.

Wendy returned with a cup and saucer that she placed in front of Joan. "Today we have a choice of jasmine, licorice, cinnamon apple, and Earl Grey. Which do you prefer?"

"I'll try the jasmine," Joan said softly, then glanced at Mildred.

"Okey-dokey." Wendy lifted the teapot with the jasmine tea and carried it over to pour into Joan's cup. "Mildred, would you mind passing the cream and sugar?"

Anne cleared her throat to get everyone's attention. "While Joan is fixing her tea, let's talk about the books. Anyone have a preference?"

They discussed the things they liked and didn't like about both selections. When asked her opinion, Joan shook her head. "I don't really care. I'm not sure if I'll have time to read it anyway."

Anne noticed a flash of disapproval on Mildred's face, but it was quickly replaced by a blank stare. "Since you don't care, let's see what everyone else thinks. Wendy?"

Wendy voiced her opinion, followed by her reasons. Everyone else nodded, including Anne.

"So let's take a vote," Anne finally said. "All in favor of this one..." She held up the book and glanced around the room and saw that all the women had their hands raised, including Joan. "Looks like it's unanimous then. I have enough for everyone to purchase it at the desk, but if you want to check it out instead, we have three copies available."

Everyone sat in uncomfortable silence until Wendy got up and took off toward the checkout desk. "I'll get everyone squared away as soon as you're ready."

Mildred hung behind. "I'll start cleaning up."

Anne had started to follow Wendy but turned around to thank Mildred. That was when she noticed Joan hovering by the kitchen door.

"I'll help Mildred," Joan said, her voice slightly louder than normal.

Mildred's hands were full, so she nodded toward the table. "If you don't mind grabbing a couple of the teapots, we can get this stuff cleared away in no time." She stopped abruptly and turned around. "When are we meeting again?"

"After Thanksgiving. Everyone will be too busy between now and then."

"Good thinking."

It appeared that Mildred was in command, so Anne smiled. "I'll be back to help finish up." Then she went to help Wendy with the selling and checking out.

After they checked out the last woman in line, Wendy turned to Anne. "I wasn't sure how it would go with Mary Zumfelde at first, but she seemed to enjoy it."

"Except for the time when she disagreed on why the heroine couldn't let go of the past," Anne reminded her.

"Yes, there was that." Wendy looked off into the distance before turning back to Anne with a soft smile. "Sort of makes me think she can relate on a personal level."

"It just goes to show that there's always something beneath what you can see in a person."

"On another note," said Wendy, the kitchen sure is getting crowded."

"It is," agreed Anne. "We might need to move it upstairs to the Reference Room soon."

"Good idea."

Anne thought about Joan and how quiet she was until she declared that she would help Mildred clean up. "Maybe I better go see how things are going in the kitchen."

Wendy gave her a nod of understanding. "Good idea. I'll cover the front until you're done."

As soon as Anne got within earshot of what sounded like an active conversation, she stopped and listened. She had to strain to hear Joan's voice.

"He keeps following me," she said. "I already told him I don't know many people in town, but that doesn't seem to matter."

"Why don't you get a restraining order?" Mildred said. "You need to show him you mean what you say."

"I don't know…" Joan paused. "He's very peculiar, and I'm not sure a restraining order will make him stop."

Curiosity welled in Anne. She wanted to barge in and ask whom they were talking about, but she didn't want them to know she'd been eavesdropping. Mildred probably wouldn't mind, but she wasn't sure about Joan. So she remained standing on the other side of the wall.

"Did you ever have someone hanging around who wouldn't leave you alone?" Joan asked.

"Yep."

"What did you do to get him to stop?"

Mildred gave her a sideways glance. "I married him."

"Oh...well, I don't think that'll happen in this case."

"I'm sure it won't," Mildred replied. "Have you ever come right out and told him that you want him to leave you alone?"

"No, not in so many words." She paused. "I've never been all that assertive. I'm thinking I might have inherited that trait from someone."

"Oh?"

"Maybe, but I'm not sure. How about you? What are the people in your family like?"

"What do you mean?" Mildred asked.

"Do you come from a loud...I mean outspoken family, or do you have some quiet people?"

Mildred didn't answer right away, so Anne decided this was a good time to make her presence known. She tiptoed a few feet away then walked as loudly as she could. When she got to the kitchen, both Mildred and Joan had their eyes focused in her direction.

"Hey, ladies." She glanced around the sparkling kitchen. "You didn't have to do everything."

"It goes fast when there are two people working," Mildred said. "Joan is a hard worker."

Anne grinned at Joan. "I can see that. Thank you for helping out."

"It's the least I could do."

Mildred patted her on the shoulder. "We had a nice conversation while we cleaned."

Anne shifted uncomfortably as she tried to act as though she didn't know. Fortunately, Mildred came to her rescue.

"Joan, I hope you don't mind if I tell Anne about the guy you mentioned."

At first, Joan appeared panicked, but she finally nodded. "I suppose that's okay."

Mildred frowned. "Some man has been following her around, and he fits the description of the guy who was outside the library checking the meters."

"Yes," Joan agreed. "That's him. In fact, he followed me here one day, and he started asking me a bunch of questions."

At least that explained why she'd seen them talking. "Had you ever seen him before you came to Blue Hill?"

Joan shook her head. "The first time I saw him was at the inn. He and Charlotte were chatting when I checked in."

"Is he friends with Charlotte and Henry?" Mildred asked.

"I'm not sure." Joan cast a nervous look in Anne's direction before turning back to Mildred. "He was there to look at some things to help save them money."

"That's what he was here for too," Anne said. "He implied that Alex sent him here to do an energy audit."

"But he was misleading you, right?" Mildred said.

Anne nodded. "How did you know?"

Mildred tapped her head with her index finger. "I'm smart." She broke into a smile and then giggled. "Actually, Alex told me and said to let him know if I spot him around the library."

Joan frowned. "You don't think he's dangerous, do you?"

"I have no idea," Mildred replied, "but I wouldn't take any chances if I were you."

"You're so smart," Joan said. "Does this run in your family?"

Mildred tilted her head and gave Joan a questioning look. "Why do you keep asking me so many questions about my family?"

"I didn't mean anything—"

Mildred held up her hands and cut her off. "Never mind. I didn't mean to come across sounding so harsh. You don't have to explain anything."

Anne found herself holding her breath, hoping Joan would explain anyway, but she didn't. Instead, she picked up her purse from the counter. "I better go now."

"Don't forget to pick up the book club selection on your way out," Mildred called after her.

Once she was gone, Anne leaned against the counter, folded her arms, and stared at the floor. "Did you enjoy your chat with Joan?"

Mildred tilted her head and narrowed her eyes before her expression softened. "Why yes, I enjoyed it very much."

The sound of Wendy's footsteps captured their attention. "Officer Banks wants to talk to you, Anne. I told him to wait by the desk and I'd come and get you."

"Thanks."

Mildred lifted an eyebrow. "Want me to stick around while you talk to Officer Banks?"

"Not unless you need to," Anne replied. "I'm sure he's just here to discuss the identity theft protection seminar we're planning."

"Then I'll leave. You can give me the details later. Want me to send Officer Banks on back?"

Mildred and Wendy glanced at Anne, and she nodded. "Yes, that'll be fine. We can talk in the kitchen."

"I'll hang out at the checkout desk," Wendy said as she followed Mildred toward the front. "Chad doesn't have football practice this afternoon, so I can stay longer. I don't want to miss anything here. From the look on Michael's face, things are about to get interesting."

Mildred's laughter faded as she and Wendy went to the checkout area. Anne wondered what Wendy meant by that last comment.

Chapter Eleven

"Coffee or tea?" Anne gestured toward the table. "I also have some leftover pastries from the Tea and Book Club meeting."

"Coffee sounds good." Officer Banks pulled out a chair and sat down facing Anne.

She quickly prepared the police officer's coffee and arranged a variety of pastries on a platter before placing them on the table. He picked one up, took a bite, and gave her a thumbs-up. "Delicious."

Anne poured his coffee and herself another cup of tea before sitting down across the table from him. "What brings you here?"

"Good news," Officer Banks said. "I'll be getting all the materials, including a short video, on how to avert most identity theft. Of course, there are still no guarantees, but if we make it difficult for the thieves, they'll move on to an easier target."

"It's such a shame that anyone has to worry about this," Anne said.

He nodded. "Blue Hill hasn't always been crime free, but concerned citizens such as yourself have been able to help us clean things up pretty quickly."

"That's good to know." She set her teacup in the saucer and leaned forward on her elbows. "So what can I do?"

"You offered the library, which is an excellent place to hold these seminars." He sighed. "Oh, did I tell you we've had a wave of people inquiring about this? I doubt we can accommodate everyone who is interested in one session."

"That's fine. I'll provide space as many times as you need it." She shifted in her seat. "We have enough room in the Resource Room for twenty-five people to sit comfortably."

He looked her in the eye. "Let's have a sign-up sheet. We can let Grace know so she can put something in the paper. This will need to be an ongoing program. After the initial set of seminars, perhaps we can have them once per quarter."

"I like that idea. The more knowledge our residents are armed with, the less likely they'll be victims."

"So how are the kids doing?" Officer Banks asked. "Ben did a nice job on his safety poster."

"You've seen it already? He just turned it in last Friday."

The officer cleared his throat. "I've already said too much. I think I'll let Ben tell you about it later. Does Liddie like her teacher?"

Anne nodded as she eyed him suspiciously. "Yes, in fact she loves everything about school."

Officer Banks squared his shoulders and lifted his head with pride. "The elementary school in Blue Hill has the best teachers in the county, and we pride ourselves in providing an education that is second to none."

Anne grinned. Officer Banks' pride ran deep since he was born and raised in Blue Hill.

"When will we have the first seminar?" Anne asked.

"Considering how many people have been affected, it's beginning to be a matter of urgency to do what we can to prevent future crime. I wondered…" He gave her an apologetic look. "Would next week be too soon?"

It was a little soon, but Anne was willing to do whatever was needed. "No, not at all. Do you think we'll have a decent turnout with such short notice?"

He shook his head. "I've already talked to some of the folks who said it can't happen soon enough. As soon as I receive the materials, I'll give you a call to set up a time for the first seminar. We'll start with those who have already been affected. I think they'll be the most motivated." He stood up and started to pick up his cup. "I need to get on back to the office and make a few calls."

Anne pointed to the cup. "Leave that there. I'll get it later."

As she walked him through the library toward the front door, he explained how he'd need the room set up. She nodded as she thought about how the Research Room was perfect since they already had a screen and a stage. The shelves were moveable so they could be rearranged as needed. The only thing they'd have to do is move a few tables to make room for the regular size chairs.

"I'm going to stop off at the bank and let Rita know what we're doing." He paused and frowned. "Her reaction was rather strange when I first told her what we had planned."

"I found her reaction strange too." Anne saw a curious look on Officer Banks' face, and she didn't want to expound on her own thoughts, so she decided to backpedal. "She's probably just feeling overwhelmed by the number of people whose accounts have been affected."

"Yeah, maybe that's it." He reached for the doorknob. "Thanks, Anne. Talk to you later."

She turned around and strode toward the desk, where Wendy stood grinning, her arms folded. "We don't waste time around here, do we? All you have to do is say 'boo,' and we send out the big guns."

Anne laughed. "And that's a good thing. We don't want to give the bad guy…or girls…more time to wreak havoc on our town."

"Absolutely," Wendy agreed.

Anne told Wendy her thoughts about using the Resource Room. "We have more flexibility and floor space."

They discussed several ideas between helping patrons. An hour later, the phone rang. Wendy answered and handed it to Anne. "Officer Banks."

"They overnighted the materials, so they were here when I got back. What do you think about holding the first seminar next Monday?"

Anne thought for a couple seconds. "We can do that. Do you want me to have flyers on the checkout desk?"

"Why don't you just put up a notice on your bulletin board? I already know of a dozen people who will likely plan to be there, and I don't want to turn any of them away since they're already victims. If more people sign up than we have room for, we can push them back to the next seminar."

"What would you like me to do besides have the room ready?" Anne asked.

"Do you have some volunteers who can help with handouts and moderating?"

Anne glanced at Wendy who was always eager to assist with whatever was needed. "That shouldn't be a problem. I'm sure we'll have plenty of people who will be happy to help."

"Fine. I'll come over and check out the logistics sometime tomorrow."

After they hung up, Anne leaned against the counter. Things were happening so quickly she needed to brace herself.

"Well?" Wendy's eyes lit up with excitement. "What did he say?"

Anne relayed the information. "Looks like this will be a quarterly program as long as people are interested, so we might as well figure out when to slot it."

"Maybe we can change it each time," Wendy said. "People who work during the week might prefer Saturdays, but some of the retirees might prefer weekdays."

"Good thinking. We can sit down with Officer Banks at a later date and plan the schedule for the next year. In the meantime, we'll need to line up several to make sure everyone who wants to attend will have the opportunity to."

Wendy glanced at the clock on the wall. "Time to head on home and start supper. Chad is a wonderful daddy, but I'm afraid he's like a kid when it comes to mealtime. He considers carrot cake a vegetable. I'm sure he's given the kids as much candy as they want already."

"Then you'd better get on home and rescue the family from all that sugar."

"See you tomorrow." Wendy breezed out of the library, leaving Anne standing there alone.

This had been an incredibly full day, with events that Anne hadn't expected. She reflected on the discoveries until Liddie and Ben came running in.

"Mommy, Mommy, guess what happened to Ben!" Liddie ran straight into Anne's arms, nearly knocking her over with the impact.

"Don't ruin it for me. Let me tell her," Ben said, the tone of his voice belying his words.

Liddie had pulled away and started jumping up and down. "You'd better hurry up, 'cause I can't wait."

Anne placed her hand on Liddie's shoulder as she looked at her son with concern. "What happened?"

His face was tinged with dark pink, and a slight smile tweaked his lips. "I won the safety poster contest."

Okay, now what Officer Banks said made sense. "That's awesome, Ben. When did you find out?"

"In morning assembly."

"I'm so proud of you." Anne let go of Liddie and reached out to Ben for a hug.

He stiffened and shuffled his feet. "It's no big deal."

"It is too a big deal," Liddie argued. "All my friends think Ben is the coolest big brother." She grinned and cut an adoring gaze over to Ben. "And I think so too."

"I agree with you and your friends," Anne said as she turned to Ben. "I'm super proud of you."

"It's no big deal." Ben shrugged. "I'm starving."

"Then let's go fix a snack…something special to celebrate your big win."

"Can I have a cookie?" he asked.

Anne winked. "Even better. We have some leftover pastries from the tea, and you can have your pick."

Liddie darted toward the kitchen, and Ben and Anne followed.

"Ben, why don't you sit at the head of the table, and Liddie and I will bring you whatever you want."

Ben's combination look of embarrassment and humility quickly gave way to satisfaction. "Got any cream puffs?"

Anne nodded. "Yes, in fact, we have two left—one for each of you. Hot chocolate, ginger ale, or tea?"

Both kids wanted hot chocolate, so as soon as the children were in place at the table, Anne heated up the milk. Days like this made her think about Eric. The Lord sure had been kind when He'd blessed them with such delightful children.

Anne poured the hot cocoa and placed it in front of the children then started to prepare herself another cup of tea when the sound of a barking dog outside the back window startled her. Normally quiet, Hershey let out a short bark in response, but quieted down when Ben rubbed his ears. As soon as Ben stopped petting him, Hershey ran to the window and let out a low growl.

Chapter Twelve

Anne went straight to the window, pulled the curtain slightly to the side, and strained to see what Hershey was barking at. "It's someone walking a dog."

"Whose dog is it, Mom?" Ben asked as he and Hershey joined her by the window. "Isn't that Mr. Parnell? I didn't know he had a dog."

"I didn't know either." Anne made a split-second decision to go out and talk to her neighbor from down the street. "You stay right here with Liddie and Hershey, while I go out there and see what's going on."

As soon as Ben nodded, she took off out the door and ran across the yard toward Mr. Parnell and the large black-and-tan dog he was walking, which Anne guessed to be a Rottweiler mix. When she got close enough to hear the dog panting, it stopped, turned to face her, and let out a series of deep rapid-fire barks. Anne's heart thudded, but then the dog stopped barking, tilted its head, and gave her a goofy look with its tongue hanging out of its mouth.

"I think he likes you," Mr. Parnell said, his voice raspy.

"Why was he barking?"

"Some fella was wandering around your backyard, went up to your door. But before he had a chance to do anything, Hank let him know we were there." Mr. Parnell lifted his chin with pride. "I've got a good watchdog here."

"Did you get a good look at the man?" Anne asked. "Could you describe him?"

Mr. Parnell rubbed the back of his neck, squinted his eyes, and pursed his lips. "Well, let's see here. He was a skinny fella. I think he was about this tall..." He held his hand up level with his own head. "On second thought, maybe he was about this tall." He raised his hand a few inches. "Yeah, I'm pretty sure he was a little taller than me. Couldn't see his hair on account of that cap he had on. He was wearing what looked like gray dungarees and a black jacket...or was it navy blue?" Mr. Parnell shrugged. "It was sorta hard to tell since there wasn't much light."

Obviously he wouldn't be much help in the description department, so Anne decided to try something else. "Did you see where he went?"

"Yeah, he took off running that way." He pointed in the direction opposite of town.

Anne squatted down to pet the dog. Once her hand touched his head, he leaned into her and let out a low moan of satisfaction. "Thanks for running him off," Anne said. "I can't imagine any legitimate reason anyone would be sneaking around here when it will be dark soon. And if they need something from the library, they should just come on in."

"Maybe it's that person who is out there robbing people blind. That's why I got ol' Hank here. I figured I needed some protection from the bad guys. I used to be able to scare the wits out of people, but now that I have a few years under my belt, I'm not as menacing."

"Have there been break-ins around here?" Anne asked.

"Nope, not as far as I know … at least not break-ins. Just people going after bank accounts and credit cards." He laughed again. "I'm not sure Hank can protect me from that, but having him sure makes me feel safer."

"Would you like to come in for some hot cocoa?" Anne asked.

"No, I better be getting on home, or the wife will worry about me. She thinks I'm just taking Hank for a walk around the block, and I'm miles away from home."

Actually, he was less than two blocks from where Anne knew he and his wife Gloria lived, but she didn't say anything. "I'd love for you and your wife to stop by sometime. We have all the classics and most of the current releases."

"These old eyes aren't as good as they used to be either. Most of the time, Gloria and I watch that big-screen television our son gave us last year."

"We have a nice collection of large-print books."

"I just might stop by sometime soon, then. My wife sure did like her romance novels back in the day."

"We have those too." Anne smiled. "I need to get back inside. Thanks again for looking after us."

He turned around with his hand waving over his head. "I'll let you know if I see anything else suspicious. We look after our own here in Blue Hill, ya know."

"I know, and I'm very happy about that."

Both children and Hershey hovered by the door, nearly tripping Anne as she went back inside. "What happened, Mommy?" Liddie asked with wide eyes.

Anne didn't want to worry either of them, so she smiled and led them back to the table. "Mr. Parnell's dog saw something and started barking."

Later that night, after the children went to bed, Anne lay awake thinking about what Mr. Parnell had said about the man wandering around the library yard. She wondered if it was the identity thief or the meter guy, but why would he be working when it was nearly dark?

* * *

The next day, as soon as the children went to school and Wendy arrived, Anne decided to get out for a while and visit some of the women from the Tea and Book Club. She started to go to Mildred's house first but changed her mind and headed toward Mary Zumfelde's house. She lived in the more exclusive area on a tree-lined street with larger Victorian homes. Mary's husband and his family owned several of the businesses in town. Aunt Edie once told her that if it weren't for the Zumfeldes, Blue Hill wouldn't be as nice as it was today.

Mary greeted her at the door, dressed elegantly as always. "What can I do for you today?" she asked.

Anne offered an apologetic look. "I'm sorry, I should have called. If you're going some — "

"I'm not going anywhere." Mary's expression softened with a smile as she stepped back. "Do come in. I'll put on a pot of tea, unless you'd rather have coffee. There's still some of that left from breakfast."

Anne followed Mary through the expansive foyer and down the hall to the kitchen in the back of the house. Mary pointed to a small table nestled in the corner, beside a very messy shelf filled with books of all sizes, papers sticking out from between them.

"Why don't you sit facing the window?" Mary offered. "We have the cutest little squirrel that likes to come up to the window while I'm sitting here." She pulled down two cups. "Coffee or tea?"

"Coffee will be fine."

"As I was saying, I keep a squirrel feeder close to the window so he won't eat all the birdseed I have out for the birds."

Anne looked out the window and saw that Mary had created a haven for small wildlife with a squirrel feeder by the window, a bird feeder hanging from a post, a couple of birdhouses on tree limbs, and a large birdbath in the center of the yard. A small flower garden in the far corner of the yard was ideal for attracting butterflies.

"Your yard is so pretty," Anne said.

"Thank you, dear. Your aunt Edie helped me plan it. Did you know that she was very good with plants?" Mary placed the coffee cups on the table and pulled the sugar bowl closer. "Cream?"

"No, thank you." Anne accepted the coffee and took a sip.

"To what do I owe the pleasure of your company?" Mary asked.

"I...well, I just needed to get out for a little while, and I thought I'd visit a few people."

Mary started to lift her cup but paused and put it down. "That's not all, is it?" She lifted her eyebrows and studied Anne.

"Does this have anything to do with what's been going on around here lately—the identity theft problem?"

"Actually, yes." Anne sighed. "Apparently someone was lurking around our yard last evening."

"Who?" Mary's face had scrunched into a scowl. "I mean, did you see whoever it was?"

Anne shook her head. "No, I heard a dog barking, so I went outside to see what was going on. Mr. Parnell was out walking his dog, Hank, and he said Hank had barked and scared someone off the property."

"I didn't know Claude had a dog."

"He said he got one for protection after this identity theft started."

Mary started to laugh, but she quickly caught herself. "I don't think a dog will do much good to protect his identity."

"He said the dog makes him feel safer," Anne replied.

"I'm sure. I would have a dog if I didn't think it would scare away the birds and squirrels." Mary leaned back in her chair. "To be honest with you, I'm starting to get concerned. Blue Hill has always been such a safe haven that we were ripe for the picking." She looked at Anne with a deep sadness in her eyes. "Our warmth and kindness make us vulnerable to someone who likes to take advantage of people."

This was exactly what bothered Anne. Anyone with a crooked streak could come into town and cause trouble before anyone had a chance to react. "I've been talking to Officer Banks at the police department about holding some seminars at the library. He has a program to teach people how to protect their identities."

"Brilliant idea. We've never had to give such things much thought in the past, but the folks in this town are smart. We can learn."

"I agree." Anne sat back and stared out the window for a few minutes as silence fell between them.

"Anne," Mary said softly.

Anne quickly turned to Mary. "Sorry, I was lost in thought."

"I know you were." Mary offered a sweet smile. "If you need any help with the seminars, please don't hesitate to call on me. I'll help you get word out to my friends, and I'm sure they'll want to get involved as well."

The offer warmed Anne's heart, especially coming from Mary. She glanced around the kitchen. It had a very homey feeling—not at all what she would have expected in Mary's house. "I appreciate that."

They chatted for a few more minutes before Anne stood up to leave. "Remember that we won't have another book club meeting for a few weeks—at least not until after Thanksgiving."

"I left before it was decided, but that makes sense," Mary said as she got up. "I'll walk you to the door."

Anne left Mary's house and drove back toward the library. She slowed down when she noticed the rental car in the inn parking lot, but she didn't stop.

The flag was down on the mailbox, indicating that her outgoing letters had been picked up, so she checked the mail before going inside. There was nothing in there, which was unusual. Until now, there hadn't been a single day since she'd arrived that either she or the library didn't receive mail.

Chapter Thirteen

Wendy greeted her with a smile as she walked into the library, but the smile quickly faded. "What's wrong?"

"Did you check the mail today?"

"No." Wendy shook her head, as she appeared confused. "I don't think the mailman has been here yet."

"I wouldn't have thought so either. I put some personal letters in the mailbox for pick up, and they're not there now."

"Oh, then maybe he came, and I didn't hear him. We've had a busy morning." Wendy gestured for Anne to follow her into the Nonfiction Room, where several of the older Blue Hill citizens were lined up at the four computers with others standing behind them. "We've had a run on computer time."

"Interesting." Anne watched the man on the end type with two fingers. "Any idea why?"

Wendy shrugged. "I haven't had a chance to ask, between folks calling, asking about the seminar, and people coming in wanting books on how to protect identity theft."

"Too bad we have to deal with this, but at least we're doing something about it."

"Yeah, I know." Wendy leaned around and grinned at someone behind Anne. "It's good to see you, Joan."

Anne spun around to greet Joan but stopped before she got a word out. Joan had a scratch across her cheek, and one side of her face was swollen and red.

"What happened?"

Joan frowned. "Nothing."

The sound of a barking dog at the front door captured Anne's attention. It sounded just like Hank. She excused herself to see what was going on.

As soon as she opened the door, Hank bounded into the library, nearly knocking Anne over. "No, Hank!" Mr. Parnell fumbled with the leash but managed to hang onto it. "Sit."

Joan's eyes lit up with fear as she took off running through the library. That seemed to give Hank a second wind. He pulled so hard Mr. Parnell couldn't hold him back.

"Stop, you crazy mutt!"

Wendy stepped in front of the man with both hands on her hips, blocking him from going after his dog that had finally pulled free. "What is going on here?"

"It's that man I saw last night." Mr. Parnell pointed toward the back of the library. "As soon as we got here, he saw that man, and I couldn't stop him."

Anne froze in place. "What man?"

"That one," he said. "The crazy one who's running from my dog."

Wendy slapped her forehead and rolled her eyes. "That's not a man. That's Joan. She's one of our Tea and Book Club members."

"Oh yeah?" Mr. Parnell stepped closer to Wendy and glared at her. "What's she doing lurking around the back of the library?"

Anne's senses returned. "I better go check on Joan and make sure she's okay." She started toward the kitchen, where Joan had run, and found her hovering behind the table holding a chair between herself and Mr. Parnell's dog, her eyes widened with fear as the big dog jumped around, trying to get to her.

"He wants to bite me," Joan said with a shaky breath.

"Of course he does," Mr. Parnell said. "He doesn't like people who run from him."

Anne opened the cupboard and pulled out one of Hershey's dog treats. "Maybe you can lure him away with one of these," she said as she handed it to Mr. Parnell.

The man took the treat, smacked his lips, and bent over toward Hank. "Daddy has a nice goody for you." He dangled it so Hank could see it. "Would you like something yummy to eat?"

Hank glanced back and forth between his master and Joan, who watched with trepidation. Finally, he pranced toward Mr. Parnell. Everyone let out a sigh of relief as the dog chose the treat over attacking Joan.

"If you keep acting this way," Mr. Parnell said with a quick sideways glance at Anne, "you won't be welcome at other people's houses."

"Why don't you take him home and come back?" Anne asked. "I'd like to show you the large-print section."

Joan still had a tight grip on the chair as she remained behind the table, so Anne took a step toward the back door. Fortunately, Mr. Parnell and Hank followed.

Once they were outside, Mr. Parnell pointed to the door. "You realize you're harboring a criminal in there, don't you?"

"I hardly think—"

"That's the problem. You aren't thinking. Look at the way she's dressed, I thought she was a man. What decent woman would go around town like that and lurk in the shadows?"

Anne offered what she hoped was a reassuring smile. "We'll be fine."

Mr. Parnell lifted his hands in surrender. "Okay, I get that you don't want my help…or Hank's. You might regret it later."

"Come back later, okay?"

He walked away without replying. Anne tried her best not to worry, but she hated the fact that she'd upset her neighbor.

When she went back inside, Wendy and Joan were standing beside the table. Anne grinned. "I think you're safe now."

"What he said wasn't true. I wasn't lurking. I knew the library was closed last night, but I saw lights on, and I thought maybe we could talk."

Wendy backed toward the door. "I need to go back to the checkout desk. If you need me, just holler."

As soon as she left, Anne turned to face Joan. "What did you need to talk about?"

Joan appeared to struggle with the right words, until she finally hung her head. "Never mind. I think I'll go ahead and buy the book for the book club."

"Is that all?" Anne stared at the woman, wondering what was going on beneath that baseball cap. "I thought you wanted to talk."

"Maybe some other time." Joan flashed a brief, forced smile. "I need to go, so why don't I just buy the book and leave?"

Anne knew she couldn't force Joan to talk when she wasn't ready, so she sighed and nodded. "Okay, let's go back up to the front. I put the extra copies behind the checkout desk."

Joan paid with cash. "I'll try to get this read before the next meeting." She stepped back and frowned. "But you never mentioned when the next meeting was."

"It'll be after Thanksgiving. I'll post a notice on the bulletin board and send you an e-mail if you have one."

With a closed-mouth smile, Joan shook her head. "I don't have access to e-mail."

"Not even on your phone?"

"No, I can only make phone calls with it." Joan glanced down at her sneaker-clad feet. "I need to go now."

After she left, Wendy turned to Anne. "That was very odd. You'd think she'd have more to say by now. What do you think is up with her?"

Anne shrugged. "I have no idea. She's obviously worried about something. Maybe she'll eventually get comfortable enough to tell us what it is."

"You don't think she has anything to do with the…" Wendy grimaced. "You know, the identity —"

"I don't know, but I certainly hope not." Anne spun around and pretended to look for something behind the counter.

"That would be just plain weird if she was the thief." Wendy shivered and rubbed her arms. "To think that we've been hanging out with the person we're looking for is something you only see in movies."

"Let's not worry about something we know nothing about."

Wendy nodded. "You're right. All we need to concern ourselves with is our patrons."

"Right."

A man came in and asked where to find information on the Revolutionary War, so Wendy left to help him. Anne added some entries to the computer catalog until Wendy returned.

"I love volunteering here," Wendy said. "One minute I'm helping a group of women find out who their ancestors are, and the next I'm searching for war books. And then some days I go from reading children's stories to recommending mystery novels to fiction fans."

"It's the best job in the entire world," Anne agreed.

Mildred walked in and headed straight for the checkout counter. "Reporting in for my volunteer work."

"You've been working a lot lately," Anne said. "Why don't you take some time off?"

"I like it here. I don't want to miss out on anything interesting."

Wendy laughed. "That's true. This does seem to be the hub for all the action these days."

"Besides, the Miller twins are gone for the day." Mildred turned to Anne. "And you mentioned that you might need to have some books shelved?"

"Yes, there are some in each of the rooms. I put the stacks by the door."

Mildred started to walk away but stopped and turned around. "The strangest thing just happened."

Wendy and Anne looked at each other then back to Mildred. "Strange?" Anne asked. "Like what?"

"Right after I left to come here, I saw Joan heading toward my house, so I turned around to see if she needed me. She'd stopped in front of my house, but when she saw me, she took off."

"Did you make eye contact?" Wendy asked.

"I thought so." Mildred tapped her chin with her index finger. "But maybe not. Now that I think about it, I'm not sure she even saw me."

"She was probably looking for something," Anne said.

Wendy lifted an eyebrow. "Or *someone*." Wendy looked directly at Mildred. "I've noticed that she seems awfully drawn to you."

Mildred forced a laugh. "I have noticed. I wonder why."

Anne noticed Mildred's look of consternation, so there was no doubt she was covering up how she really felt. "Make sure you don't tell her too much, okay?"

Mildred feigned a startled look. "You don't think—?" She dropped the pretense. "Honestly, there's not much to tell, but I promise I won't say too much. Don't forget that I have quite a bit of life experience."

After she left to do the shelving, Wendy shook her head. "She's no different from the rest of us."

"What do you mean?" Anne asked.

"She loves Blue Hill, and she's concerned about what's happening. When someone new comes along and acts like Joan is acting, she can't help but wonder if there's something we need to know about her."

Anne reared back with her eyebrows raised. "You got all that from that brief conversation?"

"Yeah, pretty much. I do read a lot of mysteries, ya know. One thing I've learned is that you have to watch what people do and how they act to fill in the blanks of what they're not saying."

"I think you might have missed your calling," Anne said. "You should have been a detective."

"Oh, trust me, I am. Like yesterday when Hannah couldn't find her shoes, I managed to track them down in Emily's room."

Anne laughed. "What were they doing there?"

Wendy maintained a grin as she rolled her eyes. "Emily still likes to play dress up with my clothes, but Chad was on the phone in our room, and he had the door locked. The only alternative was to raid her sister's closet."

"I'd love to be a fly on the wall at your house. Your family has so much fun," Anne said.

"Yeah." Wendy chuckled. "A laugh a minute. Sometimes I wish they could be a little *less* fun."

Mildred came out from the Nonfiction Room with a book in one hand and a slip of paper in the other. "Do either of you know what this is all about?"

Anne took the paper and studied it. "It looks like a series of bank account numbers." She handed it to Wendy, who agreed.

"Why would there be several account numbers on one piece of paper?" Wendy nodded toward the book in Mildred's hand. "What book is that and who checked it out last?"

Chapter Fourteen

Anne pulled up the catalog on the computer and typed in the book's title, *The Pearl*. She studied the page for a moment before looking directly at Mildred. "This book hasn't been checked out for about a month. Where was it?"

"Smack-dab in the middle of the stack of books to be shelved."

Wendy flipped through the book and stopped when she got to a page with pencil marks. "Looks like someone jotted down some notes and erased them later."

"Can you see what they wrote?" Anne asked.

The three of them leaned over the counter and tried to decipher the notes, but they'd been erased well enough to make it impossible. "Maybe we should get forensics to take a look at it," Wendy said.

"Forensics?" Mildred laughed. "Does the Blue Hill police department have a forensics department?"

Wendy shrugged. "I don't know, but I'm sure they have someone who can handle it."

Anne wasn't so sure about that, but she didn't want to assume anything. "Maybe we shouldn't handle the book any more than we already have, just in case…"

"That's right," Wendy said as she placed the book on the counter. "We don't want to mess up the fingerprints. I'll get a plastic bag and drop it off at the police department on my way home. It might be that one piece of evidence that solves this case."

Mildred tilted her head and looked at Wendy. "How do you know so much about police work?"

"She reads a lot of mysteries," Anne said.

Wendy held up a finger. "And I don't miss a police show on TV. That's one thing Chad and I both enjoy after the kids go to bed."

"Then you're the expert on this matter," Mildred joked.

"How many more books do you have left to put away?" Anne asked.

"Just a few. I wanted to call this to your attention before I continued." Mildred winked at Anne. "And good thing I did because time is obviously of the essence." She went back to the Nonfiction Room, leaving Wendy and Anne laughing.

After Mildred left the desk, Wendy and Anne chatted between phone calls and helping patrons. Finally, Anne made a decision.

"I think we need to stop trying to speculate and leave the detective work up to the professionals."

"That sounds good," Wendy said. "But you and I both know we don't have enough policemen and detectives to be everywhere at once, and they'll need our eyes and ears."

"Well, I suppose that's true, and I agree that we need to let them know when we find out anything that might relate, but..." Anne's thoughts trailed off.

"I know what you're talking about," Wendy said. "And I agree. We should present the facts to the detectives and stop trying to speculate about everyone who appears the least bit suspicious."

"Exactly."

"Now that that's settled, I need to head on home." Wendy picked up the plastic bag with the book and note. "I'll drop this off at the police department on my way."

Half an hour later Officer Banks called. "Wendy didn't have time to talk, but she said you could fill me in on this book and list of account numbers."

Anne told him everything she knew. During their conversation, Mildred came and joined her behind the counter to help with patrons so she could talk.

After she got off the phone, Anne leaned against the counter, closed her eyes, said a short prayer, and opened them to see Mildred smiling at her. "Good girl. It's always best to turn to the Lord first." Mildred leaned over and checked to see if anyone was coming before she turned back to Anne. "So what did Officer Banks have to say about what we found?"

"He seems to think it might help in the investigation, so thank you for bringing it to me."

Mildred flipped her hand dismissively. "You don't have to thank me."

"He wants to start the seminars as soon as possible."

"Did he say when?"

Anne nodded. "Saturday."

"As in this coming Saturday, the day after tomorrow?"

"Yes."

"How does he think we'll be able to get the word out to enough people?"

"He said he already has enough people for the first one—all the people who have been victims. He said every one of them will be here."

"Oh." Mildred frowned. "I wonder why Claire didn't say anything about it. I talked to her this morning."

"He just got off the phone with everyone when Wendy showed up with the evidence," Anne explained. "He's calling Rita next to let her know about the account numbers."

"So what's bothering you?"

Anne tilted her head. "What do you mean?"

"Something obviously bothers you about what you just said."

The last thing Anne wanted to do was cause a problem for Rita, but she couldn't help but hold onto some suspicion that the branch manager wasn't who she appeared to be. "I don't know. This whole thing is just so unsettling."

"You're right," Mildred agreed. "It's very unsettling, but remember Who is in control of everything."

"True." Anne took a deep breath and slowly let it out. "Okay, I'll try to take your advice again. Worrying about this won't make it go away."

"Good girl." Mildred picked up her coat and purse. "Do you need me tomorrow?"

"I think we'll be fine, but if you can come on Saturday to help out with the seminar, I'd really appreciate it. I don't know what Officer Banks will expect me to do."

"I'm sure he'll tell you, but don't worry. I would never desert you. I'll be here ready and willing to do whatever it takes to make sure it's a success."

Mildred gave her a brief hug. Anne watched the older woman walk to the door and thought about how blessed she was to be surrounded by such loving, caring people. Sometimes she had to pinch herself to be sure she wasn't dreaming.

When Anne had a free moment, she went back outside to check the mail again, and there was still nothing in the box. She knew that by now the mailman had come, so she went inside and called the local post office to ask if they knew whether or not she even had mail.

"You should have gotten a big stack today," the clerk said. "I helped sort it, and I remember that you had quite a bit. You should have also received the flyers that go out to everyone. Why?"

"My mailbox was empty."

"Uh-oh. Hold on a sec." The postal clerk covered the mouthpiece, but Anne could still hear her telling someone else in the post office about her situation. When she came back, Anne caught her crisp tone. "You need to file a report."

"Has this happened to anyone else?" Anne asked.

"Oh yes, quite a bit, especially lately. Something bad is definitely going on in Blue Hill."

Anne told her about the identity theft seminar series. "The first one is this Saturday, but I think it's already filled."

"Next time you have one, we'll be happy to post a flyer in the post office lobby," the clerk said. "And don't hesitate to ask for help if you need it. I was born and raised here, and I'll do whatever it takes to protect the town I love."

"Thanks."

"In the meantime, we'll send someone out there to talk to you tomorrow."

"What kind of information do you need?" Anne asked. "I want to make sure I have all the information available."

"It's just a form. You can fill it out online, but since this seems to be a trend lately, I'd like to have someone from the post office take the information in person," the clerk said. "Oh, another thing. Until we get to the bottom of this, I'll ask your mail carrier to deliver all your mail inside."

"That's a good idea," Anne agreed.

"Let me know if there's anything else we can do for you."

Anne sighed. "Other than the missing mail, I'm fine."

After she hung up, she tried to think about what might have been in her mailbox. She paid all her bills online, so she didn't think there would be anything that would compromise her identity. The problem was, she would never be sure unless something happened, and then it would be too late.

She was glad when her children arrived a few minutes later. Alex and Ryan were right behind them.

"How was your day?" Alex's face appeared tight with stress.

"Crazy," she admitted. "Looks like you didn't have such a great one."

He shook his head. "My day was insane. Two of my subcontractors called in because they're having to straighten out their records after having their identities stolen. One of them had his entire savings cleaned out."

"Looks like I might be the next target," Anne said. "Someone took the mail out of the box before I could get to it."

Alex shook his head. "If you want, I can install a locking mail box for the library." Alex's jaw tightened. "I really hate that someone has come into this peaceful town and shaken our sense of security."

"I know." Silence fell between them for a few seconds until Anne decided to share some of her thoughts. "We have had some new people come to town lately. I'm not saying I think one of them is the thief, but I can't help…" Her voice trailed off.

He nodded. "I've thought about that too. We have a brand new bank manager with access to all the accounts, new inn owners, and a woman who suddenly appears at your Tea and Book Club meetings."

"Don't forget about that guy who was checking everyone's meters," Anne reminded him.

"I almost forgot about him. Have you seen him lately?"

Anne shook her head. "Not in the past several days."

Liddie walked up to Anne and leaned into her, rubbing her eyes. "Mommy, I'm hungry."

"And sleepy too, I see." Anne put her arm around Liddie and turned back to Alex. "Are you coming to the seminar on Saturday?"

"Of course. I'll even be here early to help set up." Alex leaned back and got Ryan's attention. "Let's go. We still have to do some grocery shopping on the way home."

Ryan groaned but followed his uncle out the door. Anne waited until she heard the sound of Alex's truck pull away before setting out snacks in the library kitchen.

"After you're finished, put your dishes in the sink." Anne turned to Ben. "How much homework do you have?"

"Just math. Mr. Layton gave us some time to do homework before we went home."

Anne knew that some of the parents had spoken to the teacher about the volume of work, but she didn't mention it to Ben. Instead, she looked at Liddie. "Do you need a nap, or would you rather look at picture books until the library closes?"

Liddie propped her elbow on the table and placed her head on her hand. "I want to look at picture books."

Anne managed to keep a straight face. She knew that as soon as Liddie got comfortable in one of the beanbag chairs in the Children's Room, she'd fall fast asleep.

"I need to go back to the checkout desk," Anne said.

"Okay, Mom."

As Anne left the kitchen, she heard Ben talking softly to Liddie. "Want me to read you a story before I do my homework?"

"Yeah. Can you read *Winnie the Pooh*?"

"Sure."

A sense of well-being washed over Anne. Ben preferred action stories, so she knew he was sacrificing his time for his sister to give Anne a break.

About an hour before closing, someone called about the Saturday seminar. "Mildred told me about it."

"I'm sorry, but that one is filled," Anne said. "We'll be having more soon. Would you like to be added to an e-mail list?"

She jotted the information at the top of a sheet of paper. As soon as she hung up, another call inquiring about the seminar came in. By the time she closed the library, she had a half dozen people on her list who wanted to be notified about future seminars.

CHAPTER FIFTEEN

A lex arrived early Saturday morning and immediately started preparing the space for the seminar. Anne was relieved that he'd already spoken with Officer Banks to find out what was needed. She'd forgotten that little detail.

Mildred came in and got right to work, taking the handouts and placing them by the door. "I'll give these to people as they come in," she said. "Wendy said she'd sign everyone in."

Anne laughed. "Leave me something to do."

"Oh, trust me, you'll be running around doing all the important stuff." Mildred grinned. "If it weren't for you, none of this would be happening, and there's no telling how many more people would fall victim to this thief."

Officer Banks arrived and took a quick look around the space. "Perfect." He nodded toward Alex. "Can you give me a hand with some of the boxes?"

Anne got the dolly from the storage room and wheeled it toward the officer. "Maybe this will help."

Officer Banks took it and nodded. "It'll save us a few elevator trips, I'm sure. Thanks."

Anne knew most of the people who attended, but there were a couple she'd never seen before. Officer Banks had already informed her that everyone in today's seminar had either already been victims, or someone had tried to victimize them.

Everything went as planned. By the time the attendees left, Anne knew way more than she ever could have imagined about how easy it was to steal someone's identity.

Mildred pulled a handkerchief from her pocket and wiped her forehead. "Wow, that was an eye-opener. I had no idea that someone can get so much information from the Internet."

"Eric always insisted on having an unlisted number," Anne said. "Now I see that we were wasting our money because not only can someone get our phone number, they can obtain our address and find a picture of our house online."

Officer Banks stepped closer. "It wasn't so easy at first, but as more information is available to the masses, it's getting increasingly tough to protect ourselves. That's why we have to be diligent, with as many safeguards as possible."

Mildred planted a fist on her hip. "I noticed that Rita from the bank wasn't here."

"I thought she'd come," Officer Banks said. "She said she was having company from out of town, but this is still important enough that I think anyone would understand."

"Something isn't right about that woman," Mildred said, shaking her head. "She never looks me in the eye, and I don't think she comes out of her office unless it's absolutely necessary. Gary Bastille used to be all over the place. He chatted with bank customers, he went to Chamber of Commerce meetings, and he even had a float in the town parades."

"Not everyone is as outgoing as Gary," Alex said. "We shouldn't jump to conclusions about Rita just because she's more reserved." His expression belied his words. Anne knew him well enough to see that he wondered about the bank manager too.

Wendy joined them. "The one I'm suspicious of is Joan. She's one secretive lady, and she darts away the second someone tries to get to know her."

Mildred contorted her mouth. "I agree. Not only does she seem to be keeping a secret, she keeps driving by my house at all times of the day and night. I wouldn't worry about that so much if she didn't slow down in front of my house when she thinks I'm not looking and speed off when I open the door."

Officer Banks shrugged. "I wouldn't assume anything about specific people. At this point, all we can do is guess. There are so many possibilities, we need to keep open minds and be aware of everything around us."

Anne sighed. She was sad about what was happening to the innocence of Blue Hill.

* * *

On Sunday morning, Anne had a difficult time getting Liddie out of bed. Not only was it cold out, there was a light drizzle that made the warm blankets and soft pillow all the more appealing.

"Sorry, sweetie, but you really need to get up now," Anne whispered in Liddie's ear. "You can take a nap this afternoon if you're still tired."

Liddie barely opened her eyes as she slowly sat up on the edge of her bed, still clutching the blanket to her chest. "It's too cold."

"Put these on." Anne handed Liddie her slippers. "I have some waffles and hot cocoa ready in the kitchen."

"Is Ben up yet?" Liddie stuck her feet into her slippers and accepted the velour bathrobe Anne held open.

"Yes, and he's starving." Anne smiled at her daughter as she wrapped the robe around her. "C'mon so he doesn't have to wait any longer."

Anne prepared three plates with waffles and ham, and syrup on the side so they could dip their food into it. Ben started that when he was little, and Liddie followed.

"Mom, some of the guys from Sunday school are going to a movie this afternoon," Ben said as he stabbed a bite of his waffle. "Is it okay if I go?"

"Yes," Anne said. "But only under one condition. Will you have a parent with your group?"

"Zach's dad is going, and Ms. Brady is sending one of the college guys to help out."

Anne pursed her lips. Ben's habit of letting her know about things like this at the last minute annoyed her, but she didn't feel this was a battle worth fighting right now. "Yes, you may go." His Sunday school group had been good for him. The children's program volunteer didn't hesitate to ask for help from parents and other volunteers. "Why did you wait until now to let me know about this?"

He gave Anne a sheepish look. "Sorry I didn't tell you sooner, but I sort of forgot."

"That's why you need to start writing things down, Ben. Will you do that if I get you a notepad small enough to put in your pocket?"

"I can keep notes on a cell phone," he said, his voice tinged with hope.

Anne gave him her best mom look and shook her head. "I don't think you need your own cell phone just yet."

He sighed in resignation. "I'll need some money."

Anne picked up her handbag and rummaged around for the cash. "You're fortunate this time because I just happen to have enough cash on hand. Next time I might not."

He hung his head. "I know."

"Is Ryan going?" Anne asked.

"I don't think so. He and his uncle have other plans."

That was probably the reason Alex hadn't mentioned the movie. "Do I need to drive you there, or is your teacher using the church van?"

"Church van. After the movie, Reverend Tom said he'd have pizza at the church."

"Sounds like a wonderful day to me," Anne said.

Liddie put down her fork. With her cheeks still full of waffle, she looked at her mother. "Can I go too?"

"No, sweetie, afraid not."

"Why?" Liddie swallowed before pouting.

"It's just for kids in my Sunday school class," Ben said.

Anne had to think fast to get Liddie's mind off wanting to go with Ben. "Why don't you and I have a girls' day? We can watch one of your favorite movies, eat popcorn, and polish our fingernails?"

Liddie grinned, nodded, and picked up her fork. Anne let out a sigh of relief. Most of the time, Ben didn't mind too much when Liddie followed him around, but he did need some space to hang out with his friends once in a while.

Anne and the children met after the Sunday school session and found a place to sit toward the back just before the singing of the first hymn. When the pastor called the younger children up to the front for a short message, Liddie hopped off the pew and headed toward the front of the sanctuary. Ben smiled at Anne, warming her heart. Most of the time, he acted his age, but sometimes he seemed more mature than most nine-year-olds.

After the mini-sermon, the children's choir director led the younger kids to another room where they would hear a short Bible lesson, sing songs, do a craft, and have a snack. Ben scooted closer to Anne for the remainder of the service.

Grace approached her after church. "Some of us are going out for soup and sandwiches. Are you up for it?"

"Sorry, but not today. Ben's going out with his Sunday school group, so Liddie and I have plans."

"You're a good mom," Mildred said from the other side of her, patting her shoulder. "You'll be rewarded when they're older."

"Thanks. I remember Eric saying we needed to treat our children well because they get to pick our nursing home."

The corners of Mildred's eyes crinkled as she smiled. "That's one of the oldest jokes out there, but it's still funny because it's most likely true."

"Mommy, Mommy, can I go have lunch with the Pyle family and then come back here and play?" Anne heard Liddie's voice before she saw her running full steam in her direction. "I like to play with Emily."

Wendy approached, grinning. "In case you're wondering, I invited her. I think Emily likes having Liddie around, and I promised to come back and watch some choir members' kids."

"Um…" Anne noticed the hope on her daughter's face and Wendy's questioning look, so she nodded without hesitation. "That'll be fine."

"And then can I stay and play games and do puzzles?"

So much for the mother/daughter afternoon plans. "Yes, of course you may."

Grace watched with amusement as Liddie ran back toward the choir room, where some of the other children her age had gathered before turning back to face Anne. "So how about lunch with some grown-ups?"

"Sounds good, but let me go transfer the booster seat to Wendy's van."

Grace nodded. "I'll wait right here for you."

When Anne got to the choir room, Liddie was already playing on a hopscotch mat with a couple of other little girls. The choir director approached with a smile.

"Organized chaos."

Anne laughed. "I can see that. I'm getting ready to put Liddie's booster seat in Wendy's car, but I thought I'd stop by here first. What time should I be back to pick up Liddie?"

"Maybe around two thirty or three?"

"See you then."

"Oh, by the way, Grace was looking for you."

Anne nodded. "She found me." With a wave, she went back to where Mildred stood waiting with a couple more people.

"Ready to go?" Grace asked. "You can leave your car here and ride with me if you want."

"Thanks, but I'll drive." She wanted flexibility in case she needed to leave and pick up either of her children.

Anne arrived at the diner and saw that Mildred was sitting alone. She glanced at Grace who nodded. "Let's go see if she wants company."

"I saved you two a spot."

Throughout lunch, Anne listened to Mildred talk about the latest identity thefts.

Grace finally held up both hands. "Why don't we change the subject? This is Sunday, the Lord's Day. I think He would want us to concentrate on happier, more comforting thoughts and stop worrying about something we can't do anything about."

"Good idea," Mildred said.

"Hey," Grace said as she discreetly pointed toward the door. "Isn't that the girl who keeps driving by the library?"

Anne turned toward the door and spotted Joan, still wearing her baseball cap but wearing a nicer outfit—a pair of black slacks and an off-white button-front top. "Yes."

Anne glanced at Mildred whose attention had turned toward the door. Mildred stiffened before looking at Anne. Even though no words were exchanged, Anne sensed Mildred's discomfort.

Joan looked over at the table, froze for a few seconds, and turned around and walked out. Anne got up and walked as quickly after her as she could without making a scene.

When she got outside, Joan had her car door open and was about to get in. "Joan! Wait a minute."

Joan paused as her shoulders slumped. Anne didn't waste a second. She ran across the parking lot.

"Is everything okay?" Anne asked.

"Um…" Joan glanced around nervously. "I think so. Why?"

"Would you like to join us? We have another chair."

"I don't want to interfere," Joan said, sitting down.

"You won't be interfering." Anne forced a smile. "C'mon, I'm sure you'll be glad you did."

"No." Joan's body stiffened. "I think I'll just go to a drive-through and grab a sandwich."

Anne didn't want to force Joan into a situation that made her uncomfortable. However, now she wondered more than ever about the skittish woman.

Grace and Mildred watched her as she approached. She smiled as she walked, but when she got close enough, Mildred gave her a no-nonsense look. "What happened?"

"I sure wish I knew. I offered to make room for her, but she said she didn't want to intrude."

Mildred shook her head. "It sure seems awfully suspicious, doesn't it? I mean, right when she comes to town, we start having all this identity theft." She paused. "And you have to admit her actions sure are suspicious."

"Maybe so, but it might just be a coincidence," Anne replied, "and I don't want to accuse anyone if I'm not sure."

"You're right." Mildred let go of her arm. "Come sit down. Our food will arrive any minute."

Anne participated in the light discussion about the sermon, the cold weather, and the upcoming holiday, but she had a difficult time concentrating. Between Joan's odd behavior and the disconcerting things she'd learned during the seminar, her mind began buzzing in a different direction.

She was glad when it was time to pick Liddie up from church. When she got up to leave, Mildred said she'd call her later.

Liddie sat at a child-sized table coloring with another little girl. As soon as she spotted her mother, she hopped up and ran toward her. "Mommy, can my friend and her mommy come to our Thanksgiving party?"

"Yes, of course." Anne smiled at Liddie's friend. "We're having a bunch of people over for Thanksgiving dinner, and we'd love to have you. Where's your mommy?"

A woman walked up from behind. "I'm right here."

Anne smiled. "Hi, I'm Anne Gibson. And, in case you haven't heard, you're invited to our house for Thanksgiving."

"Please, Mommy? Can we go?"

The woman beamed. "Sounds great. I wasn't sure what I was going to do. My parents live out of town, but I promised to help out here with the children's programs."

"You may bring a guest too, if you'd like."

"I don't have a guest to bring, but I do make a fabulous corn casserole."

Anne smiled. "Sounds delicious. I can't wait to taste it."

Liddie jumped up and down with delight. "Let's call everyone else today, okay, Mommy?"

"Okay. Now go put everything away, and we'll go home," Anne said.

The first couple of minutes on the way home, Liddie chattered about how much fun she had had with the Pyles and then singing and coloring with her church friends. When she grew quiet, Anne glanced in the rearview mirror and saw that her eyes were half shut.

Liddie didn't argue one word when Anne suggested taking a nap before making any calls. Once she was secure in her room, Anne went to the living room and picked up the magazine she'd been trying to read for the past couple of weeks. No sooner had she gotten into an article then the phone rang. It was Ben.

"Mom, can I go to Matt's house? He wants to show me his remote-control helicopter."

"That's fine as long as it's okay with his parents, but I'll need their phone number."

"His dad's the one who invited me."

"What time do you want me to pick you up?"

"Hold on, and I'll ask." Anne could hear the muffled sound of Ben asking Matt. "His dad can bring me home."

"I'd like you home before dinner," Anne said.

After she hung up, she leaned back and closed her eyes. It seemed that as her children got older and needed her less, things never went as planned.

Liddie slept for an hour. The first thing she said when she awoke was, "Let's call people now. I wanna know who is coming so I can make something for everyone."

Anne sat down at the table as Liddie had her snack, jotting names on a sheet of paper. Then Anne picked up the phone and started calling. All but one person accepted the invitation.

"This is gonna be the best Thanksgiving ever!" Liddie exclaimed. Her smile quickly faded. "Except Grandma and Grandpa won't be here. That would make it even better."

Anne smiled as she thought about how crowded her place would be for Thanksgiving if Liddie kept inviting people. At least she had the library space if she needed more room.

Chapter Sixteen

A nother Monday, another week," Mildred said as she entered the library first thing Monday morning after the children left with Alex. "No telling what will happen next around here."

"I know." Anne smiled. "I didn't think you were coming in today."

"Donna called and said her knee was acting up on her, so I told her to get herself to the doctor, and I'd cover her shift."

Anne was amazed by the reliability of her volunteers, and she was grateful for each one. "I hope it's nothing serious."

Mildred shook her head. "She had surgery on the other knee a few years ago, and I'm afraid she might need it on this one. I sure hope not though. Recovery was rough."

"So I've heard."

The sound of footsteps entering the library silenced them. When Anne saw that it was Officer Banks, her heart thudded. "Did something happen?"

"More identity theft," he replied. "I just left the bank. Rita wasn't in yet. Apparently, her plans changed, and she went out of town over the weekend. She had car trouble and can't get back to Blue Hill."

"Too bad." Mildred frowned. "I can't help but wonder why she hasn't gotten more involved in this whole crisis. You'd think—" She clamped her mouth shut.

Officer Banks hoisted a box to the counter. "I have some brochures you can offer your patrons. They're free."

Anne pulled one from the box and studied it. The trifold flyer explained the importance of protecting your identity, listed some specifics about how to secure private information, and how quickly an unscrupulous person could take everything.

She waved it and nodded. "This is excellent. Very succinct and easy to follow. I'm sure it will help anyone who doesn't understand how thieves' minds work."

"Even if it only helps one person, it's worth it." Officer Banks stepped back and folded his arms. "Apparently, the problem gets worse during the holidays. I'd like to have more seminars between Thanksgiving and Christmas if you don't mind."

Mildred lifted an eyebrow and tilted her head. "Are you saying you think this will continue that long?"

"No…at least I certainly hope not," he replied. "However, even if we catch this person, I think we should continue with our seminars. This kind of thing is happening all over the world, not just in Blue Hill. We need to be proactive to prevent future problems."

"True." Mildred took a flyer and glanced at it. "I like the bullet points. Makes it easy to see the steps we need to take."

"That was our intention," Officer Banks said. "We looked at quite a few materials, and these seemed the simplest to follow. We're getting a DVD for the seminars too."

"A DVD?" Mildred grimaced. "Will it be packed with violence?"

"No," Officer Banks replied as he cast an amused glance in Anne's direction. "It's just a clip that shows how criminals can steal your information from a variety of places, like public and personal computers, credit card readers, gadgets they attach to ATMs, and your trash."

"Whoa, wait a minute," Mildred said. "Gadgets on ATMs?"

He nodded. "Yes, in fact, if you ever see something that looks like it isn't part of the original ATM, don't use it until you talk to someone at the bank about it."

"How do they do that?" Mildred asked.

"There are some pretty smart criminals out there, and they like to stay a step ahead of the honest people."

"Their victims. People who work hard to earn an honest living, and"—Mildred snapped her fingers—"it's gone like that."

"And that's only part of the equation," Officer Banks said. "Not only can they lose their savings, someone else can ruin their credit by taking out loans in their name with information that many people routinely give out. In some cases, all someone needs is your social security number and an address."

Mildred placed her hands on her hips and shook her head. "Well I'll be. It beats all that anyone would even think about doing such a thing. With bad guys out there spending all their time figuring out ways to dupe us, how do we even stand a chance?"

Officer Banks smiled. "By making it difficult for them. It probably won't stop a criminal, unless he—or she—gets caught, but the more people who know how to protect their identity the harder it will be for someone to ruin their lives. Unfortunately, for those who are uninformed, the thief will find them."

Mildred lifted her chin with determination. "Then let's show whoever is doing this to us that they should never mess with the folks in Blue Hill."

Anne laughed. "You tell 'em, Mildred." Then she turned to Officer Banks who by now was smiling right along with her. "So what you taught at the first seminar was basically what to do after someone steals your identity."

"Correct. From now on, we'll touch on that, but our primary focus will be on prevention."

After Officer Banks left, Anne pulled out her schedule book. "Since Thanksgiving is next week, I'm not so sure we'll have many people coming in."

"You never know." Mildred replied. "I'll be here to help out as much as you need."

"I sure do appreciate everything you do."

"I know you do, and that makes me want to do even more," Mildred said. "With Thanksgiving coming up, the other volunteers will want to be home getting ready, so it's the least I can do."

Mildred started to push the book cart but stopped. Anne noticed the pensive look on her face.

"What's wrong?" Anne asked.

"Nothing, but there is one thing that's bugging me. Do you think Smith is really Joan's last name?"

Anne pondered that for a moment and shook her head. "I wondered the same thing myself."

"The reason I asked is I overheard someone mentioning the name 'Joan Meadows' before church. I've never heard of anyone by that name, so I wondered if it was our Tea and Book Club mystery lady."

"It could very well be," Anne said. "Next time we see her, we should ask."

"We can ask, but I don't know if we'll get an answer." Mildred sighed. "She has such a way of evading direct questions."

After Mildred left the counter to put the cards in the new books, Anne turned to the computer and typed *Joan Meadows* in the Internet search box. Thousands of links popped up. She clicked on "images," and even though that narrowed the search a bit, she still wasn't sure if any of the women on the screen were Joan.

Mildred appeared. "I need to go now. I'll be back to finish putting the cards in first thing tomorrow morning." She reached for some of the literature Officer Banks had brought. "If you don't mind, I'd like to start handing these out to folks."

"Good idea," Anne said. "If we can enlighten our citizens early, maybe they won't be so shocked when they come to our seminar."

The morning was slow, but the pace picked up considerably after lunch—mostly people who'd received one of the flyers Mildred had been handing out. One of the volunteers breezed in and headed straight for the checkout desk, waving a handful of flyers.

"I don't get it," she said shaking her head.

"What don't you get, Mrs. Bultman?"

"Mildred asked me to take some of these to the bank, thinking that was a logical place to offer this information. The teller told me I had to speak to Rita, and when I did, she turned me down."

"Turned you down?" Anne asked.

"Yes. She said she wasn't interested in giving these to the bank's customers."

"That's really odd." Anne thought for a moment. "Tell you what, Mrs. Bultman. As soon as Wendy gets here tomorrow, I'll go talk to Rita and see if perhaps she misunderstood."

"I don't think she did, but you can give it a try. That woman doesn't seem to like it here much, so I can't say I'm surprised."

"Why don't you think she likes it here?" Anne asked.

"Several of the ladies' groups have invited her to functions, but she always turns us down. In case you haven't noticed, the only time anyone sees her is at the bank. She goes out of town every chance she gets."

Anne had noticed that, but she didn't respond. "I'll talk to her, but in the meantime, are you here to work, or did you just want to tell me what happened?"

"Oh, I'm here to work. I figured you would have your hands full with the holidays coming up. Mildred said she had to leave early today."

Anne didn't have much for Mrs. Bultman to do, but she didn't want to turn down any offers for help. "I would like to spend a little time with my children when they get home from school, so if you don't mind staying until closing, that sure would help."

Mrs. Bultman finally smiled. "I'll be happy to. When my children were Ben and Liddie's age, they were so precious." She sighed. "Too bad that time flew by."

"At least you have grandchildren now."

"Yes." The older woman's face lit up. "And I see them every chance I get." She waved her hand, shooing Anne away. "Now run along and do whatever you need to do to get ready for the children. I'll take over from here."

Anne chuckled to herself as she did what she was told. Mrs. Bultman could be rather bossy at times, but her intentions were always honorable. Anne didn't mind taking orders from someone who had her best interests at heart.

She pulled on a jacket and went outside to meet the children. As soon as Alex pulled in, she saw a look of concern on his face.

"Why are you out here?" he asked. "Did something happen?"

"No," Anne replied with a smile. "Well, nothing but Mrs. Bultman telling me she'd take over so I can spend time with Ben and Liddie."

Alex tilted his head back and laughed. "Okay, I get it." He leaned into the truck and helped Liddie out of her booster seat. When he straightened up, he lifted one of the identity protection flyers. "Did you know that Mildred has been running all over town distributing these?"

"Yes, I've heard."

"I was adding a wall at the florist when she came in. This is excellent information, but shouldn't we save them for the next seminar?"

Anne shook her head. "A lot of damage can be done between now and then, so we thought it would be a good idea to give people something to think about. We don't want to limit them only to library patrons."

"Makes sense." Alex started to get back into his truck but paused. "Do you need me for anything before I leave?"

"Not today, but thanks." She put her hands on Liddie and Ben's shoulders. "Let's go have a snack."

Anne prepared her children one of their favorite healthy snacks, baby carrots with ranch dressing to dip them. As they munched on them, she popped the lid off the cookie jar and pulled out three cookies — one for Liddie and two for Ben.

Liddie wanted to play with her dolls, so Anne took advantage of the time to help Ben get his homework done. She never did his work for him, but she enjoyed when he asked her to explain something she actually understood.

"You do realize it won't be long before I won't have a clue what you're doing," Anne said.

Ben gave her a look of understanding. "I know."

It took every ounce of self-restraint for Anne not to laugh at the seriousness of his tone. This was one of those times when she caught a glimpse of maturity peeking through his boyish demeanor.

CHAPTER SEVENTEEN

As soon as Wendy arrived on Tuesday morning, Anne gave her a rundown on the previous day's activities, told her about the flyers, and briefed her on what needed to be done. "I need to run a few errands this morning, but I shouldn't be long."

"Take all the time you need," Wendy said. "Chad's sister is staying with us, so I can stay as long as you like."

Anne's first stop was the bank. Before getting out of her car, she closed her eyes and prayed for guidance. She had no idea what she'd say or what Rita's reaction would be to the flyers. She just hoped they would be accepted this time.

The first teller who saw her glanced at the stack of flyers in her hands, frowned for a split second, and then forced a smile. "I'll see if Ms. Sloan can see you." She gestured toward the chairs in the waiting area. "Why don't you have a seat? It might be a little while."

"Thank you."

Anne had barely gotten comfortable when Rita appeared at her door. "I have an appointment in fifteen minutes, so I don't have long."

The abruptness of her words caught Anne's breath, but she quickly recovered. "That's fine. This won't take more than a minute or two." She got up and followed Rita back into her office.

"So what do you need?"

Anne had no doubt Rita knew exactly what she wanted since she was still clutching the stack of identity protection brochures in plain sight. She pulled one off the top of the stack and held it out toward Rita.

"Officer Banks brought these by the library, and I thought it would be a good idea for you to make them available to your customers."

Rita pursed her lips, took a quick glance down at the flyer, and looked back up at Anne, shaking her head. "No, I don't think so."

"Why not?" Those words escaped Anne's lips before she had a chance to catch herself. "What I mean is, have you looked at it? There is some really good information in there that might prevent someone from having his or her identity stolen."

Rita folded her arms on her desk and looked Anne in the eye. "I don't want to frighten my customers."

"This shouldn't frighten anyone," Anne argued. "If anything it empowers them."

Silence fell between them before Rita finally picked up the flyer, opened it, and studied it. "Hmm. It's not bad."

"So you'll make them available to your customers? You can put them on that counter by the door, and—"

Rita cleared her throat, interrupting her. "No, I'm afraid I still don't think this is such a good idea to alarm people at the bank. If anyone has any questions about how to protect their account, they can ask any of the associates, and we'll be glad to help them with their personal banking needs."

Frustration welled in Anne's chest. Rita was clearly not going to budge from her position. Anne swallowed hard and placed the stack of flyers on Rita's desk. "Why don't I leave these with you, so if you change your mind, you'll have them?"

"If that's what you want to do, fine." Rita got up but didn't walk around from behind her desk. "I have to prepare for my appointment that will be here soon. Thank you, Anne. Have a nice day."

Feeling like a child who'd misbehaved and been dismissed, Anne stood and walked out of Rita's office. She felt as though all eyes were on her as she left the bank.

When she got back to the library, she spotted Alex's truck parked in front. She quickly pulled her car into her usual spot, got out, and went inside, her heart hammering the whole time.

Alex turned around and grinned. "I thought I'd see how the display case was working out."

"Is that all?" Relief flooded Anne. "I was worried when I saw your truck."

"That's all." Alex gave her look of understanding. "I'm starting to think *Worry* should be your middle name."

"I know." Anne glanced over at Wendy who clearly enjoyed the interchange. "Anything I need to know about the library?"

Wendy shook her head. "Not a thing. Mildred came in and worked on reshelving returned books for a little while, but Claire called and asked her to run an errand for her, so she had to leave. Remi and Bella took over when she left. Other than that, it's been super slow this morning, but we did have one call inquiring about the seminar. I wrote down his name, phone number, and e-mail address."

"Good."

"Any luck at the bank?" she asked.

"No, afraid not." Anne turned to Alex and started to explain before he nodded.

"Wendy told me where you were," he said.

Wendy came around from behind the desk. "I think I'll go see if Remi and Bella need any help. Holler if you need me."

Once Anne and Alex were alone, she decided to vent, knowing he'd understand. "I don't get why Rita is being so stubborn," she said.

Alex nodded. "You know I'm not the suspicious type, but I have to admit, it makes me wonder too. She seems so detached and unwilling to bother trying to fit in here in Blue Hill."

"You don't think she's the identity thief, do you?"

"I don't think so…at least I certainly hope not, but she's not acting in a way I would think a bank manager should. Not agreeing to make the flyers available doesn't make sense to me."

Anne shuddered. "Let's hope she's not the thief. That would be a major disaster."

"I know. She has access to everyone's account numbers and other private information that could do some serious damage to a lot of people's lives." He shuffled for a moment. "I'm sure the bank checked her background before they placed her here, and they are bonded."

"Yes, and at least the police department is looking at all angles," Anne said. "I have confidence that they'll find the thief."

"Yes, so do I. However, last time I talked to Officer Banks, he said it might take a while."

"That's why we need to arm everyone with what they need to protect themselves…and I'm not letting Rita's resistance get in the way." Anne lifted her chin.

"As long as you let Officer Banks know what you're doing and don't overstep the safety boundaries, I'm right there with you."

They exchanged a friendly look and smiled, sealing their resolve to continue doing their part in protecting Blue Hill.

Wendy returned, waving a sheet of paper around. "All done with the reshelving. We're in good shape now—at least until the next batch is returned."

"It's a never-ending cycle, isn't it?" Anne asked.

"You're right about that." Wendy nodded then tilted her head. "So how about the next book club selection?"

"I thought we could find one of the books we have multiple copies of here."

"Good idea."

Alex gestured toward the display case. "Mind if I take a look and see how the case is holding up?"

"Go right ahead," Anne said. "From what I can tell, it's built like a tank."

After he walked away, Wendy put the sheet of paper on the desk and leaned against it with her arms folded. "I couldn't help but overhear some of what you two were discussing. You don't really think Rita might be the thief, do you?"

Anne cringed. "We shouldn't have said anything since we have no proof she's even remotely involved."

"True, but I've been wondering about her for a very long time. One of the women in my mom's group at church lives down the street from her. She said Rita is an odd bird."

"How so?"

Wendy shrugged. "She's rarely home, and when she is, she stays inside. Most weekends she goes out of town to visit family and friends. I'm sure it hasn't been easy moving here and not knowing anyone. Occasionally she has guests from somewhere else come and stay with her. All her neighbors—" Wendy stopped. "Okay, sorry, I'm starting to spread gossip, and that's not good."

Anne understood, but she agreed with Wendy. It wasn't good. "Let's talk about something else. I don't want to be consumed by this identity theft thing."

"You and me both," Wendy said. "Ya know, I really like the idea of getting the children involved in putting together the displays. Have you thought about one for Christmas yet?"

"A little bit, but I'm open for suggestions."

Wendy's eyebrows shot up. "Good, because I have plenty of them."

Anne giggled. "Why am I not surprised? So tell me what you've been thinking."

By the time Alex joined them again, Anne had heard more than a dozen of Wendy's ideas—all of them different and disjointed but still very good and interesting. Anne wanted to use as many of them as she could, but she knew she'd have to organize them and incorporate them into an overall plan.

"So far so good," Alex said. "The only things I was concerned about were the hinges. I got a good deal on them several years ago, and they've been in my work shed since then."

"They're working just fine," Wendy said. "And they don't even squeak."

The corner of Alex's lips twitched into a slight smile. "That's good. We wouldn't want a lot of squeaking in the library."

The library phone rang, so Anne excused herself to answer it, leaving Alex and Wendy still chatting about noisy hinges. It was Claire.

"Do you still want us to come for Thanksgiving?" Claire asked.

"Yes, of course I do."

"Then we'd like to accept. What would you like me to bring?"

"Do you have a favorite dish you enjoy cooking?" Anne asked.

"Well…" Claire paused. "I do make a good squash casserole. Think anyone would eat it?"

Anne laughed. "I don't know about everyone else, but I sure will. I love squash."

"I'll bring some rolls too." Claire's voice sounded lighter and more joyful than when she first called. "Thank you so much for thinking of us, Anne. You're such a sweet girl."

Alex was still talking to Wendy when she hung up. "That was Claire. She and her husband are coming for Thanksgiving."

Wendy and Alex exchanged a glance that seemed mildly suspicious.

"What?" Anne narrowed her eyes. "What's going on?"

Alex stepped back with his hands up as if in surrender. "Nothing. I have to get back to work so I can finish up before I pick up the kids."

"Want me to do it?" Anne said. "Wendy said she can be here as long as I need her."

Alex nodded. "That'll be good. I'll pick Ryan up here. Thanks." He waved. "I still have to run. See you after school lets out."

Anne turned back to Wendy who had begun studying her fingernails a little too closely. "Okay, so what gives?"

Wendy blew on her nails before looking back at Anne. "I have no idea what you're talking about."

Anne let out a grunt of exasperation. "All right. So don't tell me. It's okay for you and Alex to have secrets."

"Secrets?" Wendy wiggled her eyebrows. "That sounds very mysterious."

"It is." Anne feigned a frown. "One day everything seemed so normal in Blue Hill, and now everything and everyone appear shrouded in secrecy."

"That's just your perception."

"Maybe." Anne glanced around the room. "At least I have the familiarity of the library, even when Blue Hill changes before my eyes."

"It's not really changing that much," Wendy said. "So who else has accepted your invitation for Thanksgiving?" Wendy asked.

Anne held up her fingers and rattled off all the names. Wendy listened attentively.

"Why do you ask?"

Wendy shrugged as she picked up a pad of paper and pencil. "I need to go do something in the Children's Room for a minute. I'll be right back."

Anne couldn't imagine what Wendy needed to do in the Children's Room. Apparently there were even secrets in the Blue Hill Library that she still hadn't discovered.

Wendy came back out in time for Anne to go pick the children up from school. "Want me to have a snack ready and waiting?" she asked.

Anne laughed. "You are such a mom."

"Well, yeah, with seven kids, I think you're pretty safe in saying that."

"I would love for you to do that, but don't feel you have to. I mean, if you get busy, don't worry about it."

"You know me," Wendy said. "I never worry about the small stuff. As for being busy, based on how things have been so far this week, I don't think that's going to happen."

"True."

Wendy made a shooing gesture. "You better get going, or you'll find yourself at the end of the carpool line."

Anne grabbed her keys. "See you in a little while."

Twenty minutes later, Ryan looked confused as he walked toward her car. "Where's Uncle Alex?"

"I told him I wanted a turn picking you all up from school, and he's letting me have it."

"Mom," Ben said as he slid into the backseat beside Liddie, "do you think Mrs. Farley would be willing to talk to my class about history?"

Anne made eye contact with him in the rearview mirror. "I don't know. Why don't you ask her?"

Ryan got in on the other side of Liddie in her booster seat. Anne waited until everyone was buckled in before pulling away.

"Mommy, we played the funnest game during recess," Liddie said.

"Tell me about it," Anne said as she drove toward the library.

From that moment on, Liddie dominated the conversation in the backseat. Anne smiled as she wondered if this normally happened when Alex drove.

Back at the library, the children greeted Wendy, and she pointed toward the kitchen. "Snacks are ready and waiting. Enjoy."

"Whoa," Ben said as he plopped down in his chair. "Sandwiches, fruit cups, and cake." He grinned up at Anne. "Mom, can we have this every day?"

"I don't think so."

Alex arrived when they were almost finished with their snacks. He looked at the table and lifted his eyebrows. "We might just have soup for dinner," he told Ryan. "Can I help clean up?"

"No thanks, the kids will take their own plates to the sink, and then all I have to do is rinse them and stick them in the dishwasher."

Ryan shoved the last bite of cake into his mouth, stood, and cleaned his area. Ben and Liddie followed right behind.

"Thanks for picking them up today," Alex whispered on his way out. "I got quite a bit accomplished."

"Maybe I can do that more often." Anne enjoyed joining the carpool crowd, and she loved seeing the children's faces as they waited for their parents.

CHAPTER EIGHTEEN

By noon on Wednesday, everyone Anne invited for Thanksgiving dinner had accepted. When Liddie got home from school, she was delighted to learn that so many people would be there.

"I need more paper so I can make their placemats." She scrunched her sweet little face. "Can you write down their names so I can copy them? I don't want to spell them wrong."

Anne printed the names of the guests and handed the list to Liddie. Then she glanced over at Ben, who had his book open but didn't appear to be reading it. His look of consternation reminded Anne of herself when she had to work through a problem.

"Having trouble with something, Ben?" she asked.

He shook his head. "Not really."

"Mommy, do we have any stickers?"

"A few," Anne replied, "but I think everyone would like your drawings more than stickers."

"Okay, I'll draw some pretty pictures." She frowned. "What kinds of pictures should I draw?"

"Why don't you draw some flowers and butterflies?" Anne suggested.

Ben glanced up. "Shouldn't she draw turkeys and pilgrims?"

"That's too hard," Liddie said.

"Ben has a good point, since flowers and butterflies are more for spring. How about leaves and pumpkins?"

Liddie nodded and rummaged through her crayon box. She pulled out an orange crayon. "I'll make a really pretty pumpkin."

Anne leaned over. "And you can use other colors to make designs around the pumpkins."

"Okay." Liddie put down the orange crayon and looked back in the box. "What is Mrs. Daniels' favorite color?"

"I have no idea," Anne replied.

Ben snickered and opened his mouth but shut it when Anne gave him a warning glance. He rolled his eyes as he turned back to his book.

"How about pink for her 'cause she's a girl and blue for Mr. Daniels?" Liddie said.

Anne nodded. "Sounds perfect. And for the rest of them, just pick a color you think they would like. I'm sure they'll love whatever you choose."

Mildred popped her head into the library kitchen. "There's a call for you, Anne."

"Can you take a message?"

"It's Rita from the bank."

Anne rose. "I'll take it."

"I thought you would." Mildred smiled down at Liddie. "Want me to hang out in here?"

"If you don't mind."

Mildred leaned over and gave Liddie a hug. "Not only do I not mind, I'm thrilled to spend time with your wonderful children."

Anne went to the checkout desk and picked up the phone, which Mildred had placed on a stack of papers. She heard dead air. Obviously Rita didn't like waiting.

She glanced at the caller ID and returned the call. Rita answered on the first ring.

"Do you have any more of those flyers?" she asked. "We've run out, and people are asking for them."

Anne decided not to mention the fact that Rita said she wasn't planning to use them. "We have a few left here, but I'm sure Officer Banks can get more. Would you like for me to ask if he can drop some off at the bank?"

"Yes, please."

When an uncomfortable silence fell between them, Anne spoke up. "We're planning another seminar a week after Thanksgiving, and I'd love for you to attend."

"Maybe."

"I'll make sure to save you a spot," Anne said. "Did you need anything else?"

"Not now," Rita replied.

After Anne got off the phone, she thought about the conversation and how strained it was. At least Rita had changed her mind about the flyers, which lowered her a few notches on Anne's suspicion list.

She went back to the kitchen and saw Mildred bent over Ben's book, with him looking at her in awe. Mildred grinned and pointed to a page.

"Mom, did you know that Mrs. Farley remembers when some of these things actually happened?" Ben looked at the older woman with adoring eyes. "That is so cool."

"Some of it was cool, but there were quite a few tragedies too." Her reflective expression reminded Anne of how her mother looked when she spoke of life-changing events.

"One of my professors in college told us that history is always being made," Anne said. "Most of us didn't think much about that, but now I do."

Mildred nodded. "I still can't believe so much of my life is in history books these days. It kind of makes me feel..." Her voice trailed off.

"Say no more. I know exactly what you mean," Anne said. "I think that happens to all of us."

Mildred grinned. "Yes, I suppose that would be logical. Those days are like another lifetime."

Ben asked her some questions related to what he was studying, and Mildred gave him a different, more personal perspective than he could get from his books. Anne was grateful to have Mildred there to make these events more real.

Later that evening, after Liddie had been asleep for a while, Anne sat on the edge of Ben's bed. "You're not sleepy, are you?" she said.

"That's because I can't stop thinking about Mrs. Farley and how she actually lived through all that stuff. Life must have been hard with so much going on."

Anne nodded. "Sometimes maybe, but remember that it didn't happen all at once. It was spread out throughout her life."

They bowed their heads, and Ben said his bedtime prayer. After he said, "Amen," he opened his eyes and smiled at Anne. "Mom, I think I like history. It's way cool when you think about how real people did all that stuff."

"Yes," Anne agreed. "It is *way cool*." She bent over, gave Ben a kiss on the forehead, and stood up. "Love you. Good night."

"G'night, Mom."

She left his room and closed the door on her way out. It seemed that every day Ben became more and more like her. History had always been one of her favorite subjects for the very reason Ben just mentioned.

Anne walked down the hall to her bedroom. Her cell phone, which she'd left on her dresser, buzzed to indicate she had messages.

The first one was from Mildred, letting her know that something had come up, and she'd have to cancel her Thanksgiving plans. Liddie would be so disappointed. The second message was from Claire Daniels, asking her to call her back tomorrow.

Anne jotted the messages on the notepad she kept on the nightstand before getting ready for bed. Her mind raced with all the events over the past couple of weeks, so she picked up a book and started reading to clear her head. She could easily get annoyed by everyone changing their minds at the last minute, since she'd already purchased quite a bit of the food.

She awoke the next morning with the nightstand light still on and the book she'd been reading face down on her chest. She smiled. It had been a while since she'd done that. At least she'd gotten a good night's sleep.

Alex arrived right on time to take the children to school. "Two more days before break," Alex said. "Need any help with them next week?"

"I'm having a special Thanksgiving children's Story Time on Monday, but I doubt it will interest Ben."

"Then why don't I take him and Ryan somewhere?" Alex offered. "That way you won't have to find something for him to do here."

"Thanks."

"I should be thanking you. Ryan enjoys hanging out with Ben."

After they left, Anne called Claire to find out what she wanted. "I'm so sorry to do this to you at such late notice," Claire said. "But I'm afraid I'm going to have to cancel our plans to attend your Thanksgiving dinner."

She'd only accepted a couple days ago, but Anne understood how Mr. Daniels' health could go from good to bad and then improve again from one day to the next. "Thanks for letting me know. If things change, we'd still like to have you. I'll have plenty of food, I'm sure."

As Anne hung up, her first thought was how disappointed Liddie would be. She'd painstakingly made placemats and decorated napkin rings for each person who'd originally accepted the invitation.

Wendy and Mildred walked into the library together, gabbing and laughing, until they looked at Anne. Mildred closed the distance and put her arm around her. "What happened?"

Anne didn't want to make Mildred feel bad, so she just shook her head. "Nothing, really. Just a little bit of disappointing news. We've had another cancellation for Thanksgiving dinner."

Wendy cut a glance over at Mildred who cleared her throat. She grinned at Anne. "That stuff happens to me all the time. Did I ever tell you about my oldest daughter's fifth birthday party? We invited everyone in her class at school and her Sunday school class. They all said they'd be there. Unfortunately, that was also flu season, so one kid after another canceled until we only had a few who actually showed up."

"That must have been awful for her," Anne said.

Wendy shrugged. "At the time, yes. She was upset with her friends, but when she got the flu a week later, she understood a little better."

"As I told Ben," Mildred interjected, "when an event is actually happening, you don't see the big picture. But when you look back, you see it with a whole different perspective."

"Good point," Anne said as the words from her friends sank in. "It's just one Thanksgiving dinner. There will be more."

"That's right," Mildred said as she patted Anne's shoulder. "Lord willing, many more." She winked at Wendy before looking back at Anne. "You'll have a wonderful Thanksgiving anyway, I'm sure."

CHAPTER NINETEEN

Anne wished she knew the secret between Wendy and Mildred, but before she had a chance to ply them with questions, a patron came in looking for books on how to build a birdhouse. Mildred motioned for the man to follow her. "I know exactly what you need. Come with me."

As they walked away, Mildred chattered about the many birdhouses she had built over the years. "Don't make it too fancy because the birds don't care. All they want is a place to get out of the elements."

Wendy nodded her agreement. "That's pretty much the case for many of us. The elements can be pretty rough sometimes."

"Is there a hidden message somewhere in that statement?" Anne asked.

"Not really. I'm just feeling rather overwhelmed with the holidays coming up."

"That's not like you," Anne said. "I've always known you to be cool, calm, and collected, no matter what."

"See? That's just a façade. And I'm obviously a pretty good actress if you actually believe it." She paused. "Besides, you're seeing me through the lens of friendship, which tends to be rather rose colored."

Since traffic in the library was sparse, Anne spent most of the day wrapping up loose ends. Mildred left at noon, so she and Wendy were alone for lunch.

"Want me to whip up something really good, or do you want me to go pick up something from the diner?" Wendy asked.

"I'm not all that hungry," Anne replied. "Some of that leftover soup in the fridge will be good."

After lunch, they cleaned up and headed back to the checkout area, where they stood chatting for almost an hour before Wendy finally said she might as well go on home. "I'm not doing much good around here," she said. "And I'm sure you're getting tired of having me yacking your ears off."

Anne laughed. "I've actually enjoyed it."

"Me too. It's kind of nice having a slower pace for a while."

An hour after Wendy left, Alex brought the children in. "Any news?" he asked.

Anne gave him a questioning look. "About what?"

"I think I just got my answer."

"Ben, why don't you and Ryan go on into the kitchen and have your snack? Mrs. Pyle left some homemade cookies. Have a piece of fruit first."

"Mommy, can I go over to Cindy's house tomorrow after school?" Liddie asked. "Her mommy said it's okay with her if you don't mind." Her smile widened as she put down her backpack, opened it, and pulled out a piece of paper with a phone number on it. "She wants you to call her."

Anne took the paper and nodded. Liddie knew Cindy Jacobs from school and church, so Anne had chatted with her mother Yvette several times.

Alex stepped up. "Why don't Liddie and I join the boys in the kitchen while you call Cindy's mom?"

"Thanks."

Anne waited until they left the area to call Yvette. "Cindy has been asking to have Liddie over for several weeks now, so I thought it was about time we did it."

"Liddie loves playing with Cindy," Anne said. "Why don't you bring her and Becca over for a special holiday story time on Monday? She can stay for lunch afterward."

"Sounds like an excellent plan." Yvette cleared her throat. "I've been hearing some things about the identity protection seminars you're planning at the library. Is this open for anyone?"

"Absolutely."

"One of my neighbors had her identity stolen, so I thought it might be a good idea for my husband and me to find out more about how we can protect ourselves."

"We're starting the seminars for the general public after Thanksgiving, but in the meantime, we're handing out flyers with some helpful tips. I'll put one for you in Liddie's backpack. If she forgets to give it to you, remind her."

"That'll be great."

"What time do you want me to pick Liddie up?"

"The library closes at five, right?"

"Yes," Anne replied.

"You can come after you close. That'll give them plenty of time to play."

Anne went straight into the kitchen, where Alex had the boys and Liddie laughing. "What's so funny?"

"He told us a joke," Liddie said.

"A joke, huh?"

Ben nodded. "It was a really lame elephant joke...but it was funny."

Alex folded his arms and pretended to be offended. "Lame, huh? I'll have you know that it's the funniest elephant joke I ever heard." He winked at Anne. "Well, except maybe the second funniest. Want to hear the funniest?"

"Yes, please." Liddie swung her legs in excitement. "I love elephant jokes."

After Alex told his joke and the laughter died down, Anne walked up behind Liddie and placed her hands on her shoulders. "I talked to Cindy's mom."

Liddie turned around, her face lit with anticipation. "Can I go play with her tomorrow?"

"Yes, and I'll pick you up after the library closes." She bent over and hugged Liddie. "And then on Monday, Cindy is coming to Story Time and lunch."

Liddie bounced around her chair, eliciting laughter from Ben and Ryan. "I'm gonna have so much fun with Cindy. I can't wait."

Alex looked amused, but he didn't say a word. He didn't have to. Anne knew he liked children as much as she did, and he was simply enjoying the experience of watching Liddie's excitement.

Later that evening after dinner, Ben said he wanted to hang out in his room and read a little bit of the book he'd started a few days earlier. Liddie asked Anne if she'd read her an extra story.

"Yes, but you need to go to sleep right afterward so you can get plenty of rest for tomorrow. I don't want you to be grouchy when you go to Cindy's house."

Liddie scrunched her face and shook her head. "I don't wanna be Miss Crankypants."

Anne cracked up. "*Miss Crankypants*? Where did you hear that?"

"I heard Mrs. Pyle call one of her kids that."

Anne should have known. Wendy Pyle said the funniest things — especially when she wasn't trying to be funny.

"Okay, let's get you ready for bed, and I'll read you a couple of stories."

Anne read Liddie two stories, listened to her prayer, and gave her a hug. "Love you, sweetie."

"Love you too, Mommy." Liddie smiled, pulled the covers to her chin, and closed her eyes.

After pulling Liddie's bedroom door almost closed, she went to Ben's room. He glanced up from his book.

"Want me to listen to your prayer tonight?" Anne asked. It had been a while since she'd tucked him in, and she missed it. She thought that would be a less babyish way to do it.

"Sure." He picked up a bookmark, tucked it into the book, and placed it on his nightstand as Anne walked across the room and sat on the edge of his bed.

As Anne listened to his prayer, she was amazed by how mature he sounded. She'd heard that children went through phases where one day they acted like kids, then they behaved more like adults, and the next day they went right back to being kids. She smiled down at him, her heart longing to scoop him into her arms and rock him.

"Mom, you are awesome," he said.

Her eyes misted with tears. "So are you, Ben."

"I really mean it. After Dad died, I was so scared something terrible would happen to us, but you've made sure Liddie and I are fine."

She had to swallow hard to erase the lump that formed in her throat. "Any mother would do the same." She stood up, bent over and kissed his cheek, and backed toward the door. "I want you to know that I'm very proud of you." She closed the door and let the tears stream down her cheeks. This was one of those moments she'd never forget.

The next morning, Anne put an identity protection flyer in Liddie's bag and gave instructions to give it to Mrs. Jacob. Liddie nodded with excitement.

"I can't wait to play with Cindy!"

"I know. Just make sure you thank her mother for everything."

"I will."

Alex appeared at the door. "Ready, kids?"

Ben and Liddie followed him to his truck, while Anne headed back to the checkout desk. She wondered what she'd do all day, but she didn't have to think about it long. Officer Banks arrived with boxes of flyers and materials for the seminar.

"I know it's early, but these arrived, and we don't have any place to store them at the station. I thought we might keep them in a corner here."

Anne gestured toward the stairs. "There's a nearly empty closet on the second floor if you don't mind carrying them up there."

"Perfect. They're not all that heavy."

They put them on the cart and took them up to the second floor. After they had all the boxes put away, Officer Banks hovered near the checkout desk. She could tell he wanted to talk.

"Have you received all the materials yet?" she asked.

"I think so." He glanced over his shoulder before turning back to face her. "This whole situation is continuing to get worse. Three more people contacted us this morning about having their identity stolen." He shuffled nervously as he looked around.

His behavior was so odd Anne had to ask about it. "Are you okay?"

"Yes, but for the past few days, I've had the feeling that I'm missing something important."

Anne leaned over and glanced behind him. "There's no one in here but us."

"I know. I've never been paranoid before, but I'm afraid this whole situation has me confused." He sighed. "Everyone at the station is baffled."

"That's understandable. Blue Hill isn't the type of place that kind of thing happens to . . . at least not until recently."

"What's so frustrating," Officer Banks said, "is that every time we get a lead, we follow up on it, only to find ourselves hitting a dead end."

"I know. It's been frustrating for everyone." She recalled Ben's words about how she had protected him and Liddie, and resolved to continue keeping her eyes open for clues. "Let me know if there's anything I can do."

"Offering to let us use the library is a big help," he said. "Eventually, we'll find whoever is doing this, and the citizens of Blue Hill will be able to relax again." He rocked back on his heels. "And I'll be back to issuing parking tickets, following up on whoever's spread toilet paper on someone's lawn, and patrolling after football games to make sure no one gets overly enthusiastic."

Anne laughed. "That's the Blue Hill we all love."

"You know my number, so call me if something happens. Otherwise, I'll see you after Thanksgiving." He turned to leave.

"Oh, Officer Banks. I know this is late notice and all, but we're having some friends over for Thanksgiving dinner, and I want to invite you, Jennifer, and the kids."

He spun around with a curious look on his face. "But I thought…Oh, never mind." He stared at his feet and shuffled nervously for a few seconds before glancing back up at her, a guilty expression plastered on his face. "I would, but Jen and I have made other plans. Thanks anyway. I really need to leave now."

Before she had a chance to say another word, he was out the door. His odd behavior after she mentioned Thanksgiving confused Anne, but she finally just chalked it up to his frustration over the identity theft crisis.

To Anne's delight, not much else happened the rest of the day. Alex called and asked if Ben could spend the night with Ryan. She said that was fine, but he needed to come home and get his things first.

"We'll come straight there after school. Ryan has been after me to take him to the new theater with special effects over in Deshler, and I thought Ben might enjoy it as well."

"Thanks, Alex."

"My pleasure."

Mildred called shortly afterward. "You didn't give me any volunteer hours today, but if you need me, I'll be glad to come in."

"Thanks, but I don't even think I'm needed here today. It has been incredibly slow."

Mildred laughed. "That's a good thing. You need a little down time. Call if things pick up. I have to run over to Claire's, but I'll have my cell phone with me. Try to enjoy the quiet."

After they hung up, another call came in, this time from Donna. "Sorry to cancel out on you, but something has come up, and we won't be able to make it for Thanksgiving."

Not again, Anne thought. She sat down at the computer and read an e-mail from Suzanne from church, letting her know she wouldn't be attending Thanksgiving dinner either. At this rate, Anne and the children might be spending the holiday without anyone else. Then she remembered the Parnells. They hadn't canceled — at least not yet.

Alex brought Ben home after school to pick up some things. Ryan plopped down in front of the computer while he waited for Ben.

"I fed Hershey," Ben said as he came running down the stairs.

"Do you have your toothbrush?" Anne asked.

He stopped in his tracks and dropped his bag. "I'll go get it."

Alex didn't say a word until Ben came back. "Are you sure you have everything?" Alex asked.

Ben nodded and then smiled sheepishly at Anne. "Have fun, sweetie," she whispered as she hugged him.

He tossed his overnight bag over his shoulder. "Where's Ryan?"

"I'm right here," Ryan said as he came out of the computer area. "Let's go."

It seemed like forever before time to close the library. Anne was finally able to go pick up Liddie from Cindy's house.

She pulled up in front and took a long look around, her gaze settling on the familiar truck parked in the driveway next door to the Jacobs' house. Anne pondered what to do as she got out of her car. Before she had a chance to decide, she spotted the energy audit man coming around from behind the neighbor's house. His gaze locked with hers, but he quickly glanced away and started walking at a faster pace.

CHAPTER TWENTY

Anne started up the sidewalk and noticed that the man was doing something on the side of the house. She trudged toward him.

He glanced up and pursed his lips. Anne forced a smile.

"Hi there. Are you still doing energy audits?" she asked.

He nodded. "I've been pretty busy."

"I told Alex about you, but he said he didn't know anything about an energy audit."

"He probably forgot we'd spoken," he said. "He seems like a busy man." He lifted a screwdriver and tapped something on the side of the house.

"What are you doing now?" Anne asked.

He pulled his bottom lip between his teeth and shook his head. "I'm sorry, but I'm really busy, and I don't have time to chat. Maybe later?"

"Okay, I won't keep you." Anne backed away from him and went on up to the Jacobs' front porch. She knocked and then turned around to see where the man was now. He'd gotten into his truck and appeared to be writing something down.

The front door opened, and Yvette greeted her. "Come on in. The girls are playing in the kitchen while I cook. Would you like something to drink? We have tea, soda, or coffee."

"No thanks…" Anne stopped, and Yvette turned to face her with a curious look. "Are you aware that there's a guy from the energy company working in your neighborhood?"

"I know." Yvette shivered. "I'm sure there's nothing to worry about at all, but I still called the girls inside." She gestured toward the kitchen. "I need to check on dinner."

"Oh, of course." As they entered the kitchen, Anne spotted Liddie who glanced over her shoulder grinning. "I really appreciate your having Liddie over. Did she give you the identity protection flyer?"

"Yes." Yvette pointed to the counter. "It looks interesting. You can't be too careful anymore, can you?"

"No, but I never thought anything like this would happen in Blue Hill."

"I think in today's world, it happens everywhere." Yvette shook her head. "It's just so sad, though."

Anne went over to Liddie. "Ready to head on home, sweetie?"

Liddie nodded as she started piling Barbie clothes into a plastic container. "I had so much fun!"

Cindy grinned. "Me too. Can you come over and play with me again sometime?"

"Next time," Anne said, "you can come over to our house and play." She turned to Yvette. "Are we still on for Monday?"

"Yes, but I'm afraid I forgot to tell Cindy."

Before either of the moms had a chance to explain, Liddie started talking about Story Time. "This is a special story hour for Thanksgiving. You get to come over and listen to really fun stories and look at pictures and make puppets talk and have lunch with me."

She put the last of the clothes into the container and hopped out of the chair, taking Anne by the hand. Yvette picked up her backpack and walked them to the door.

"We'll see you in church on Sunday," Yvette said before she closed the door.

After Anne buckled Liddie in her seat, she straightened and caught another glimpse of the man she'd spoken to earlier. She quickly slid into the driver's seat and turned around to face her daughter.

"See that man over there?" she asked.

Liddie nodded.

"Do you know how long he's been there?"

"A long time. He was there when we got home from school."

"Did he say anything to you?"

Liddie shook her head. "Cindy's mommy made us go inside right away. We wanted to play in the backyard, but she said we had to stay indoors."

Anne was glad Yvette was being so protective.

When they arrived at the library, the door was standing open. Anne's heart thudded. She didn't remember locking the door, but she was certain she'd pulled it shut.

"Liddie, honey, why don't you stay in the car while I go make sure everything is okay."

Her daughter's eyes widened. "Don't go in there, Mommy. I don't want a bad guy to get you."

Good point. Anne pulled out her cell phone to call the police when Claude Parnell stepped out onto the porch and waved. A breath of relief whooshed from Anne's mouth as she got out of her car and walked toward him.

"I came looking for you," Claude said.

"Liddie was at a friend's house. As soon as the library closed, I went straight there to get her. What's up?"

Claude's demeanor changed. He looked uncomfortable as he nervously swung his arms and looked everywhere but at her. "I, uh…" He gave Anne an apologetic look. "I'm sorry, but I'm afraid the wife and I are going to have to back out of Thanksgiving dinner. Something has come up."

Anne's heart sank. She didn't want to be nosy, but she felt the urge to salvage the last of her dinner party. "Would it help if we changed the time? I mean, if you can make it later, I'll be glad to—"

"Nope." He cleared his throat and shook his head. "Can't do it. Sorry. I need to get on home now."

Anne went back to the car and got Liddie out. "Mommy, what's wrong? Why are you so mad?"

"I'm not mad, sweetie. Just disappointed."

"Why are you dis–pointed?"

Anne was tempted not to tell Liddie, but she had a policy to be open with her children, so she blurted, "Looks like it's just going to be the three of us for Thanksgiving."

Liddie's chin dropped, but she quickly recovered. "Don't be upset, Mommy. We can still have fun." She reached up and placed both hands on Anne's cheeks. "I promise."

That simple gesture touched Anne's heart more than anything her daughter could have done. Her eyes moistened. "I know we will. I was just hoping we could share the fun with some of our friends."

"Can we go out to eat?" Liddie asked. "I have some money in my piggy bank if you already spent all your money on the turkey and stuff."

Anne helped Liddie out of the car and took her hand. "Yes, we can go out to eat, but we don't need to use your money. I have enough for dinner and a special treat afterward."

"Ice cream?" Liddie asked, her face beaming up at Anne.

"Isn't it a little too cold for ice cream?" Anne couldn't help but giggle.

"No, Mommy, it's never too cold for ice cream."

The seriousness of Liddie's voice was so funny Anne couldn't help but laugh. And once she started, Liddie joined her, laughing so hard she snorted, making them both laugh even harder.

Anne finally settled down. "I'm not sure the ice cream shop will be open on Thanksgiving, so why don't we have ice cream tonight?"

As Liddie put her backpack away and washed her hands, Anne made reservations for Thanksgiving dinner at the children's favorite restaurant and then returned a few phone calls. Ten minutes later, they were on their way to the diner.

Anne enjoyed the rare time alone with her daughter. *Girl time.* A chance to talk to Liddie about things that wouldn't interest Ben.

After dinner, Anne and Liddie set off on foot toward Thrifty Drugstore for ice cream. As she expected, the place was deserted. The soda jerk glanced up from the counter where it appeared he was working a crossword puzzle. He looked surprised.

"What's bringing you two lovely ladies out on such a cold evening?" he asked.

"We are craving ice cream." Anne lifted her chin and squeezed Liddie's hand.

The young man behind the counter gave Anne a knowing glance. "Now that's my kind of craving." He bent down over the counter and looked Liddie in the eye. "What kind of ice cream can I get for you, little lady?"

"Chocolate and peppermint," she said as she held up two fingers. "That's one scoop of chocolate and one scoop of peppermint."

Anne and the soda jerk exchanged a look of amusement before he glance back down at Liddie and nodded. "Double scoop of chocolate and peppermint coming right up. Sugar cone?"

"Yes, please," Liddie replied.

"Such a polite girl," he said as he scooped the ice cream. "Here ya go." He turned to Anne. "And how about you? Same?"

Anne started to order a single scoop but changed her mind. "Yes, that would be wonderful."

The young man nodded and scooped hers. After he finished, he pulled another sugar cone from the stack. "That sounds so good I think I might have it too."

Liddie's gaze turned up to Anne's. "Looks like I started something."

"Yes, you most certainly did, sweetie." Anne had a feeling this wouldn't be the last thing her thoughtful little girl started.

* * *

Alex called early Saturday morning, before Anne had time to go downstairs and open the library. She'd thought about closing since it was so close to Thanksgiving, but even if one person wanted to use the library, she figured it would be worth unlocking the door. "Mind if I keep Ben here until after lunch? The guys are having so much fun I'd hate to interrupt them."

"Sure, that's fine, as long as he's not too much trouble."

"Are you kidding?" Alex said. "Having him here is keeping Ryan busy, so I can finish my paperwork without interruption."

"Do you have a minute?" Anne asked.

"Sure, what's up?"

"Remember that man who is doing energy audits and mentioned your name?"

"Yes, why? Is he there again?"

"No, I saw him at the Jacobs' neighbor's house." She told him about the short conversation they'd had. "Since I've never seen him around before he started doing these energy audits, I thought he might be a long way from family. Maybe someone should invite him to have Thanksgiving dinner."

"Are you considering inviting him to your place?" he asked.

"I don't know; it would be awkward to have a strange man over, but everyone else is canceling."

"Yeah, I understand," Alex said. "If I see him again, I'll see if he has a place to go."

"Thanks."

Fifteen minutes before the library was due to open, Anne went to Liddie's room and sat down on the edge of her sleeping daughter's bed. She gently reached out and brushed the hair from her face.

Liddie's eyes fluttered opened, and she smiled. "Mommy, I had a good dream."

"Want to tell me about it?" Anne asked.

"Uh huh." Liddie sat up in bed, rubbing her eyes. "I dreamed that Cindy and I were playing with my toys, and there were ponies, and they told us we could ride them."

Anne grinned. "That sounds like a fun dream."

"It was fun. The ponies could go anywhere." Liddie's eyes widened. "They could even fly."

Still smiling, Anne stood. "Maybe next time you can include me in your dream. I would love to ride on a flying pony." She opened Liddie's closet. "I have to open the library in a few minutes, so why don't you get dressed and come on downstairs?"

"Okay." Liddie ran over to the closet and pointed to her purple outfit. "Can I wear that?"

"I don't see why not." Anne pulled the outfit off the hanger and handed it to Liddie. "Can you put this on by yourself, or do you need help?"

"I can do it." Liddie took the outfit and started changing. "Can you make waffles?"

"Sure. I'll take them down to the library kitchen, and you can eat there."

After Liddie ate, she played with some of the puzzles in the Children's Room while Anne worked at the desk. Business was slow, so Anne didn't need help and was surprised when Mildred came in anyway.

"I'm finished with everything on my to-do list." Mildred brushed her hands together. "So I'm ready for something else to do."

"Sorry, but there's nothing here."

"Where are the children?" Mildred looked around. "I can play with them."

Anne laughed. "Ben is still at Ryan's, but Liddie is doing puzzles in the Children's Room."

"Good. I'll go help her with that."

After Mildred left, Anne couldn't help but smile. Mildred never failed to amaze or amuse her with her lighthearted kindness.

Ben came home while Liddie was having lunch. "Want a grilled cheese sandwich?" Anne asked.

He started to shake his head but changed his mind. "I had lunch, but I would like a grilled cheese sandwich."

"Soup?" Anne held the spatula midair as she held Ben's gaze.

"Yes, please." He sat down in his regular chair and propped his face in his hands. "Mom, I've been thinking about something..."

Uh oh. Last time Ben started thinking they wound up with Hershey. "What have you been thinking about?"

"You know, dogs are social animals, and we only have one." He looked up at her with a hopeful expression.

"Ben." She gave him one of her no-nonsense looks. "The answer is no."

* * *

On Sunday morning, Anne found a seat near the front of church. The sanctuary was packed, so Anne couldn't tell if any of her friends were missing. Normally, the first person to greet her was Mildred, but she wasn't at the door this morning.

The organ began to play, so she sat back and placed her arm around Liddie who sat between her and Ben. She nearly jumped out of her seat when someone tapped her on the shoulder.

She glanced up and saw Mildred motioning for her to scoot over. "Sorry I'm late," Mildred whispered as she grabbed the hymnal from the pew pocket and glanced up at the hymn board.

Warmth from being surrounded by people she cared about in the midst of other believers flooded Anne. Mildred grinned and winked at her as Liddie took off toward the front when the pastor called up the younger children for their mini-sermon. Ben scooted closer to Anne. Throughout church, Anne reflected on the pastor's words and how they related to her many blessings.

During the final hymn, she heard the door to the side of her opening and whooshing shut. She glanced over in time to see Joan's face on the other side of the window to the hallway leading to the classrooms. Joan's gaze was fixed on Mildred.

When Joan realized Anne was looking at her, she quickly darted away. Anne turned to Mildred. "Did you see Joan looking at you?"

"Who?"

"Joan...You know, the mystery woman from the Tea and Book Club." Anne pointed to the window. "She was on the other side, watching you."

Mildred looked up and then back at Anne. "Are you sure? She's not there now."

"She ran away when she realized I noticed her." Anne jumped up. "Ben, stay right here with Mrs. Farley. I'll be back in a few minutes. I want to go see if Joan needs anything."

"Take your time," Mildred said. "Oh, and see if she wants to join us for lunch."

CHAPTER TWENTY-ONE

Anne took off in the direction she thought Joan might have gone. She went up and down the hallways, but found no sign of her.

One of the elders stopped Anne. "Looking for someone?"

"Yes." Anne described Joan.

"As a matter of fact, I did see a woman who fits that description. I think she left." He pointed to the side door leading to the parking lot. "Is she new in town?"

"Yes," Anne replied. "Reverend Tom has already spoken with her, and I think he might know more about her than I do."

The man laughed. "You look eager to find her, so why don't you see if she's still in the parking lot?"

Anne ran outside and stood there looking around. She didn't see any sign of Joan's rental car. Feeling defeated, Anne slowly went back into the church. Mildred and both children stood in the church foyer.

"They both have something to ask you," Mildred said. "I told them you'd be right back."

Ben spoke first. "Mom, a bunch of the guys are going to Matt's to hang out. Is it okay if I go?"

Mildred touched her arm. "Matt's dad is checking out one of the movies from the church library for the boys to watch."

"Sure, Ben," Anne replied.

"Can you pick me up at four?"

"Yes, of course." Anne glanced down at Liddie. "Did you have a question?"

Before Liddie had a chance to speak, little Juliana came skipping up. "Did your mommy say you can come with us?"

"Where?" Anne asked.

Liddie looked up at Anne, her eyes wide. "Juliana's house. Her mommy wants me to come over and help her bake cookies."

Juliana's mother approached. "We have an extra car seat, now that Howie has outgrown it, so she can go straight home with us."

"Okay," Anne said. "You may go." She wrote down their phone number and put it safely in her purse. "What time should I pick her up?" she asked Juliana's mother. "I'm picking Ben up from Matt's at four."

"How about four fifteen?"

Anne nodded. "See you then."

Liddie squealed with delight as she jumped up and down, holding Juliana's hand. "I love to bake cookies."

After the children headed off with their friends, Mildred took Anne by the arm and led her to the fellowship hall for the post-service fellowship time. "I wonder why Joan took off so quickly," Mildred said. "She should have hung around to discuss the pastor's sermon and his text from Leviticus." She sighed. "Without fully understanding the holiness of God, it's difficult to understand our relationship with Him."

"Isn't that the truth." Anne said.

After the fellowship time ended, Mildred took off with some of her friends. Anne went out to her car and got in. As she stuck her key into the ignition, she spotted a note tucked beneath the windshield wiper.

She slid partially out of the car until she could reach the note that had been folded in half. She unfolded the note and read the words, "Call 555-4321 ASAP."

Anne had no idea who the number belonged to, although she suspected that the number belonged to Joan. There was only one way to find out.

She pulled her cell phone from her purse and punched in the number. No one answered, and when the voice mail came on with the automated message, she was tempted to hang up. But she didn't. She left her name, cell phone number, and number at the library. After she punched the Off button, she leaned back in her car and closed her eyes.

All this secrecy was taking its toll on her, and at the moment, she felt like going home, crawling into bed, pulling the covers up to her chin, and staying there until everything returned to the way it used to be. *Too bad that may never happen,* she thought as she opened her eyes and shook herself back to the moment.

Her mind raced with all the possibilities of what could possibly be going on. Even though she believed the note was from Joan, she wouldn't know for sure until she spoke with the person. Still, the fact that Joan took off so abruptly made her worry about the timing. Could Joan be in some kind of trouble?

Anne pondered what to do next. She couldn't very well ignore some of the warning signs. Maybe if she found Joan, she could get some clarity on the big picture.

She drove to the inn, hoping someone would be able to talk to her. Joan's rental car wasn't in the lot, but Charlotte's SUV was parked out front. She pulled up beside the SUV and went inside.

Charlotte smiled until she realized it was Anne. Then her lips twitched nervously as she said, "How may I help you?"

"Is Joan still staying here?" she asked.

A suspicious expression blanketed Charlotte's face. "I'm sorry, but you know I can't discuss anything about our guests." The tightness of her tone let Anne know something was awry.

"Look, Charlotte, even though we don't know each other well, I think you know me well enough to know I'm not a bad person. I'm concerned about Joan, and I'd like to talk to her."

Charlotte pursed her lips. "Let me go talk to my husband for a second. I'll be right back."

After she left, Anne looked down at the desk and noticed an open register with a list of names. She turned her head to the side and saw the name *Joan Meadows* twice on the same page. It appeared that she had checked out and then checked back in a few days later. The town she listed as her home was Lancaster. At least that gave Anne more information to search.

Charlotte returned and slowly shook her head. "I can't."

Anne sighed. "This is very important."

"Please stop," Charlotte finally said. "You're only making things more difficult for both of us."

With that, Anne decided to stop pressing. "Okay, but please, if you see her, tell her to call me. I think she has the library phone number, but just in case she doesn't…" She pulled a slip of paper from her purse and jotted down her numbers. "I included my cell phone and library numbers. She can call me at either."

Charlotte didn't reach for it. Instead she just stared blankly at Anne. She was obviously not going to say anything that would indicate whether or not she would see Joan.

Anne walked toward the door. "Thanks anyway, Charlotte."

The inn owner gave her a half smile before turning her back. Anne scurried out to her car and got in. Charlotte's demeanor was so different from that of most people in Blue Hill. Why would someone purchase a business in such a friendly town yet not even try to fit in?

The dull gray sky felt heavy as she pulled out of the inn's parking lot. By the time she turned onto the street, a light snow had started. She knew the weather forecast called for several inches by the next morning, so it wasn't a surprise, but she'd hoped it wouldn't begin until night time, when she and the children were all safely tucked inside.

She pulled into the next parking lot and called the numbers where her children were. Juliana's mom said her husband had a large truck with snow tires, and he could take her home later. Matt's dad said that since the kids were out of school on Monday, Ben and the rest of the boys could stay overnight. That gave Anne some relief, so she turned back out onto the road.

As she drove, the snowfall grew heavier and denser. Her windshield wipers flopped back and forth, but as the snow descended, it became more difficult to see.

She'd barely gotten out on the main road when she spotted a light blue car with its hood up on the side of the road. Beside the car stood a woman in a bright red jacket. Anne slowed down and saw that it was Rita Sloan, the bank manager.

Anne pushed the window button to lower it as she came to a stop. "Car trouble?" she asked.

Rita stepped toward her and nodded. "I called a mechanic, but he can't get here until tomorrow. Apparently there are only two tow trucks in Blue Hill, and both of them are busy with emergencies."

"Would you like a ride?" Anne asked. At least Rita's car was far enough off the road that she didn't think it would obstruct what little traffic would be out in inclement weather.

Rita hesitated. "I'm not so sure I should leave my car here. What if someone steals it?"

"That might be difficult if it doesn't start," Anne reminded her.

"True." Anne saw a glimmer of a smile tweak the corners of Rita's lips.

"But I understand your concern." Anne pondered what to do. "Let me call the police station and ask for advice."

One of the weekend people answered. "We have quite a few stranded vehicles, so we're recommending finding shelter and dealing with the cars after the snow stops."

Anne relayed the information to Rita. The shivering woman finally opened the car door and got in.

Anne cranked up the heater. "I thought it was supposed to snow later, but this caught me by surprise."

"Yes," Rita said, her chin quivering. "Me too."

"Want me to take you home?" Anne asked.

Rita nodded as she looked out the window at her car. "I guess it's better to leave it than stand there and freeze to death." She turned to Anne with a bigger smile. "Thank you for stopping."

"Glad to do it." Anne pulled away. "I'm not sure where you live, so you'll have to give me directions."

Rita told Anne where her neighborhood was, so Anne went in that direction, creeping along very slowly, since the salt trucks hadn't been there yet. "Driving in this mess is rough," Anne said.

"I'm not used to driving in snow," Rita admitted. "In the city, I mostly used public transportation."

"How do you like Blue Hill?" Anne asked.

Rita shrugged. "It's been an adjustment."

"I can imagine." Anne had quite a few questions she wanted to ask, but she didn't want to come across as nosy. "I used to live in New York, so I understand what you're saying about driving."

"New York? What brought you to Blue Hill?"

The sincerity of Rita's question surprised Anne. Until now, she felt as though Rita didn't much care about anyone else.

"My aunt left me her old house that's now the library." Anne went on to explain how she'd lost her husband and then her job. "I prayed that the Lord would show me some direction because none of my plans were working out as I'd hoped."

"I know what you mean," Rita said. "That happened to me too. I asked for a promotion, hoping to get one in the city. When I was called in for some good news, I had no idea I'd be offered something so far away."

"I'm sure you miss all your friends," Anne said softly.

"Yes, I really do. We visit each other sometimes on weekends, but it's not the same."

"Maybe..." Anne paused. "Have you considered joining some groups here so you can get to know people?"

She pulled up to a stop sign and turned to look at the bank manager. Rita smiled shyly and shrugged. "It's a little scary joining a group where I don't know people very well."

"That's the best way to get to know people."

"In case you didn't notice," Rita said, "I don't always know what to say. I've always been the quiet one...maybe even a little on the shy side. My old friends know that about me, so I don't have to explain anything to them."

So she was shy. That revelation made sense, and Anne saw Rita in a whole new light. "One of the things that might help is if you find one person and get to know her. Then when you join a group, it won't seem so intimidating."

"Sort of like how I'm getting to know you now?" Rita asked.

"Exactly." Anne smiled. "Is this your street?"

"Yes." She pointed. "I'm renting that red brick house over there."

Anne pulled up in front of the house and stopped, but Rita didn't make a move to get out. Instead, she fidgeted, looked around, and finally settled her gaze on Anne.

"You know, I'm starting to worry about all this identity theft."

Anne didn't express her thoughts—that it was about time Rita became concerned. She nodded. "It's becoming a serious problem."

"I know. We've had dozens of bank customers with issues, many of them being completely wiped out." She cleared her throat. "At least the bank is insured for that kind of thing, so we are able to put the money back into their accounts."

"That's good." Anne had wondered about that.

"For the customer, yes, but the bank is still on the hook. I got a memo last week that I need to be more diligent in protecting our customers from the thieves." Her expression changed. "I have to admit that I'm in over my head this time. I'm good at administrative things, but this is out of my realm of understanding."

"Well, you can start by participating in the seminars we're hosting at the library," Anne said.

Rita held out her hands. "Would I be expected to talk to all those people? I wouldn't have any idea what to say."

"You don't have to say a word. Officer Banks is conducting the seminars, so it would be nice to have you on hand just to show your support. I think that would show goodwill from the bank."

"I agree." Rita nodded. "I'll do that. When is your next seminar?"

"We have several coming up. Why don't I e-mail you with a list of dates and times?"

"I'll try to come to all of them. Some of our seniors have been distraught over what has happened, and I don't know what to tell them."

"Have you given a list of all the cases to the authorities?" Anne asked.

Again, Rita nodded. "Yes, and they told me they were aware of them already, and they're working on them. I thought I could talk to each customer and help them protect their accounts, but it looks like we're dealing with a professional thief here, and I'm out of my league."

"Yes, I agree with you. It's been happening so much and so quickly, there's no doubt in my mind that the thief knows what he...or she is doing."

Rita opened the car door. "I guess I better get on inside. Thanks for stopping for me and..." She gave Anne a sheepish look. "And for taking the time to talk with me."

"It was my pleasure," Anne said. "Please don't hesitate to call me if you need someone to talk to."

"Thanks." Rita got out, closed the car door, and walked as quickly as she could up her sidewalk.

Anne waited until Rita was inside before pulling away from the curb. Although she still wasn't sure about Rita's innocence, Anne wasn't quite as nervous around her as she once was. She made a mental note to visit the bank next week.

CHAPTER TWENTY-TWO

By the time Anne expected Liddie to come home, the snow was so deep she had to use the snowblower to clear the sidewalk. Fortunately, the snow had stopped. She'd barely finished when she heard a truck coming up the street.

She met the truck at the curb and opened the passenger door so Juliana's dad didn't have to get out. "Thank you so much for bringing her home."

"It's rough out there," Juliana's dad said. "I'm happy to do it. Have a happy Thanksgiving."

"You too." After he pulled away, Anne glanced down at Liddie whose bottom lip quivered. "What's wrong, sweetie?"

"Juliana said her grandma and grandpa and aunt and uncle and cousins are coming to her house for Thanksgiving." She looked up at Anne as a tear trickled down her cheek. "I wish my grandma and grandpa were coming."

"I know." Anne took Liddie by the hand. "Me too. Just remember that there will be many more Thanksgivings when you'll get to see them."

"Did anyone call and say they changed their mind?" Liddie asked.

Anne sighed and tried to lighten her voice. "Sorry, sweetie. Looks like it's just going to be the three of us."

Liddie didn't respond. Anne should have suspected that Liddie had been working hard to put up a happy front about both sets of grandparents not being able to visit.

"Did you have fun with Juliana?" Anne asked.

"Yes."

Since she'd cleared the sidewalk, they used the library entrance. Anne opened the front door and gently guided Liddie inside. "Let me help you with your jacket."

"I'm tired," Liddie said. "Can I watch a movie?"

"Sure. Let me set one up, and you can lie down on the sofa."

After she had Liddie situated in front of the television with her favorite children's movie, Anne went to her computer to do some more research on Joan, now that she knew where she was from.

She typed the name *Joan Meadows* and added *Lancaster* to the search. Several articles popped up, and Anne couldn't tell if they were about the same person. She clicked on *images* to see if they resembled the Joan she knew.

The first one was a different person but gave credit to a photographer named Joan Meadows. She backed out of that and clicked on several more—all of them grainy and hard to see.

This was extremely frustrating, but Anne's thoughts kept popping back to all the people who had been affected by the identity thief, so she continued. She tried enlarging the clearest one of the photos, but that didn't help. However, she could sort of make out the shape of the eyes, nose, and mouth.

She stepped back from the computer and squinted at the screen to see if it gave her a better perspective. As she studied it, she thought it might resemble the Joan she knew. However, she'd only seen the woman wearing a baseball cap, including that morning in church.

The baseball cap was throwing her off. Anne pondered the reasons anyone would wear one all the time, and what she came up with gave her chills. She was obviously trying to hide something.

Anne clicked on the information behind the picture and saw that the woman had a long history of nonviolent crime. She'd been found guilty of check forgery and impersonating a law enforcement official. Goosebumps formed on Anne's arms.

The sound of another truck rumbling up the street caught her attention. The front bell rang.

Anne went downstairs and opened the door to see Alex kicking the snow off his boots. "Hey there. What are you doing out in this weather? Is everything okay? Are you freezing?" She noticed that he was alone. "And where's Ryan?"

He laughed. "Whoa there. I'm here because I wanted to check on you and see if you needed anything, and Ryan is still at Matt's."

"Sorry I pounced on you with so many questions. Come on in. I'll fix you some hot cocoa." She led the way to the stairs. "Liddie's watching television, and I'm doing a little research on the computer."

"Always working," he said as he followed her. "What kind of research?"

When she reached the landing, she turned and waited for him. "I can't stop wondering about Joan."

"Why don't you just ask her whatever you want to know?"

Anne shrugged. "She keeps skittering away when things start to get personal. Did you see her this morning at church?"

"She was at church?"

"I guess that answers my question." Anne smiled as they walked past Liddie who had fallen asleep on the sofa. "Let's sit at the kitchen table. I'll get my laptop."

She poured some milk into a pot, added several teaspoons of cocoa, and turned on the burner. Then she opened her laptop and found the picture of Joan.

"Do you think this might be her?" she asked as she leaned away so Alex could get a good look.

He did the same thing she did — squinted his eyes — but backed away and shook his head. "I don't think so. The woman in the picture has bangs."

"Hair is easy to change. Besides, the Joan here in town just might have bangs. We can't tell because she always has that baseball hat on."

"Want me to grab it off her head next time I see her?" he teased.

"Only if you want to face the wrath of a woman who doesn't want you to see something she's trying to hide."

"Excellent point." He looked at the picture again. "There's really no way we can tell whether or not this is her."

Anne folded her arms, pursed her lips and shook her head. "Did you see what it says about her?"

"No, not yet. Why?"

She tilted her head toward it. "Then take a look. You'll see why I'm so worried."

Alex turned back around and read the article, scrolling all the way to the bottom. "I have to admit this is concerning." He clicked back on the picture. "I still can't tell if this is her. According to the article, the woman isn't actually from Lancaster. That's just where she got caught. Is the Joan who showed up here *from* Lancaster?"

"Yes," Anne replied. "At least that's what the register at the inn said."

He grinned. "So were you snooping around the inn?"

"No." Her voice came out defensive. "It was right there on the counter, and when Charlotte left me standing alone while she went to talk to her husband, I just happened to look down, and…"

"I was just kidding." Alex held up his hands to calm her down. "I get the picture." He leaned back in the chair. "Even if this isn't the same woman, I think you should show it to Officer Banks. It's probably as good as any other leads they've gotten on this case."

"But wait. There are more pictures."

"Can we have our hot cocoa first?" he asked.

"Sure. Do you want marshmallows?"

His smile widened. "Is there any other way to have it?"

After she put the mugs on the table, she sat down across from Alex. "So do you think that might be her?"

"It's so hard to tell, but there are a lot of factors that point in that direction. First, you have the Lancaster connection. Next, the Joan we've seen here in Blue Hill has similar shaped features." He paused and held her gaze. "And then there's the issue of similar crimes."

"To think we've welcomed her to our Tea and Book Club meetings." Anne shuddered. "You have to admit it's pretty creepy to think about a criminal hanging out with our God-loving group."

He tilted his head. "Yes, but what better group for her to be with? Even if she is guilty, she's experiencing the goodness of these people."

"True." His comment didn't make her happy about the situation, but it did ease some of her anxiety. "But since we're not one hundred percent sure, I don't want to tell anyone else our suspicions."

"I agree. No point in pointing fingers until we know for certain." He nodded toward the phone on the wall. "Why don't you go ahead and call Officer Banks?"

"Right now?"

Alex tipped his head toward the phone. "Might as well so he can start following up."

"One of the weekend receptionists answered when I called earlier. I doubt he's there."

"I just happen to know he's at the station now because I saw his car in the lot on my way here."

Officer Banks was not only at the station, he answered the phone. "I didn't expect you to answer," she said.

"The receptionist is taking another call. What can I help you with?"

After Anne told him about finding the picture and information on the Internet, he said he'd check it out immediately. She gave him the Web address.

After she hung up, she sat back down. "I'm having mixed feelings about this. On the one hand, I hope it's not her because she's been with our group a couple of times, and I don't want to frighten the other book club members. On the other hand, if it's her, then we can get back to living our normal lives without worrying about people stealing our identity."

Alex gave her a comforting smile. "I'm praying for an answer soon."

"Me too. I think we also need to include Joan in our prayers."

Anne sighed. "I wonder what Aunt Edie would have done."

Alex leaned back and looked off into the distance before meeting her gaze again. "Probably exactly what you're doing."

His compliment touched her heart. "Thank you, Alex."

"There's something I need to ask you, but I don't want you thinking I'm just being nosy."

Anne laughed. "Don't worry about that. Plenty of people have asked some very nosy questions, and it hasn't bothered me yet."

"Something seems to be bothering you lately." He paused. "Are you sad about something?"

"Of course. I'm concerned about all this identity theft."

"No, I think there's something else."

"Well…" Anne sighed.

"Does it have anything to do with the holidays coming up?" he asked.

Tears stung the backs of Anne's eyes, so she bit her lip and nodded. She swallowed hard and opened her mouth, but no words came out.

"Are you sad about family not being here?"

She nodded and glanced down at the table. "Sort of…" She forced a smile. "And I don't get why people are canceling plans after saying they'll come for Thanksgiving dinner."

"After this coming week is over, you'll be so busy with the upcoming seminars and getting ready for Christmas you won't have time to even think about Thanksgiving."

"Are you sure you can't join us?" Anne had asked him to share their Thanksgiving meal as soon as she learned her in-laws weren't coming, but he had declined, saying he and Ryan were heading out for an extended guys' weekend.

He nodded, then stood up, looked around the kitchen, and stretched. "I'm sure. Say, I'd better get on home before the roads get any worse. Besides, you probably need to start dinner soon, and I don't want to get in the way."

She walked him downstairs and to the door. After watching him pull away, she closed the door and thought about his odd reaction to her question.

By the time she returned upstairs, Liddie's eyes were open, but she was still snuggled up beneath the blanket on the sofa.

"Where were you, Mommy?"

"Mr. Ochs stopped by. I was just walking him to the door. Did you get a good nap?"

Liddie propped up on one elbow and rubbed her eyes with her other fist. "Yes, but I missed the movie. Can I watch it again?"

"Okay, but just for a few minutes while I cook dinner. Try not to fall asleep again, or you might have trouble sleeping tonight."

Liddie sat all the way up. Anne rearranged the blanket around her before going back to the kitchen. "How does spaghetti sound?"

"Yummy! I love s'getti!"

After dinner and a couple of stories, Anne tucked Liddie into bed. "Sleep tight, sweetie."

"I will." Liddie snuggled deeper beneath the covers. "I can't wait until Story Time tomorrow 'cause I get to see Cindy again."

Anne left Liddie's room and headed for the living area on the third floor. The note that had been left on her windshield popped into her mind, so she got her purse, pulled out the note, picked up the phone, and punched in the number again. She didn't expect an answer, but she felt the urge to try again.

This time, after three rings, someone answered with a very scratchy, unfamiliar voice. Anne identified herself and said she was calling the number on a note.

"Are you the one who put that note on my car?" Anne asked.

"Yes, I'm the one."

"What can I help you with?"

Silence fell over the line, and Anne held her breath. Finally, the woman spoke up. "I can't discuss it over the phone. It's kind of sensitive and personal." A hint of familiarity came through, but Anne couldn't tell if it was Joan.

"Would you like to come here to the library? I'll be here most of the day."

"No, I'd rather meet somewhere more discreet."

Anne was tired of trying to figure out who she was talking to, so she decided to come right out and ask. "Who is this?"

"I—I'd rather not say…at least not yet."

"Okay," Anne said, trying to hide her frustration. "How about meeting at the sandwich shop near the police station?"

"No, I'd rather meet somewhere else."

Anne suggested a couple more places. The woman definitely wasn't making it easy to meet her request.

"Never mind," the woman said. "It was probably a bad idea anyway."

"Tell you what," Anne said. "You let me know where you want to meet, and I'll be there."

"How about the Castle Diner?"

Anne vaguely remembered the place from when she was growing up in Blue Hill. It was on the other side of town in an area where she didn't know anyone. "Can't we meet someplace closer?"

"No." The woman paused. "I knew this was a bad idea. Why don't we just forget about this conversation?"

"I'll meet you at the Castle Diner. What day and time?"

"How about Tuesday afternoon at three?"

Anne thought about who could watch Liddie and Ben. Surely someone would stay with them. "Okay, but if I can't find someone to watch my kids, I'll have to cancel."

"That's fine. I don't want anyone else there," the woman said. "I'm very uncomfortable about this."

The irony of the situation wasn't lost on Anne. The woman claimed to be uncomfortable, yet she was calling all the shots.

"I'll see you at three on Tuesday," Anne said. "Unless I can't find someone to watch my children."

"Why don't you ask Wendy? I'm sure she wouldn't mind."

"You know Wendy?"

The woman gasped. And then she hung up.

CHAPTER TWENTY-THREE

Monday morning seemed brighter, starting when Anne first awoke. The snow still glistened on the grass, but the roads had been cleared and salted. She called the police station to find out whether or not it was safe for people to drive to the library for the program. The receptionist said it should be fine as long as everyone drove slowly and heeded conditions.

Liddie woke up excited because she'd get to see her friend Cindy again. "Can I wear my sweatshirt and blue jeans?" she asked. "Cindy is wearing red, and I want to dress like her."

Anne laughed. "Yes, sweetie, that's fine." She remembered wanting to dress like her friends at Liddie's age too.

After getting dressed, they went down to the library kitchen for breakfast so Anne could be available if people arrived early. Wendy was the first one there.

"You really didn't have to come out in this weather," Anne said.

"I'm fine. I wouldn't want to miss anything." She lifted a box to the kitchen counter. "I brought some goodies for the children. I hope we have a good turnout."

"Some of the parents from church said they were bringing their kids, but that was before the snow. I'm not sure if they'll want to get out in this or not."

"The conditions aren't all that bad now. Someone got up before the chickens and made sure of that."

Anne laughed. "You have a way with words."

"She always has." The sound of Betty Bultman's voice grabbed their attention. "Good morning, ladies. I hope you enjoyed the beautiful snow we had yesterday evening."

"Always," Wendy said. "I love snow."

Betty smiled. "Yes, I remember that time when we all went on a sleigh ride. You had the best time of everyone."

Wendy chuckled. "Yes, I always loved sleigh rides." Her eyebrows shot up. "In fact, it's such a blast maybe we can do it sometime this season. Liddie and Ben would love it."

"I'm sure they would," Anne said.

Betty held up a finger. "I hate to change the subject, but Story Time will be starting soon, and I wondered about the agenda. Do you want me to read the first story?"

"Yes, if you don't mind."

"I'd love to." She walked over to a shelf and pulled out a book. "I was looking at this one last time I was here, and I thought it would be a fun one to read aloud."

"It's one of my favorites," Anne agreed.

"Then it's decided," Betty replied.

"What would you like for me to do?" Wendy asked Anne. "I can read or prepare snacks or do both."

"You're making the rest of us look like slackers," Mrs. Bultman said. "I've never known anyone who can do all you do and keep such a high energy level. What's your secret? Even when I was younger, I didn't have half the energy you have."

Wendy shrugged. "I guess it must be in the genes. I take after my dad."

"Your dad must be quite a guy."

"He is." Wendy pulled out a book and held it up. "I'd like to read this one. It's a favorite among my kids."

Anne grinned. "Looks like I'm not needed in here today."

"Oh, you're definitely needed," Wendy said. "But if you have something else you need to do, go ahead. You mentioned something about going over to the bank and talking to Rita."

"That's what I was hoping to do."

Mrs. Bultman wandered off to prepare for her reading and Wendy remained standing beside Anne.

"Speaking of being needed, I have a question for you." Anne lowered her voice. "Something has come up, and I need a favor tomorrow afternoon."

"Sure." Wendy's eyebrows came together. "Is something wrong?"

"I don't know."

Wendy took Anne by the arm and gently pushed her toward the library kitchen. "Okay, what's up?"

Anne relayed the phone conversation to Wendy. "I'm a little uncomfortable about this since she wouldn't tell me who she was, but my curiosity is piqued."

"So is mine."

"If you don't mind watching Liddie, I'd like to see what she wants."

"Of course I don't mind watching Liddie. The kids are enjoying having Chad to themselves. How about Ben? Do you need for me to go pick him up?"

"I think I'll ask Alex to take him for an hour or so."

"Make sure you tell Alex where you'll be. Want one of us to call your cell phone to make sure everything is okay?"

"That's not a bad idea," Anne replied.

"We can have a code. If you say certain words, we'll call the cops."

Anne let out a nervous laugh. "You've been watching way too many crime shows."

"Probably." Wendy shrugged. "But that's what Chad likes to watch, and if I want to spend time with him after the kids go to bed, that's what I have to do." The corners of her eyes crinkled as she grinned. "And since I'm willing to do that for him, he watches romantic movies with me."

Anne called Alex and told him about her meeting with the stranger.

"Would you like for me to go with you?" he offered.

"She told me I have to come alone, or she won't talk to me."

"If you change your mind, I don't mind going with you."

"I appreciate that. I'll be meeting with her in a public place in broad daylight. Wendy is going to call me fifteen minutes after I get there. We even have some code words."

He laughed. "Now this is starting to sound interesting."

"It's not funny." Anne couldn't help but belie her own words with a nervous giggle. "But I do have a favor to ask."

"Would you like for me to have Ben come over to hang out with Ryan?"

"Yes, how did you know?"

"It's logical, and logic is one thing I understand. What time do you want me to bring him home?"

"Any time before dinner. If I'm not back, Wendy will be here."

"Okay, that sounds good. Please promise me you'll be careful."

"Of course I will be."

"Oh, before you go," he said, "I wanted to tell you that Rita is having an identity protection seminar at the bank tomorrow."

"I wonder why she didn't tell me," Anne said.

"Probably just an oversight."

"Yeah, you're right." Anne hung up still wondering how Rita could have kept the seminar from her, since she was doing the same thing at the library.

Anne went into the Children's Room and listened for a few minutes. Wendy had the rapt attention of all the little ones. She changed voices for each character and showed pictures after she read each page. It put Anne at ease to see how well things were going. As she stood there, she thought about how she needed to get past the hurt feelings and perhaps offer a helping hand to Rita. After all, she could share her own experiences.

Wendy glanced at her, and Anne mouthed, "I'll be back soon."

"Take your time," Wendy mouthed back.

She didn't waste any time driving straight to the bank. The front parking lot was already full, so she drove around until she found a spot on the side of the building. As she got out of her car, something in the distance caught her eye. She turned and spotted the meter man doing something on the side of the building.

She scurried around to the front, pulling out her cell phone as she ran. She called Alex and held her breath.

Fortunately he answered before the first ring ended. "Hey, what's up?"

"Remember that energy audit man?"

"Yes, the one who mentioned my name."

"That's the one. He's doing something on the outside wall of the bank."

"How close are you?" Alex asked.

"I'm on the other end of the building."

"Can you see what he's doing?"

"I'm not sure, but he's standing between the meters and the trash bins."

Alex sighed. "I'll be there in a few minutes. It's time I had a chat with the guy who has been dropping my name around town. In the meantime, why don't you go on inside the bank?"

"That's exactly what I plan to do." Anne opened the door with her other hand. "And now I'm in."

"Good. Stay there for a while if you can."

She headed up to the teller desk and handed over the deposit wallet. The teller quickly counted the money and checks before handing her the wallet and wishing her a happy Thanksgiving.

Anne turned around and saw Rita standing at the door of her office. They made eye contact. Rita smiled and motioned for Anne to follow her into her office.

Still smiling, Rita closed the door behind Anne. "How's everything at the library? Have you been busy?"

"Yes, but my volunteers graciously offered to cover for me so I could come here and talk to you." Anne took a breath. "By the way, did you know that some guy is out there? I think he might be doing something to your meters."

Rita nodded. "Yes, he came in with some paperwork letting me know he's here to do an evaluation on our energy usage. The bank is all about saving money wherever they can."

"Did you actually look at that paperwork?" Anne asked.

"Yes. In fact it was on bank letterhead and had the CEO's signature on it." Rita frowned and tilted her head in confusion. "Why do you ask?"

"That same man was at the library not long ago. He implied he knew Alex, but Alex denied ever talking to him."

"That's odd." Rita gestured toward a chair on the other side of the desk. "Why don't you have a seat?"

"I called Alex, and he said he'd be right over to talk to the guy."

Rita nodded. "I also think I should call the home office to see if they know anything about the energy guy."

"Good idea." Anne sat back in her chair as Rita punched in the number. She was put on hold, so she spoke to Anne. "They are swamped with account questions, holiday loans, and…" She grimaced. "And identity theft problems. This is something the bank is dealing with in all locations."

"I can imagine."

Rita's attention was diverted to someone on the other end of the phone. "Yes, I can wait." She widened her eyes and shook her head. "Until the past week or so, I've never had to hold this long."

"Have you had any more incidents of people having their accounts broken into?" Anne asked, hoping Rita would tell her about the seminar.

Rita held up her finger to indicate someone was on the line. She listened and said, "I understand. I'll try again later." Rita hung up. "Apparently, there are quite a few other people ahead of me, some of them branch managers. I'll call back later, after you leave." She folded her hands on the desk. "So where were we?"

"I just wondered how many of the bank's customers have had money stolen from their accounts."

Rita glanced up as she thought about it. "So far, about a dozen have come forward—all of them senior citizens. There might be more who haven't alerted us yet."

"That's terrible. Whoever this horrible person is should be prosecuted for taking advantage of so many vulnerable people."

"Oh, I agree," Rita said. "I fully intend to do everything in my power to make sure we catch him…or her."

"Or them," Anne added.

"Is that all you need to discuss? I have a meeting with one of our investment people in a half hour, and I have to prepare."

"I needed to get out of the library for a little while, and I needed to make a deposit. I figured while I was here, I could see if you were interested in having one of the seminars here at the bank for your customers. We've had so many people calling the library, I don't think we have enough space or time to do it."

Rita nervously fidgeted with a pen before looking back up at Anne. "Actually, we're having a seminar tomorrow morning. This one isn't advertised, though. It's for people who have already had their accounts compromised but missed the first seminar at the library." She offered an apologetic half smile. "Any helpful hints to make it go smoothly?"

"Basically, all you have to do is provide the room, and for future seminars when you invite everyone else, let people know. Officer Banks will take care of everything else."

Rita lifted her eyebrows and nodded. "Sounds like a good plan. I'm sure we'll have more for the rest of our customers. There's no point in limiting everything to the number of people we can cram into the library, is there?"

Anne laughed. "I totally agree."

"Since we're not expecting more than a dozen or so people tomorrow morning, I plan to hold it in the main meeting room. If more people sign up for the next one, we can hold it in the lobby. I think we can fit approximately thirty or forty people in there."

"Easily," Anne agreed as she stood.

"Did you need anything else while you're here?" Rita asked.

"No, I already made the deposit, and now I need to get back to the library. I just thought it would be a good idea to stop by."

"I'm glad you did. If you can get away tomorrow morning, please feel free to join us. It's early, though."

"What time?"

"Before the bank opens. Officer Banks said to plan for an hour, so I have it ending fifteen minutes before we open the doors to the public."

"I'll try to make it," Anne said as she took a step back.

Rita got up and followed her to the door. "I'll get back on the phone and try to find out if an energy audit was ordered. I appreciate the warning that this guy might not be legitimate."

Anne glanced in the direction where she'd seen the man, and he was no longer there. Then she looked around the parking lot and didn't see any sign of Alex's truck. She wondered if he'd been there and had a talk with the man and perhaps scared him off.

She started for her car when she heard someone calling her name. She spun around and saw Charlotte running toward her.

"Hey, Anne, I'm glad I caught you. I tried calling the library, and the woman who answered said you might still be here." Charlotte nervously glanced over her shoulder before looking back at Anne.

"What do you need?" Anne asked.

Charlotte leaned toward her and whispered, "Henry doesn't want me talking about this because we have a policy about not giving out information about our guests."

"That's what you said." Anne wasn't sure what was happening, but she was curious about Charlotte's actions.

Charlotte's eyes darted around, and she shifted nervously from one foot to the other. "But I wanted to let you know that the boarder you've been asking about has checked out. We think she might have gotten her own place."

Now Charlotte had her full attention. "You think Joan might have decided to move to Blue Hill permanently?"

Charlotte shrugged. "I don't know about permanently, but I don't think she's finished with whatever she had planned for her stay in Blue Hill."

A shiver of alarm crawled down Anne's spine. "So you and Henry think she had something planned? Any idea what?"

CHAPTER TWENTY-FOUR

It's hard to say." Charlotte shook her head. "I don't like doing this because Henry told me I'd best leave things alone and stay out of everyone else's business, but I know how hard you're trying to find out who is stealing so many people's identities. I want to help if I can."

Anne smiled. "Thank you, Charlotte. I really appreciate that."

"Even Henry thinks whatever she's doing seems mighty fishy."

"Thanks for finding me," Anne said. "Since you're concerned about this identity scam, why don't you and Henry plan to attend one of our seminars?"

"I just might do that. Henry isn't one for going to events with big crowds, but I can go without him."

"That would be fine," Anne agreed. "I can drop off some flyers for the inn if you'd like."

"Perfect." Charlotte backed away. "I better get back. He knows I came to the bank to make a deposit, but I don't want him to wonder what's taking me so long."

After she took off, Anne glanced down at her watch. She still had a little bit of time left to stop off at a couple more places before going back to the library, as long as she moved quickly. Since Joan had moved out of the inn, Anne thought maybe she could learn something new about the woman. If she signed a lease on an apartment or house, surely she'd need utilities and other services.

Her first stop after the bank was the town newspaper office. The young receptionist for the *Blue Hill Gazette* grinned. "Hey, Anne. How's the library these days?"

"Mostly slow, but today some of my part-timers and volunteers are holding Story Time."

The young woman's ponytail bobbed as she nodded. "I remember taking my niece and nephew to one of those when I visited them in Philly. I'm glad you started them here. So what can I do for you?"

"Do you know if there have been any new subscribers in the past couple of days?"

"We always have stops and starts. What's the name?"

"Joan Meadows."

The receptionist shook her head slowly, setting her ponytail in motion again. "I don't recall anyone by that name starting a new subscription. Why?"

"I just wondered. I'm trying to track down one of the new members of the Tea and Book Club."

"That sounds like fun. I might see if I can come to one of your meetings. What days do you hold them?"

Anne gave her the information. The young woman said she would try to take a late lunch so she could attend the next one.

On Anne's way back to the library, she stopped off at the power company and the city water and sewer office to ask if anyone by the name of Joan Meadows had ordered new service. No one seemed to be familiar with that name.

"Trust me, Mrs. Gibson," Mr. Diggers at the water and sewer office said. "I'm good with names, and when we get new customers, I don't forget them for a very long time."

"I remember that about you," Anne said with a smile. "Thanks anyway."

Mr. Diggers grinned. "I'll let you know if I run into this Joan Meadows woman."

On her way back to the library, Anne's mind raced with all the different people she'd encountered that morning. Until now, she suspected Charlotte and Henry, but after the offer of information, it didn't seem likely that they'd be involved in the theft. Based on what Charlotte had told her, it was more probable that they wanted to stay out of anything that made Henry uncomfortable.

She still wondered about the timing of the identity theft starting shortly after Charlotte and Henry purchased the inn. That was probably a coincidence, but she still wasn't about to take a chance. The thief was obviously smart to have gone so long without getting caught.

She pulled into her parking spot at the library and scurried inside. A couple of the moms had arrived to pick up their children from Story Time.

"Thanks for holding it this week," one of the mothers said as they walked toward the Children's Room. "I had a few last-minute things to do before Thanksgiving, and this gave me a chance to get it done."

"Glad we were able to help." Anne nodded toward the room where the children remained riveted as Wendy turned the page.

Wendy's gaze darted to Anne, and she waved. "We just finished snack time, so I thought I'd read them one more story," she said before turning her attention back to the children.

Anne told the other parents to go on into the Children's Room and wait. She went into the library kitchen and pulled out the pots and pans to prepare lunch for Liddie and her friend. Then she sliced some leftover chicken, dropped it into a pot filled with water, added carrots, celery, and some seasoning. Once it came to a boil, she dropped in some noodles.

After the story time, Liddie and Cindy ran into the kitchen and scrambled up into the chairs. Anne placed bowls of her fresh homemade chicken noodle soup in front of the girls.

Liddie tilted her chin upward. "My mommy makes the best-est chicken noodle soup in the whole entire world."

Cindy scooped some soup into her spoon and tasted it. "This is delicious!"

Anne laughed. "I'm glad you like it. Now how about grilled cheese sandwiches?"

"I like cheese sammiches," Cindy said. "But not grilled. Can I have mine regular?"

"Sure," Anne said. "How about you, Liddie? Grilled or" — she winked at Cindy — "regular?"

"I'll have mine regular too." Liddie took another spoonful of soup. "Cindy and I are doing everything the same today."

Anne loved every minute of time with the girls. As they ate lunch, she reflected on her old life back in New York. When she first lost her job, she thought it was just another horrible tragedy, but now she saw it as a blessing.

After lunch, the girls played for a couple of hours before Cindy's mom arrived to take her home. "Let's do this more often," she said. "They seem to enjoy each other."

"Sounds good."

"Our house next." Yvette took Cindy by the hand and led her toward the front. "Have a wonderful Thanksgiving."

Liddie's chin quivered, but she kept the tears from falling until after her friend left. The moment the door closed behind her, the floodgates opened. "I don't wanna have Thanksgiving by ourselves."

Anne knelt down to Liddie's level. "Sweetie, we won't be by ourselves. We have each other."

"And the Lord," Wendy said from behind her. "As long as we remember He is there, we never have to feel alone."

"That's right, Liddie," Anne said. "Maybe we can do something really special."

Liddie sniffled. "Like what?"

"How about if we start making Christmas cookies after dinner?"

Liddie blinked and wiped her eyes with the back of her hand. "Can I put rainbow sprinkles on them?"

"If that's what you want to do. We can decorate them however you'd like."

"Can I take some to Cindy?"

"Absolutely," Anne said as she looked up at Wendy.

Wendy bent down and touched Liddie's cheek. "I better get on home now. See you tomorrow afternoon. You and I are going to do something really fun tomorrow afternoon while your mommy goes someplace."

Liddie's eyes lit up as she looked at Wendy. "What are we gonna do?"

"It's a surprise."

A wide grin replaced Liddie's frown as she clapped her hands. "I love surprises."

Anne looked at Wendy in amazement. "You are good."

"Remember I have seven children. Lots of practice."

After Wendy left, Anne and Liddie finished cleaning up the Children's Room. It didn't take long.

"I still have to work," Anne said. "Why don't you color here at the desk for a while? I'm sure Ben won't mind reading you a story when he gets home."

"When is he coming home?" Liddie asked. "I miss him."

"Pretty soon."

* * *

An hour later, Ben came walking in looking as though he'd pulled an all-nighter. "Tired?" Anne asked.

He nodded as he let go of his backpack smack-dab in the middle of the floor. "I'm going to get something to eat and play some video games."

Anne nodded toward his backpack. "Pick that up, Ben. I don't want anyone to trip over it." She paused and waited for him to obey. "And before you play any video games, you need to take Hershey out, and then I want you to read Liddie a story."

"But—" One look at Anne, and he stopped. "Okay, but it has to be a short one."

Anne didn't argue with him. Instead, she gestured toward Liddie.

"While you walk Hershey, Liddie and I will put together your snack."

Ben started for the stairs, but when Anne cleared her throat, he turned around, picked up his backpack, and lugged it upstairs. A few minutes later, Anne heard Ben and Hershey going down the outside stairs at the back of the house. When he came back in, Liddie announced that their snacks were ready.

"Okay." Ben glanced down at his little sister.

Anne watched as Liddie eagerly followed her brother into the kitchen. As much as she wanted to ask Ben about his time at Matt's, she knew he needed a little bit of time to relax first. If she asked now, he'd give her short answers. If she waited, he was more likely to provide details.

Over the next half hour, she went back and forth between the kitchen to check on the children and the checkout desk to see if anyone needed assistance. Very few patrons came through the door, but the ones who did had quite a few questions.

The phone rang a couple of times — once from a person who wanted to know if the library had a book with Christmas plays and the other time from someone asking about the next identity protection seminar. This was one of those days she wasn't sure what to expect.

Alex called right before she closed the library. "I just wanted to check on you and make sure everything is okay."

"We're fine, but Liddie is sad about everyone canceling on Thanksgiving dinner."

"I'm sure it's hard for her to understand now, but she'll be fine," Alex said.

"I know." Anne sighed.

"I have a favor to ask you. Would you mind if Ryan hangs out with Ben in the morning? I need to give an estimate on a renovation."

"Of course I don't mind. What time?"

"I have to be there at ten, so I thought I could drop him off around nine thirty." He paused. "Or if you want to attend the seminar at the bank, I can come early and hang out with the kids so you can go."

"Are you sure you don't mind?" Anne really did want to go, but until now she didn't see how she could.

"You've known me long enough to know that I wouldn't offer unless I meant it."

Anne let out a nervous laugh. "True. Yes, that would be nice."

"Why don't I plan to fix them some of my famous French toast?" Alex offered.

"Famous?"

"Well, famous in our house." He laughed. "Ryan likes it."

"Sounds good. Both of my kids like French toast."

They made plans for Alex to get to the library in time for Anne to attend the seminar. After they hung up, Anne told Ben that Ryan would be there early in the morning. Liddie seemed delighted, but Ben just shrugged and said, "Cool." His droopy eyelids let her know he wouldn't be good for more than one story for Liddie.

CHAPTER TWENTY-FIVE

The next morning, Alex and Ryan arrived right on time for Anne to leave. She bent over and gave Liddie a kiss on the forehead. Ben wasn't close enough, so she just looked at him and smiled. "Have fun. I'll be back as soon as it's over."

Before she got to the door, she heard Alex. "C'mon, kids. Let's go make a mess in the kitchen."

A sense of peace flowed through Anne as she walked out to her car. Alex's easy, relaxed manner with the children was the total opposite of her hands-on fussy approach, but both methods seemed to work. She had no doubt her children were in excellent hands, and she wouldn't have to worry.

When she arrived at the bank, she was surprised to see so many cars since Rita had said only the people who'd had their accounts hacked were invited. She went inside and offered to assist Rita.

"I have some of the tellers handing out materials," Rita said. "Why don't you sit on the side, and if I need an extra pair of hands, I can grab you?"

Anne did as she was told. There were already almost twenty people packed into the meeting room. If many more showed up, they'd have to move out into the lobby. She reached into her handbag and turned her cell phone on silent.

"Mind if we sit with you?"

Anne glanced up and saw Charlotte with Henry right behind her. "Of course not." She moved her legs so they could slip past.

Once they were seated, Charlotte leaned over and whispered, "Officer Banks convinced Henry to attend when he delivered the flyers."

"I think he'll be glad he came." Anne spotted Rita chatting with someone she'd never seen before. She nudged Charlotte. "Do you know who that woman talking to Rita is?"

"I think she's one of the bank executives. She told us several of them were coming from the home office in Pittsburgh to show their support."

That explained why some of the people in the room were wearing business suits. Officer Banks came in through the side door and scanned the crowd. His gaze settled on Anne, and he waved and smiled.

He picked up a microphone at the podium. "Since we have to be finished by opening time, we need to go ahead and get started. Does everyone have one of these?" He lifted a flyer. "If not, raise your hand, and someone will bring you one."

Rita and one of her tellers delivered the flyers to the people with raised hands as Officer Banks began his program. Anne picked up some new tips.

"There are so many ways the bad guys can steal your identity, you must never let down your guard," Office Banks explained. At this point, Anne knew what came next. "Before you leave town, make arrangements with someone you trust to pick up your mail and newspaper. One of the ways thieves know you're not home is when your mail stays in the mailbox for several days, and the papers pile up in the driveway. And identity thieves will look for bank statements, credit card statements, and credit solicitations to get personal information about you."

Anne saw folks nodding as he spoke. The man in front of her nudged his wife and whispered, "See? I told you that long ago."

Officer Banks continued. "If you ever see someone digging through your trash, call the police so we can send a patrol car to make sure everything is okay. Even though it's not illegal for people to curb shop, our presence might deter someone with bad intentions. That's another way someone can steal your identity. I recommend purchasing a personal shredder and using it before discarding any documents. The smaller the shred, the better."

"Why can't we just rip it up?" someone sitting in the front row asked.

"Good question," Officer Banks said. "Larger pieces can be taped together."

He continued explaining things like phishing scams where someone claiming to be a bank, credit card company, or a representative from any other financial institution sends an e-mail, asking for personal information. He went on to advise everyone to never click on an e-mail link unless they were one hundred percent certain where the message came from. "Some Web sites are designed to infect your computer," he explained.

Officer Banks spoke for another ten minutes before he opened it up for questions. Most of the people had already spoken to him, so this segment didn't last as long as it had at the library.

After it was over, Henry stood up, shaking his head. "I don't know about all this. I thought technology was supposed to help people, not hurt them."

"Unfortunately, the bad guys will use everything to get what they want," Anne said. "But I have to admit I'm still amazed by what thieves are willing to do in order to access a person's information."

"You and me both," Henry said.

Anne thanked Rita for inviting her. She was glad she'd sat in on another seminar because she learned so much more this time.

As she left the bank and made a final turn onto her street, she spotted Joan's car. She blinked. She'd been thinking about Joan, so maybe her mind was playing tricks on her.

But no, as she got closer, she was certain Joan was behind the wheel. And she was pulling out of the library parking lot.

Alarm bells went off in Anne's head. The library wasn't due to open for another ten minutes. If Alex hadn't been in there with her children, she would panic, but she knew they were as safe as they could possibly be.

Joan left before Anne got close enough to stop her. Anne quickly pulled into her parking spot, got out, and ran inside. She heard voices in the Children's Room, so she went straight there.

Alex glanced up and grinned. "How was it?"

"Good," Anne replied. "Did you talk to Joan?"

His puzzled expression told her everything she needed to know. "Not today."

She held up a finger. "Stay right here with the kids. I need to check something." Before he had a chance to respond, she took off running through the library, glancing around to see if everything was in place. The computers hadn't even been turned on yet, and she'd recently changed the password, so she wasn't worried about that.

After she felt confident that everything was in order in the library, she opened the front door and walked outside onto the porch. That was when she noticed that the trash cans had been moved. She'd put them about twenty feet from where they currently were. One of the lids lay on the ground, and the top bag appeared to be open.

She went out to get a better look, and she saw the slit in the bag. It was a clean, straight cut, obviously done with a tool.

The image of Joan's car leaving the library parking lot popped into Anne's mind, and she realized this couldn't possibly be a coincidence. Officer Banks had emphasized the importance of shredding documents because identity thieves could easily piece together statements to get the information they needed.

Anne's shoulders felt heavy as she turned around and trudged back to the library. Alex stood at the door, watching her with concern.

"What just happened?" he asked.

"Where are the children?" She wasn't about to tell him the details if they were nearby. Scaring them would make it worse.

"Ben and Ryan are taking turns reading to Liddie." He grinned. "They're even doing voices." His expression changed back to worry. "Now I'm worried about you."

Anne rubbed the bridge of her nose. "I'm not the one you need to worry about."

"What?" He stepped down off the porch and walked toward her. "You're confusing me now."

"It's Joan."

"What are you talking about?" He tilted his head as he continued studying her face. "Start from the beginning and tell me what's going on."

She explained what Officer Banks had said about identity thieves stopping at nothing to get private information. "They even rummage through the trash and look for financial statements to piece together." She pointed to the trash can with the cut bag. "And look at that. Someone has gotten into the library trash."

He glanced over then turned back to her. "Maybe it was birds. I've had grackles get into my trash. They make a huge mess."

"No, it's not birds. The bag has been cut."

His eyebrows came together, and he rubbed his chin. "So where does Joan factor into all this?"

"When I turned the corner, I spotted her car pulling out of the library parking lot."

A look of understanding came over his face as he nodded. "Oh, now I get why you asked about her. But still, that doesn't mean anything. Maybe she was just looking for you."

"You have to admit this is probably more than just a coincidence," Anne said.

"Maybe, but don't be too sure."

Anne spread her arms in dismay. "What now?"

"Why don't you start by calling Officer Banks and tell him what you just told me?"

"Yes, of course." Anne started walking toward the library. "That goes without saying."

"I'll check on the kids while you make the call." Alex took off toward the Children's Room, while she went to the checkout desk and picked up the phone.

Officer Banks seemed happy to hear from her, until she explained why she called. "Did you see any footprints, or do you remember the exact time you saw her car?"

"I didn't notice any footprints, and I can't remember the exact minute, but I came straight here after I left the bank. And I've only been back for about fifteen minutes."

"I'll be right there," he said. "I want to have a look at the trash."

After Anne hung up, she shivered.

Officer Banks arrived a few minutes later. "I took a look at the trash, and I agree with you. It's been cut. I called to have someone come out and dust for fingerprints, but I doubt we'll get anything. Whoever is doing this hasn't left fingerprints anywhere else, so he's probably wearing gloves."

"Or maybe it's a she," Anne said.

"Could be," Officer Banks said. "Want me to take a look around here and make sure everything is okay?"

"I don't think that's necessary. I left the kids here with Alex, and he said he didn't see anyone."

"In that case, I best get back to the station. From the time this identity theft started, we've been getting calls every day. Everyone is pretty worked up over this."

"Understandably so," Alex said as he approached. "Hi, Officer Banks." He looked at Anne. "I told Ryan he needed to finish his story so we could leave."

Officer Banks turned back to Anne. "Let's go over everything one more time to make sure I have all the information."

After she relayed everything she remembered about Joan— the way she slipped into town and started asking questions, keeping her cap low on her forehead, driving by Mildred's house, peering through the window into the church sanctuary, seeing her pulling out of the library parking lot today, and finding the trash bag slit—his cheeks puffed as he blew out a long breath. "That's some evidence," he agreed. "Seems suspicious."

"The thing is, I've never seen her do anything wrong," Anne said. "I don't want to accuse the wrong person."

"You haven't accused anyone," Officer Banks reminded her. "You're just telling me some of the things you've observed. It's all important if we ever hope to wrap up this case."

Anne knew he was right, but it still felt odd to admit that she suspected a specific person when she wasn't one hundred percent certain. He jotted everything down in his notebook before leaving. Alex and Ryan took off a few minutes later.

"Mom, I know you don't want to worry us," Ben said, "but I sort of know what's going on. Kids in school are still talking about a crook breaking into bank accounts." His frown deepened. "Is that why Officer Banks was here? Did that happen to us?"

"No." Anne glanced down at her son with as reassuring of a look as she could manage. He was growing up fast. It wouldn't be much longer before she had to look up to see him face to face.

"Then why was Officer Banks here?"

Anne pulled him away from where Liddie was playing with her paper dolls. She'd made it a policy to never lie to her children, and with such a direct question, she knew that not answering it could frighten him even more than telling him exactly what was going on. She explained how she'd noticed that the trash cans had been moved and that one of the bags was slit.

"I don't want to worry Liddie, so please let's not discuss this in front of her, okay?"

He shoved his hands in his pockets and nodded. "Yeah, I think that's a good idea." He chewed on his lip for a few seconds. "At least it happened outside and not inside the library."

"Yes." She pulled him into an embrace and gave him a brief squeeze. For the first time in a very long time, he didn't pull away. A lump formed in her throat. Not only would he grow taller, he would eventually want to protect her. The very thought of that tweaked her heart.

"You're a good big brother, Ben."

The little-boy look returned as he shrugged. "We have to make sure Liddie is safe." He took a step back. "Mom, I know you want to talk and all, but do you mind if I go watch some of the Saturday morning cartoons we recorded?"

Anne grinned. "Of course I don't mind. I'll send Liddie up when she gets tired of playing with her paper dolls."

Very few patrons came into the library all morning. Liddie played by the checkout desk until about a half hour before lunch. "Can I go watch cartoons with Ben now?" she asked.

Anne nodded. "Just for a few minutes. I'm going to fix lunch, so tell Ben that it'll be ready in about half an hour."

"Okay, Mommy." Liddie started skipping toward the stairs.

"Be careful going up, sweetie. Slow down and hold the rail."

A little after two o'clock, Wendy arrived with a tote bag filled with what she called emergency items—granola bars, children's puzzles, stickers, and a new praise-and-worship CD. "It's a little harder to find something Ben will like, but Christian likes this CD, and they're close in age," she explained as she held it up.

"You didn't have to bring anything," Anne said. "They have plenty of things to do around here."

"I know, but I want them to look forward to the times I hang out with them. I love Ben and Liddie."

"I know you do. And they love you too. I need to fill you in on the latest." Anne spent the next few minutes telling her about what she'd seen when she got home from the bank.

"That's pretty strong evidence," she said.

"I know." Anne sighed. "It really bothers me that we might have welcomed a thief into our book club."

"Not knowingly, so it doesn't count."

Ben and Liddie came out of the Children's Room and grinned at Wendy. She held up her tote. "I have some goodies in here."

Liddie clapped her hands and squealed while Ben merely grinned. Wendy leaned toward Anne and whispered, "I'll call you at a quarter after three, so don't forget the password. If you don't say it, I'll send someone after you."

"Okay." She ran her hands over her jeans. "I'm very nervous."

"That's understandable. It's not too late to change your mind...or at least have someone go with you."

Anne shook her head. "I'll be fine."

"Okay. Just don't take off in someone's car or put yourself into a dangerous spot."

"I promise I won't."

Chapter Twenty-Six

Anne's nerves remained a jangled mess as she drove to the other side of Blue Hill. Castle Diner was a small single-story concrete block building with a poorly marked asphalt parking lot. The exterior of the diner hadn't changed since Anne had last been there when she was in high school, but the instant she stepped inside, she was surprised at the improvements. The fluorescent bulbs had been replaced by ultramodern drop lighting. The wallpaper above the chair rail had been stripped and painted white, while the lower part of the wall had been painted a soft taupe. Framed sepia-toned photos of Blue Hill dotted the walls, creating a nostalgic but fresh ambience.

She glanced around the diner, looking for someone who appeared to be waiting. When she spotted the woman in the corner, she narrowed her eyes. Even without the baseball cap, she knew it was Joan. Her heart began to beat double time.

All sorts of things flickered through her mind. Should she turn around and leave? Should she ask the manager to call the police?

When she looked directly at Joan, she noticed even more fear in Joan's eyes than Anne felt. Not knowing the right thing to do, she decided to continue with her original plan and not let Joan see her suspicion. Besides, there wasn't much Joan could do here in public.

Anne started walking toward Joan, who appeared even more nervous the closer she got. When she finally reached the booth, Joan lowered her head. "I was afraid you wouldn't come."

"Why all the secrecy?" Anne did her best to keep the accusing tone from her voice, but she wasn't sure she was successful. "Why didn't you tell me who you were?"

Joan slowly lifted her gaze to meet Anne's. "Because I was afraid."

"Afraid of what?"

"I don't know." Joan fiddled with her spoon.

Anne decided to take the bull by the horns. "What are you really doing here in Blue Hill?"

Joan shrugged, closed her eyes for a few seconds, and then opened them. "I needed to find some answers." She pursed her lips.

"What kind of answers?" Anne glared at her.

"This is really hard for me with your looking at me like that."

Frustrated, Anne decided to soften her gaze as she tried other questions. "Are you married? Do you have a job?"

Joan shook her head. "No and no. I did have a job, but I was let go about a month ago."

"So you came here to Blue Hill. Are you looking for a job here?"

"No." Joan pulled her lips between her teeth.

Anne racked her brain, trying to think of a question that would at least get the conversation started. "Where is your hat? I've never seen you without it."

Joan reached up and touched her head. "I wanted to be as inconspicuous as possible." Her gaze darted around the room, and she looked everywhere but at Anne.

"Okay, this is making me very uncomfortable," Anne admitted. "Tell me what is going on."

"*You're* uncomfortable?" A light gurgle erupted from Joan's throat. "I've been uncomfortable...no, make that miserable since I arrived in Blue Hill."

"Then why did you come here, and why have you stayed if you're so miserable?"

"Please, Anne, this is more difficult than you can imagine...but I need your help." Her voice cracked, and Anne could hear the anguish.

No way would Anne help a thief, but she couldn't let on that she suspected anything. "If you don't tell me, there's no way I can help you."

"I'm looking for my family," Joan blurted.

"Your family?" Anne asked. "I'm confused. Does someone in your family live in Blue Hill?"

"Yes...well, at least I'm pretty sure." Joan's shoulders lifted and sagged as she sighed. "I was adopted, and I think my birth mother lives in Blue Hill."

"Your birth mother?" Anne thought back to all the times Joan had come around the library, and then her mind wandered to what Mildred had said. Alarm bells sounded in Anne's head. "Is that why you kept driving past Mildred's house?"

Joan nodded. "Yes."

"Are you saying you think Mildred might be your birth mother?" Anne asked.

"No...." Joan met her gaze for a split second before looking back down at the table. "But I'm pretty sure we're related." She shredded the napkin in front of her as she spoke.

Anne sat there still stunned. She didn't know what to expect of this meeting, but this was the farthest thing from her mind.

"So why did you want to meet with me?" Anne asked. "I would think that Mildred would have been a more likely person for you to talk to."

"I was hoping you might help me." Joan looked back at her, offered a faint smile, and sighed. "In case you haven't noticed, I'm kind of shy, and talking to Mildred makes me very nervous."

"Yes, I did notice." Anne left out the fact that she was suspicious of her intentions. Now she wasn't so sure what to think. Perhaps this was a ruse.

"I know that I need to talk to Mildred about this, but I don't know what to say or how to begin. I was hoping you might have some suggestions. I have so many questions." Sadness filled her eyes. "Even if I don't like the answers, there are some things I really need to know."

The memory of Joan grilling Mildred after the first Tea and Book Club meeting popped into Anne's head. "Is that why you were asking her so many questions that day you met?"

Joan nodded. "It was very awkward, and when I realized others were listening, I felt like running away and never coming back."

"What exactly do you want me to do?" Anne asked.

"I'm not sure. I thought you might have some ideas."

"I—" Anne glanced down at the table as her mind whirled with all kinds of conflicting thoughts. "You just sprang this on me. There's really nothing I can do."

"Please."

Anne's cell phone rang. She glanced at it and saw Wendy's cell phone number. "I have to take this call."

Joan nodded.

"Hello," Anne said as she thought about how silly the code words sounded. But she needed to say it, or Wendy would worry. "I like sugar in my coffee." She allowed herself a glance at Joan who didn't appear to notice her random comment.

"Are you okay?" Wendy's voice sounded tight.

"I'm fine. How is Liddie?"

"She was tired, so I told her she could read quietly in the Children's Room, and when I checked on her five minutes later, she was sound asleep in the beanbag."

"How about Ben?"

"Alex called here and asked if he could go out to dinner with him and Ryan. I hope you don't mind that I gave him permission."

"I don't mind."

"How's everything going with Joan?" Wendy asked. "Or can you not talk now?"

"We'll be wrapping up soon," Anne replied.

"Okay, I get it. But don't feel as though you have to hurry. Take your time. Chad and the kids are having a blast without me there to keep them in line."

"Thanks." Anne smiled as she hung up. "Looks like everything is going well at home."

"That's good." Joan cleared her throat. "Could you...well, would you mind arranging for us to talk? I mean Mildred and—"

Anne picked her cell phone back up. "Why don't I call her now?"

"No!" Joan's abruptness startled Anne. "Not now."

"When?"

Again, Joan sighed. "I don't know. I'm not sure yet that I'm ready to talk to her about it. I mean, I'm still wrestling back and forth, trying to decide if I really want to open this can of worms or not. I've read about people who've met their birth parents and they end up being disappointed. Once it's done, it can't be undone, if you know what I mean." She dropped her gaze and studied her hands.

"I can understand why you'd be nervous, but knowing Mildred and her family like I do, I don't believe you really have anything to be afraid of, Joan."

"That's another thing," Joan said as she lowered her head and averted her gaze.

Anne's stomach lurched. Another thing? How much more could there be? "What other thing?"

"My name isn't Joan."

"So you lied about your name? What else did you lie about?" She paused. "What is your real name?"

The mystery woman's lips twitched into a shaky smile. "Yes, I lied about my name, but that was only so no one would start looking for me or try to find out anything about me."

"Why didn't you want anyone to know anything about you?" Anne asked.

"Please, one question at a time." The mystery woman chewed her bottom lip. "I needed to move slowly, and I didn't expect people to be so curious. Normally I just blend in."

Anne thought about how much time she'd spent searching for something about Joan Meadows. "Then what is your real name?"

"Cassandra Brown." The woman blinked then held Anne's gaze. "And that's my real name. Want to see my driver's license?" Without waiting for an answer, she opened her purse and dug through it before producing a driver's license with a picture of a slightly younger looking woman than the one sitting across the table from Anne. "That was me three years ago."

"What else have you lied about?" Anne looked up from the driver's license and directly at Cassandra.

"Nothing…at least nothing I can think of at the moment." Cassandra shifted in her seat. "I've never been a very good liar, so I almost slipped a few times."

"You're better than you think," Anne said. "You almost had me convinced. So how about telling all this to Mildred? She's the one with the most vested interest—at least according to what you've said since you've been here."

The look of sadness on Cassandra's face touched Anne's heart. "What if she tells me she never wants to see me again when she finds out why I'm here?"

Anne shook her head. "First of all, I know Mildred, and she won't do that. However, even if she did, what do you have to lose? It's not like you've been close to her all these years."

"True."

Silence fell between them. Finally, Anne pulled out her wallet to pay for the coffee. "I can't stay out too long."

"I thought you said everything was fine."

"It is, but there's no point in Wendy having to stay at the library with Liddie when we don't have anything left to discuss."

Anne started to stand when Cassandra reached out and touched her arm. "Wait."

Anne turned and looked at her. The expression on Cassandra's face looked like a mixture of pain and trepidation.

"You're right," Cassandra said. "I have nothing to lose. Can you arrange something?"

"Yes, when?"

Cassandra swallowed hard, grimaced, and looked directly into Anne's eyes. "Now?" A hiccough escaped her throat. "If I wait, I might chicken out. Can you call her now?"

"Okay, what exactly would you like for me to tell her?"

"Can you just say I'd like to see her? Don't tell her why." She blinked. "At least not yet."

Anne took a deep breath and slowly let it out as she thought it over. "Okay, but I'm not so sure she'll drop whatever she's doing unless I tell her what's going on."

"You better go ahead and call her before I change my mind."

"Okay." Anne speed-dialed Mildred who didn't answer until after the third ring. "Do you have some time to meet with…" She glanced at the woman across the table from her. "Can you meet with Joan today?"

"What does she need?" Mildred asked.

"This isn't something I can discuss over the phone."

"Oh, so she's back to being the mystery woman, huh?" Mildred said.

"This is pretty serious." Anne glanced at Cassandra, who sat there watching her with an expectant but fearful expression.

"How serious?"

"Very," Anne replied. "Can you do it?"

"I'm sure I can work it out," Mildred replied. "When would be a good time for her?"

"How about now? Can you come to the Castle Diner?" Cassandra's wild gesturing captured Anne's attention. "Hold on a sec, Mildred. Cass—I mean, Joan wants to tell me something." She put her hand over the mouthpiece. "What's wrong?"

"I don't want to meet her here," Cassandra said. "Can I go to her house?"

"I'll see." Anne let go of the mouthpiece. "Joan wants to know if she can go to your house so she can talk privately."

"What is going on, Anne?" Mildred asked.

Anne wasn't going to allow anyone to pull her into a lie, but this definitely wasn't something she needed to reveal over the phone. "It's…complicated, and I think you should agree to see her."

Mildred didn't answer right away, and when she spoke, her voice cracked. "Will you be with her?"

Anne thought about Wendy's offer to take her time. "If you want me to be."

"Okay, then, yes. But I hope you understand that I'm going to call Officer Banks and let him know that if he doesn't hear from me soon, I want him to come over and check on me."

"Yes, I absolutely do understand. That's very smart of you to do that."

After Anne hung up, she turned back to Cassandra and forced a smile, hoping Cassandra wouldn't ask for details of the conversation. "She said you may come over but only if I'm with you. I'll follow you there."

"You don't have to go," Cassandra said. "As a matter of fact, I'd rather—"

"I'm going." Anne leveled her with the sternest look normally reserved for her children when she meant business. "And so are you," she added as she picked up her purse, dropped some money for a tip on the table, pulled out enough to pay for their coffee, and walked toward the cash register.

Cassandra stared at her for a few seconds, but she didn't argue. That was a relief to Anne. She quickly called Wendy and let her know she'd be a little later.

"Please be careful," Wendy advised.

"Can you call Alex and let him know where I'll be?" She saw Joan's rental car leaving the parking lot. "I need to go now."

As she followed Cassandra through Blue Hill to Mildred's house, she let her mind wander over events of the past several weeks. Each time she saw the mystery woman, she noticed something different. Without her hat, her thin, mousy brown hair made her look much less conspicuous than with the hat. She also wasn't wearing a T-shirt and jeans. In spite of the crumpled plaid shirt and khaki pants, Anne could now see that Cassandra was an attractive young woman.

CHAPTER TWENTY-SEVEN

Cassandra slowed down as soon as she turned onto Mildred's street. Anne parallel parked in front of the house, since Joan had pulled into the driveway.

Mildred opened the front door and stepped out onto the porch. She wasn't wearing her standard smile. The lines across her forehead revealed her concern.

"Hey, Mildred," Anne said, keeping her voice as light as possible. "I'm glad you were able to see us on such short notice."

Mildred nodded and turned toward Cassandra who had just gotten out of her car. "What is this all about?" she asked in a low tone.

Anne glanced over her shoulder and saw that Cassandra remained standing beside her car. "This is something you'll need to sit down for."

"Should I be worried?"

"I don't know for sure, but I don't think so. In fact, it might even be a good thing."

"Please tell me."

Anne shook her head. "I think I've already said too much." The sound of Cassandra's boots crunching through the snow let Anne know she was coming.

"Hi there, Joan." Mildred's lips quivered as she took a long look at the woman. "My, don't you look nice without your hat? Come on in. Can I get you some tea?"

"No thank you, ma'am," Joan said. "We just had coffee."

"All right then." Mildred swept her hand toward the sofa. "Let's all have a seat, and we can chat."

The awkwardness wasn't lost on Anne. She sat on one side of the sofa, and Cassandra chose the other side. Mildred lowered herself onto the edge of a chair adjacent to Anne. She clasped her hands and looked back and forth between Anne and Cassandra, who was shredding a tissue as she fidgeted.

"So, Joan, I understand you have something you would like to discuss with me."

"Yes." Cassandra nervously looked at Anne, who nodded. She turned her attention back to Mildred. "I'm here looking for my birth family."

Mildred narrowed her eyes. "Your birth family? Who might that be?"

Cassandra licked her lips and cleared her throat. "I was given up for adoption when I was a baby. I think I might be related to you."

A *whoosh* of air escaped Mildred's mouth as she flopped all the way back into her chair. "I didn't see this coming."

Anne found herself looking back and forth between Mildred and Cassandra, who couldn't take their eyes off each other. Some unspoken communication was flowing between them, and she halfway wished she wasn't there.

The ringing of her cell phone startled her. It was Wendy.

"Sorry to keep bugging you. Is everything okay?"

"Everything's just fine. Sorry I'm taking so long." She looked back at the other two women who still hadn't said anything since the big revelation. "I think I can leave now."

"You really don't have to if you're needed there," Wendy said. "Chad ordered pizza, and they're doing just fine."

"I'm not needed here anymore."

"Okay, see you in a little while," Wendy said.

After she clicked the Off button, Anne got up. "Ladies, it looks like the two of you can carry on here without me."

"Wait a minute," Mildred said. "I have a few things to say, and since you were involved with this, I'd like you to stick around for a few minutes."

Anne turned to Cassandra, who nodded. "Okay." She sat back down.

Mildred's bottom lip quivered as she smiled at Cassandra. "I should have known. Your eyes look so much like my niece's." She took a shaky breath. "We were all heartbroken when she decided to give you up for adoption."

Cassandra remained silent as she kept her gaze fixed on Mildred. Anne's heart pounded. This was a life-altering moment for these two women.

"Joan…" Mildred began.

Anne darted her gaze over to Cassandra. "You need to tell her your real name."

"Real name?" Mildred's forehead crinkled. "Your name's not Joan?"

Cassandra shook her head. "My real name is Cassandra Brown. I didn't want anyone looking for me."

"You're not some kind of fugitive, are you?" Mildred asked. "Because if you are, there's no way I'll hide you, even if you are related to me."

"N—no, I'm not a fugitive. I'm just a very normal person with a confusing past."

Mildred's shoulders rose and fell a couple of times before she stood up. "I have to go make a phone call to let Officer Banks know I'm fine. I'll be right back."

While she was in the kitchen, Anne gave Cassandra what she hoped was a comforting smile. Cassandra appeared to be close to tears.

"She took it quite well, I think," Anne said.

Cassandra sniffled and nodded. "I'm the one who's falling apart."

"You did just fine."

"I just wish I knew more, like why my birth mother gave me up for adoption."

Anne nodded toward the doorway where Mildred had appeared. "Why don't you ask the only person here who might know?"

Mildred slowly walked back to her chair, appearing exhausted. "What do you need to ask?"

Cassandra clamped her eyes for a few seconds then opened them. "Why did your niece give me up for adoption?"

Mildred glanced down at her hands that were folded in her lap. "This is a difficult question for me to answer, since she's not here to explain it herself."

"Do you even know?" Cassandra asked.

"Yes, I know." Mildred took a deep breath and slowly let it out. "I suppose that after all these years it's okay to tell you. My niece Janet was very young when she became pregnant. My widowed sister had been sick for quite some time." Her hands shook as she unfolded them and gripped the arms of the chair.

"If this is too difficult—" Anne said.

Mildred shook her head. "No, it's something Jo...I mean Cassandra needs to know about, and since Janet isn't here to explain, it's my place to tell her." She turned back to Cassandra. "Janet was still in high school. In late spring, she got special permission to take her exams early so she could go to Philadelphia and give birth. She'd lined up an adoption agency who assured her they'd place you with a very nice family." Mildred's eyebrows shot up. "Was that the case? Did you have a nice family?"

Cassandra nodded. "Yes, a very nice family. My parents were quite a bit older, and they weren't able to have children. They made sure I had everything I needed."

"Did you feel loved?" Mildred asked.

"Oh yes," Cassandra said as she nodded. "Very much."

"And how about the most important thing? Did they take you to church?"

Cassandra pursed her lips as she started to nod then shook her head. "Yes."

"That's good," Mildred said.

"But now I feel bad about lying to Reverend Tom. It's bad to lie to anyone, but somehow it seems even worse to lie to a pastor."

Mildred shook her head. "It's not any worse than lying to the rest of us, but I'm sure he'll forgive you. Reverend Tom is a very kind man who understands human nature better than anyone else I know."

"I hope you're right," Cassandra said.

"Now, back to the family situation. My niece originally wanted to maintain contact with you and your adoptive parents, but the social worker advised her against it."

"Why?" Cassandra asked.

"She said that Janet was so young, and based on the agency's experience with teenage pregnancy, she'd have a more difficult time starting over with her life." Mildred sank farther back in her chair. "Unfortunately, that's not the way it worked out. She never could get past the fact that she'd given up an important part of herself."

Anne vaguely remembered meeting Janet when she'd first arrived in Blue Hill, but she hadn't seen her since then. "Does she go to church?"

Mildred turned to Anne and shook her head. "No, in fact, she became angry with God after all this happened. I tried to get her to talk with Reverend Tom, but she didn't want any part of him or the church."

"Would she...I mean, do you think she might want to see me?" Cassandra asked.

"After all these years, I honestly don't know," Mildred replied. "But I'll see what I can do." She started to stand up but stalled. "Do you mind if I call her now?"

Cassandra's eyes widened. "Do you think you should?"

"Yes, but I'm not sure how to handle this. I'd like to ask her to come over, but I don't want her to be too shocked when she sees you for the first time. By the same token, I don't think this is something I can tell her on the phone."

"Can you go see her while I wait here with Cassandra?" suggested Anne. "You could tell her and give her the opportunity to decide whether or not she's ready to meet her daughter."

Mildred appeared energized as she bounded from her chair. She turned to Cassandra. "She doesn't live here in Blue Hill, but I'll call her so you can talk to her on the phone."

Janet was home, and after a few moments of what Anne surmised must be shock on Janet's part, Mildred put Cassandra on the phone.

Cassandra's voice sounded scratchy as she tentatively answered questions. Anne couldn't help but smile as she thought about the significance of this moment.

Mildred leaned toward Anne. "This is one of the biggest days of my life. I never thought it would ever happen." She nodded toward the kitchen. "Let's give Cassandra a few minutes of privacy."

Once they stepped into the kitchen, Mildred chattered about all kinds of things, from the sound of Janet's voice when she told her about Cassandra to the fact that Janet had never married. Anne realized how this would change the course of the lives of both Janet and Cassandra.

"I knew there was something about Cassandra," Mildred admitted. "And I'm ashamed of myself for thinking she might have had something to do with the identity scam."

Anne nodded. "I know. I thought the same thing."

"Now that I know she's family, I'll stick by her no matter what." Mildred lifted her chin.

Anne smiled. "You're amazing."

"And so are you." Mildred reached for her hand and squeezed it. "And together we are awesomely amazing."

"I need to check on Wendy and the kids," Anne said. "So I'll go out on the front porch while the two of you talk some more."

Mildred immediately turned to Cassandra and started chatting again, so Anne pulled out her cell phone and went onto the porch to make her call. Movement at the side of the neighbor's house caught her attention.

Someone was bent over, rummaging through the garbage can. She darted back inside the house, closing the door as gently as she could. Instead of calling Wendy she punched in the number of the police station.

She spoke softly as she asked for Officer Banks. He was on the line in a matter of seconds.

"I'm at Mildred Farley's house," she said barely above a whisper. "There's some guy going through her neighbor's trash."

CHAPTER TWENTY-EIGHT

D oes he know that you saw him?" Officer Banks asked.
"I don't think so. I was on Mildred's porch, but now I'm inside."

"Are you near a window that overlooks where you saw him?"

Anne took a couple of steps into the dining room. "I am now."

"Look outside and see if he's still there."

She leaned over to where she could barely see the side of the neighbor's house. He had an envelope sticking out of his back pocket, and he was in the process of shoving something into his other pocket. "He's there, and he's taking some papers out of the trash."

"Okay, I'll be there in a few minutes. Stay inside until I have a chance to talk to him."

"Anne, is that you?" Mildred called out.

"Yes." Anne tiptoed back toward the other women.

Mildred tipped her head to the side. "Why are you tiptoeing?"

In a soft voice, Anne explained what had just happened. Mildred nodded. "He's been there before, but when I spotted him, he always appeared to be doing something to the meter."

Anne thought a moment and realized that every time she spotted that guy doing something to electric meters, there was a trash can nearby. "I think he's using the meters as a cover."

"A cover?" Mildred asked. "I'm confused. Do you think he's stealing electricity?"

"No," Anne said slowly. "I suspect he's going through our trash cans looking for paperwork with account numbers and other personal information."

"He's the guy I talked to about having electricity turned on when I found an apartment," Cassandra said. "First he asked me all these questions about where I was moving from and what kind of work I did, and if I had a checking account and good credit history...all things he said the company would need to know before authorizing a new account...then he said he didn't handle new service connections and that I'd have to call the company to set up an account. I felt like some of the questions he was asking were a bit too personal. So, of course, I didn't give him any information. He made me uncomfortable. I excused myself as soon as I could and walked away."

Mildred covered her mouth with her hand. She slowly shook her head.

Anne tried to soften her expression as she placed a hand on Mildred's shoulder. "I can't say for sure, but I have a hunch he just might be connected somehow to our identity thief."

Cassandra gasped. "You mean the one who has the whole town in an uproar?"

"Yes," Anne replied.

Mildred moved her hand from her mouth to her chest. "Oh my. That is frightening." She started to walk to the front of her house, but Anne stopped her. "I want to see him," she argued.

"No, I've already called Officer Banks. He said to stay inside until after he has a chance to check things out."

All three of them went into the dining room and clustered by the window until Officer Banks arrived. The guy digging through the trash tried to take off, but another police officer came around from behind the neighbor's house and caught him. Officer Banks snapped some handcuffs on him as he said something.

"Think it's safe to go out there now?" Mildred asked. "I'm dying to find out the details."

"Let's wait another minute or two," Anne said. "I don't want to interfere with law enforcement."

Cassandra shook her head. "Is it always this exciting in here?"

In unison, Anne and Mildred replied, "Never!"

Cassandra gestured toward the window. "Looks like they're taking him away. I think it's safe to go out there now." Anne was surprised that Cassandra led the way to the door, but then she stopped and waited for Anne and Mildred.

Anne opened the door and gestured for Mildred to go first. "Thank you, dear." Mildred didn't waste any time moving past Anne and out onto her front porch, where she stopped and shaded her eyes as she looked in the direction of the action.

Officer Banks walked over to Mildred's sidewalk, and the three of them joined him. He gave a thumbs-up as he smiled at Anne. "I think we have our guy, thanks to your call."

Anne let out a sigh of relief. "So you think he's the identity thief?"

"I'm pretty sure. He had some incriminating evidence in his pockets. The envelope in his possession had a list of account numbers, just like the list Wendy dropped off at the station."

"Why would he keep pretending to be doing energy audits?" Mildred asked.

Officer Banks spoke up first. "He claimed to be doing energy audits and water meter checks, depending on what was closest to the trash cans."

Anne nodded. "The library's meters are right beside the slab where we keep our trash cans when it isn't garbage day."

Her phone rang. She pulled it out and saw that it was Wendy.

"Not that I'm complaining or anything, but I expected to hear from you by now. What's going on?"

"Sorry," Anne said as she stepped away from the other people. "This has been one crazy afternoon. You'll never believe what happened."

"Based on the sound of your voice, it must be a doozy." Wendy cleared her throat. "I need to get on home soon, but if you need to stay a while longer, Alex said he and Ryan can come over."

"No, I think I can go home now, but thanks."

"Okie dokie. See you soon."

"If you don't need me, I need to get back," Anne said as she rejoined the group. "Wendy's been with the children all afternoon."

Cassandra cast a nervous glance at her and then at Mildred, who closed the distance between them and placed her arm around her great-niece's shoulder.

Mildred spoke up. "We're just fine here. My—my…great-niece, and I…" She choked up as she gave Cassandra a loving glance. "We have quite a bit of catching up to do."

Officer Banks had been typing something into his cell phone, so he didn't appear to be paying much attention to their conversation. He glanced up. "I'll probably have more questions for you later. Mind if I stop by sometime tomorrow?"

"That would be fine," Anne said. "I'll be working on Thanksgiving dinner."

An odd look came over Mildred. "I'll call you later. Thank you so much for bringing Cassandra to us."

Anne smiled and waved. She left with mixed emotions—glad to get back home to a place where things made sense but still curious about the details of Cassandra's life. As soon as she walked into the library a few minutes later, Wendy pounced on her. "I can't wait to hear all about it. What happened?"

"Don't you have to go home to your family?" Anne teased.

Wendy placed her hands on her hips and widened her eyes. "You know I'm not leaving until you at least tell me something."

Anne shrugged. "Okay, so Joan isn't really Joan, and we caught the identity thief."

Wendy's chin dropped, and her eyebrows rose higher. For the first time since Anne could remember, Wendy was speechless.

"That's pretty much it in a nutshell." Anne turned slightly and took a step away from Wendy.

"Oh, no you don't," Wendy said as she reached for Anne's arm. "You're not going to get away with teasing me like that. I need details."

Anne tilted her head. "What about your family?"

"They can wait another ten minutes."

"Where are Ben and Liddie?"

Wendy pointed toward the Children's Room. "Ben already left with Alex and Ryan. Liddie is playing with her dolls."

"Okay." Anne gestured toward the table by the door of the Nonfiction Room.

Once they were seated, Wendy leaned forward on her elbows and locked gazes with Anne. "Spill."

"Brace yourself. This has been a very surprising afternoon."

"I'm as braced as I can get. So who is Joan really?"

"Her name is Cassandra Brown, and she came to Blue Hill to find her family."

Wendy's eyebrows came together. "Now I'm confused. I thought you said she was the identity thief."

"No, I said Joan wasn't Joan, and we caught the identity thief."

"So if Joan aka Cassandra isn't the identity thief, who is?"

"Remember the meter man?"

Wendy thought for a couple of seconds and then nodded. "Yes, the guy who was supposed to be helping us save all that energy?"

"He wasn't really looking at our meters. He was going through our garbage."

Wendy flopped back in the chair. "This is really strange."

"I know," Anne agreed.

"So what's the connection between this guy and Cassandra?"

"There doesn't appear to be one. The timing of both of them arriving so close together is purely coincidence."

"But didn't you see them talking outside the library?"

Anne nodded. "She was asking him how to contact the power company when she found an apartment."

Wendy pushed back her chair and stood. "I really do need to go now, but at least I know the basics. Maybe things will get back to normal, now that these two mysteries have been solved." She took a step toward the door before stopping. "I wonder why Cassandra told us her name was Joan."

"Apparently she didn't want us to go digging for more information," Anne replied. "At least now I know why I couldn't find anything about her on the Internet."

After Wendy left, Alex called and said he'd be dropping Ben off in about an hour. Anne went into the Children's Room to get Liddie so they could eat dinner and clean up before Ben got home. Liddie quietly followed Anne into the kitchen.

Seeing Liddie so sad broke Anne's heart, but she knew that nothing would help except the passing of time. They ate dinner with very little conversation. After they finished, Anne asked Liddie whether she wanted to watch a movie or read.

Liddie shrugged. "I want to play in my room."

Anne helped Liddie into her pajamas and left her alone to play. Ben arrived home a few minutes later.

"Where's Liddie?" he asked.

"She wanted some quiet time, so I left her in her room."

"That's weird," Ben said. "She never wants quiet time unless she's sleepy. I'll go see what's going on."

Anne smiled and nodded. She went into the living room and settled down with a magazine. After a half hour of silence, she decided to check on the children. She knocked and then pushed Liddie's door open. "Everything okay in here?"

"Hi, Mom." Ben turned to face her from his position on the edge of his sister's bed. "Liddie is worried about eating out for Thanksgiving. She's afraid they won't have all the things we normally have."

Anne squatted down between her children. "They're serving turkey, dressing, gravy, green beans, sweet potatoes, and pump-kin pie—all the food you love."

"Will they have cranberries?" Liddie asked.

"I'm sure they will."

Liddie continued to frown. "How about later? You know how I like turkey sandwiches and turkey soup and turkey casserole."

Anne nodded. "I'm cooking a turkey here so we'll have all the leftovers you like."

Ben looked at Liddie. "See? Nothing to worry about."

Anne's heart melted at how grown up Ben was trying to be. "That's right. There's absolutely nothing to worry about." She stood. "I need to check on the library before we go to bed."

"We'll go with you," Ben said.

Over the next few minutes, they turned off all the lights downstairs, except the one by the door that they always kept on for security. They also made sure the doors were all locked, and made their way up to their living space. Ben picked up the leash and took Hershey down the back stairs for a walk without being asked.

When Ben and Hershey returned, Anne decided it was time to tell her children what was going on, so they wouldn't be surprised by anything they heard. She sat down at the kitchen table with Ben and Liddie.

"Since I'm sure people will be talking, I think it's best for you to hear this from me." Anne took a deep breath, and began a children's version of how the identity thief had been caught.

Ben's eyes lit up. "Mom, you're a hero." He paused. "A superhero."

"I wouldn't call myself a hero. I just saw something suspicious and did what anyone would do. I called the police."

"But if you hadn't done that, the guy would still be out there stealing people's information."

"Mommy, I don't understand," Liddie said. "Why would someone steal garbage?" She made a face and plugged her nose. "That's just gross."

Anne started to explain, but Ben spoke up. "You'll understand one of these days…" He glanced over at Anne and then back at his little sister. "When you're older."

"But I wanna know now."

Anne knew that Liddie's pout had more to do with disappointment over Thanksgiving than what Ben had said, so she spoke up. "Bad guys don't care how gross something is. If they want it, they go after it. And now we don't have to worry about that bad guy anymore because the police took him away."

"Is he in jail?" she asked.

"Yep," Ben said. "Right, Mom?"

Anne wanted to end this discussion to prevent Liddie from worrying even more, so she nodded and stood. "Why don't we finish decorating tomorrow and make this house more festive so Thanksgiving will be more fun?"

Liddie nodded, and Ben gave her a knowing look. "I'll read you another story," he told Liddie. "Mom needs her rest."

CHAPTER TWENTY-NINE

Anne had to tamp back her uncharacteristic melancholy mood throughout Wednesday, but she managed to get through the day with more smiles than frowns. Every now and then she caught Liddie pouting, so Anne forced a lilt into her voice to cheer up her little girl. Ben, however acted pretty normal. He went back and forth between playing games and helping with the decorations and baking when Anne fussed at him.

When the day was finally over, Anne tucked Liddie into bed. "Mommy, let's try to have some fun tomorrow, okay?"

Anne smiled down at her angel. "Okay, sweetie. Let's do that." She kissed Liddie and left the room, closing the door behind her.

Ben was allowed to stay up another half hour. Anne found him sitting at the kitchen table playing with some of the toothpicks they'd used to check the cupcakes.

"Be careful," she said out of habit. "Those are sharp."

"Mom." He gave her one of his preadolescent looks that he was starting to use. "I'm not a baby."

"So are you excited about Thanksgiving?" She pulled out a chair and sat down across from him.

He shrugged. "I guess. We'll eat a bunch and then come back here and eat some more until we're stuffed."

Anne sighed. "I'm really sorry about how everything happened, but you realize it was out of my control, right?"

Ben nodded. "It would be nice to see Grandma and Grandpa, but I understand."

They chatted about past holiday seasons and what they might do next year. Finally, Ben stood up and stretched. "I think I'll go on to bed and read for a little while."

Anne gave him a few minutes to change into his pajamas and get into bed before going in there to say good night. She pulled the blanket up to his chin and tapped him on the nose with her finger. "You're growing up, Ben, but you'll never be too old for me to tuck you in."

His lopsided grin tweaked her heart. "I love you, Mom."

She left his room before the first tear fell. After she got to the kitchen, the tears came in streams, until they eventually dried up.

Lord, I pray for protection for my children and that we will never forget the blessings that You have provided.

When she opened her eyes, she took a deep breath and slowly let it out. Not having Eric here with them was still difficult.

She flipped through a magazine until she was sure both children were sound asleep. Then she went to bed without setting her alarm clock. Usually she awoke at the crack of dawn, but even if she didn't tomorrow, it didn't matter.

* * *

The sound of the phone ringing on Thanksgiving morning woke Anne. She reached over and picked up the phone.

"Good morning, dear."

"Mom?" She sat up in bed.

"Yes, it's me. Come downstairs and let us in."

"What?" Anne rubbed her eyes. "Where?"

"Downstairs. We're standing on your front porch, and we're freezing."

Anne kept the phone to her ear with one hand as she pulled on her fluffy robe with the other. "I'll be there in a minute."

She ran down the stairs straight for the door and flung it open. Her parents scooted in with their arms wide open. They both gave her a hug.

"Grandma!" The sound of Liddie's voice behind Anne caught everyone's attention.

"How's my little sweetie pie?" Anne's mom said as she gave Liddie a giant hug.

Her dad lifted Liddie high, making her giggle. "You're almost too heavy for me to do this anymore."

Ben joined them a few minutes later. At first, he blinked, and then a slow grin spread across his face. He didn't resist hugs or kisses from either grandparent.

After her grandfather put her down, Liddie bounced all over the place. Ben tried hard to act cool, but he couldn't stop smiling. Anne couldn't remember ever being so happy to see her parents.

"Anyone want coffee?" Anne asked.

"Yes, that would be nice."

"This is such a wonderful surprise," Anne said. "When Eric's parents' plans changed and they weren't able to come, we were all really disappointed."

"We know, and that's why we kept checking airfare several times a day," Anne's dad said. "You should have heard your mother's excitement when she found a last-minute bargain." He shook his head but smiled. "So here we are."

"And I couldn't be happier," Anne said. "If I'd known you were coming, I would have had Thanksgiving here, but since everyone we invited canceled, I made reservations for the kids and me." Anne gave her parents an apologetic look. "I'll call and ask them to add two more."

Anne's mother gave her a conspiratorial smile. "Call the restaurant—but to cancel your reservations. We have other plans."

"But—" The look on her mother's face stopped her from finishing.

"Just call and cancel," her dad said, smiling. "You'll find out soon enough."

Anne did as she was told. Now that her parents were here, she relaxed. Liddie and Ben showed more excitement in the short time they'd been awake than they'd shown in the last few weeks leading up to Thanksgiving.

Liddie tugged on Anne's sleeve. "Mommy, can Ben and me show Grandpa and Grandma the library?"

"'Ben and *I*.' But yes, that's a great idea, honey," Anne said. She turned to her parents. "You're going to love it."

"I can't wait," Anne's mother said. "Let's go see it. And then when we get back upstairs, I'll fix you and the kids something light to eat for breakfast," her mother said. "Your father and I will clean the kitchen while you get dressed. Oh, wear something nice."

Anne narrowed her eyes. "How nice?"

"Sunday nice." Her mother turned around and opened the refrigerator.

Liddie and Ben led their grandparents down to the library, with Anne close behind. The family took the grand tour, as Anne moved ahead and turned on the lights in each of the rooms, accompanied by the oohs and ahhs of her appreciative parents. When the tour culminated near the old elevator, Anne's father hugged her and said, "Anne, you've done such a beautiful job of bringing Aunt Edie's vision to life. She would be so proud of you. Now, how about some eggs and toast?"

"I thought you said something light," Anne replied as they entered the elevator and made their way upstairs again and emerged into the family living quarters

Her mom made a beeline to the refrigerator, opened the door and reached in, and then straightened up with a carton of eggs in one hand. "Where are your bowls and frying pan?" She looked at Anne and winked. "You need to relax and let someone else take care of you for a day."

Anne showed her mother where to find everything before sitting down at the table with her dad. Ben and Liddie took turns telling their grandpa all about school, and when they appeared to wind down, he'd ask another question to get them started again.

After they finished eating, Anne's mom shooed her and the children upstairs. "Go get ready now."

Anne knew that it was pointless to argue, so she reached for her children's hands. "Come on. Let's do as we're told."

"That's funny, Mom." Ben grinned at her. "I've never heard anyone tell you what to do."

A half hour later, the three of them joined Anne's parents in the squeaky clean kitchen. Her dad put down the magazine he'd been reading.

"Ready?" he asked, but before anyone could answer, he started for the door. "Let's go."

"Let me get Liddie's booster seat."

She got it out of her car and handed it to her dad who placed it in the center of the backseat of their rental sedan. Anne, Ben, and Liddie piled into the car with her parents. Once everyone was buckled in, they took off.

Liddie chattered about how fun it was to ride in Grandpa's car. Ben was silent as he stared out the side window, but Anne knew he was happy by how he paid attention to everything.

When her dad turned on to Alex's street, Anne's mother turned around and grinned. "Surprised?"

"Um…what are we doing here?"

"I called the library one afternoon when you were out, and Wendy said everyone would be here. They were planning to surprise you, so I talked her into letting us do it instead."

Her dad laughed as he looked at Anne in the rearview mirror. "Your mother and her surprises."

Her mother playfully swatted at him. "You didn't exactly argue with me."

He nodded as he pulled to a stop, put the car in park, and turned off the ignition. "True. So let's go in and join the party."

They'd barely made it to the first porch step when the front door opened. Alex motioned for them to hurry inside.

Anne walked in and took a long look around. Everyone who had canceled on her was here, including Mildred, Cassandra,

Janet, Claire and her husband, Grace, Rita, the Parnells, Wendy and her family, and a few more people from church.

"Surprised?" Alex said as he ambled up to her side.

She playfully jabbed him in the side. "Now this was sneaky." She took another look around the room. "But truly the nicest surprise I've ever had."

"Happy Thanksgiving," Mildred said. "I hope you'll excuse me so I can get back in the kitchen and put the finishing touches on the casserole before I put it in the oven."

Anne's mother followed Mildred. "I'll help."

"What can I do?" Anne asked.

Wendy motioned for her to join them in the playroom that Alex had built onto the back of his house when he got custody of Ryan. "You can help me. I'm in charge of children's entertainment."

Since the older children had gone into the family room to play video games with Ryan, Wendy and Anne had everyone under the age of eight. "How long has this been in the works?"

"About a week and a half," Wendy said as she pulled another game from the stack. "Who's up for a game of Candyland?"

Throughout the day, Anne learned about the scheme in bits and pieces and how Alex had sworn everyone to secrecy. The rest of the morning, some of them played board games, while others prepared food in the kitchen. When it was time to serve, Alex stood with his hands up to get everyone's attention. "With so many people here, there's no way we can all sit at the dining room table, so we're doing this buffet style. After you fill your plate in the kitchen, find a spot anywhere in the dining room, family room, or kitchen." He paused. "But first, I'd like to say a blessing. Please bow your heads."

As Alex thanked God for the food they were about to eat, the fellowship, and the safe travels for Anne's parents, Anne felt a sense of peace wash over her. Blue Hill truly was a special place, and this holiday season would rank right up there with the best.

ABOUT THE AUTHOR

Debby Mayne and her husband, Wally, live on the west coast of Florida. They have two beautiful daughters, two handsome sons-in-law, and two delightful granddaughters.

Debby has published more than thirty books and novellas, four hundred print short stories and articles, more than one thousand Web articles, and a slew of devotions for women. She has also worked as managing editor of a national health magazine, product information writer for HSN, a creative writing instructor for Long Ridge Writers Group, and a copy editor and proofreader for several book publishers. For the past eight years, she has judged the *Writers Digest* Annual Competition, Short-Short Contest, and Self-Published Book Competition. Three of Debby's books have been top-ten favorites by the Heartsong Presents book club. *Love Finds You in Treasure Island, Florida*, received four and half stars and was named a "Top Pick" by *Romantic Times Magazine*.

A Conversation with the Author

Q. *Describe your writing process.*

A. For most of my books, I start with a character interview and a basic plot outline. My most creative time is first thing in the morning. As I drink my coffee, I read what I wrote the day before and fix any obvious errors. Then I write until around noon. If I have a close deadline, I write for a couple of hours after lunch and a light workout. After I finish the first draft of a complete novel, I read and revise it right away. Then I put it aside for at least a week or two — longer if I have more time — and revise it again before I turn it in to my editor.

Q. *When you are not writing, what are your favorite activities?*

A. My first love is family, and doing anything with my grandchildren makes me happy. I also like reading, so I try to set aside a little bit of time each day or evening to do that. I enjoy a wide variety of other activities, including crocheting, beading, cooking, and fitness.

Q. *What advice would you give an aspiring novelist?*

A. First, be a reader because you need to relate to people who spend money and time on your books. Second, write books you would enjoy reading. Third, be patient and know crafting a novel isn't an overnight thing. After that, my advice is to take time to study craft, be brave, and know that you'll run into a variety of people with different opinions. If being a published author is something you really want, don't give up. You might take some time off to regroup after a rejection, but if it's your calling, you need to keep on trying.

Q. *How did you get started as a writer?*

A. After I had my first child, I started writing informational articles for regional parenting publications. I did this for several years before my husband commented on how many novels I read and challenged me to try writing one. I'm always up for a challenge. It took me five years to sell my first book to Avalon. Ten days after I got the call from that editor saying she loved my book, the editor at Barbour called and offered a contract for a novella. After that, I was hooked.

Q. *Anne Gibson likes to drink her coffee without cream or sugar. What are your coffee-shop favorites?*

A. I like all flavors of coffee—sweet or unsweetened, cream or no cream. What I generally do when I go to a coffee shop I'm not familiar with is ask if they have a house special and order that. I generally like hot coffee, but during the summer, I prefer cold coffee drinks.

Recipes from the Library Guild

Thanksgiving Squash and Zucchini Casserole

1 pound of fresh squash, sliced into rounds

1 pound of fresh zucchini, sliced into 2-inch spears

2 eggs

½ cup of melted butter

½ cup of diced onions

⅔ cup of milk

½ cup of grated cheddar cheese

1 teaspoon of mustard

½ teaspoon of garlic salt

½ cup of breadcrumbs (or cracker crumbs)

Preheat oven to 325 degrees. Steam squash and zucchini until tender. Drain and transfer to a large bowl. Set aside to cool.

In a separate bowl, mix eggs, butter, onions, milk, cheese, mustard, and garlic salt. Pour egg mixture into the squash and zucchini bowl. Mix well.

Pour the mixture into a greased 9 × 13 casserole dish. Sprinkle the breadcrumbs over the top. Bake at 325 degrees for approximately forty minutes. The crumbs should be brown. Serve hot.

From the Guideposts Archives

The following "His Mysterious Ways" article by Katy Brown originally appeared in the July 1982 issue of Guideposts *magazine.*

The hot summer days of 1979 seemed to crawl by. My husband and I were waiting for our county adoption agency to complete the long process of clearing us so we could adopt a baby. We'd already gone through months of being interviewed and investigated — and we were told we would have another long wait even after we were approved.

Early one July morning, before dawn, I was startled awake by a vivid dream about a baby. What a happy dream that was — surely we'd have our baby soon!

But August passed without any developments, and September came before we even received our letter of clearance. Still, though our "credentials" were established, nothing happened. September dragged into October, and then November plodded by.

At last, two weeks before Christmas, the telephone call came. A woman at the adoption agency told me that the mother of a baby girl had reviewed the records of people who wanted to become adoptive parents and had chosen us. She gave me various details about the baby's birth and made an appointment for my husband and me to see her.

I hung up the phone and got out my desk calendar to mark the date and time. Riffling through the pages, I saw a notation in my handwriting.

A prickle ran up my spine.

On the calendar page for July 20, I'd written "dreamed about baby."

That was the very day God had chosen for our adopted daughter to be born.

Read on for a sneak peek of another exciting book
in *Secrets of the Blue Hill Library*!

The Christmas Key

C ome on, Mommy!" Liddie Gibson wormed her way through
the post-service coffee hour crowd to grasp her mother's
hand. "They're going to open the Advent cabinet!"

"The Advent *cabinet*?" asked Anne with a laugh, as she
allowed herself to be dragged off. The parishioners around her
smiled indulgently. Besides, they were all drifting in the same
direction Liddie was tugging her mother.

Anne's son, Ben, appeared at her side. At nine, Ben was four
years older than his sister and was often a solemn child, but Anne
could tell he was excited as well. As she was herself, truth be told.
Though she still had trouble envisioning what they meant by an
Advent cabinet, many of the parishioners had assured her that the
church's special Advent ritual was one of the highlights of the
holiday season. And now she would finally have the chance to
see what they were talking about. A crowd was gathering at the
far end of the community room, and Anne could see that Reverend
Tom was already there, standing next to what Anne guessed must
be the Advent cabinet.

When Anne got closer, it became apparent that the people of
Blue Hill Community Church had been quite literal in their

appellation. It was an Advent calendar built in the form of a cabinet. It stood about five feet high, although most of that was in its legs. The case atop those legs was perhaps two feet tall and three feet across. There were four ranks of six drawers each for a total of twenty-four. To her librarian's eye, it looked like an old-style card catalog cabinet.

Except, she realized, those weren't drawers. They appeared to be little doors, each hinged to swing out and each with a small keyhole and a key in its lock. Anne wondered what was behind those doors. Some sort of cubbyhole? She noticed that, despite the cabinet's height, the piece had little depth—perhaps only eight inches or so. The wood was painted in festive red-and-green colors with pictures of Christmas-related scenes on each of the small doors.

"Friends." Reverend Tom's resonant voice carried through the room, quieting the coffee-hour chatter. "Once again the Advent season is upon us, and as part of our celebration in this joyful time of the year, we enjoy our church's unique tradition of the Advent cabinet!" With a flourish of his hand, he indicated the odd card catalog.

"Now, today is only December second," he continued with a twinkle in his eye, "so we have only two doors to open. But next Sunday, we will have a full week's worth. Shall we begin?" He stepped up to the cabinet, solemnly turned the key in the first door, and opened it. Anne could see that there was something inside the small space, but she couldn't make out what it was.

Reverend Tom removed it and held it up for all to see. "A Matchbox car," he announced. "Who has put it here and what is its message for us?"

"I did," said Helen Smith, on the far side of the crowd from Anne. "I put it there." Helen was the president of the church's board, and she stepped forward now. "It's to represent all the people who will be traveling during the holidays and to remind us to pray for their safety." Many heads nodded, and Anne recalled that Helen herself had a large and far-flung family who would be among those travelers.

Tom delivered a brief, impromptu message that began with the traveling wise men of the Christmas story and ended with the joys of seeing family and friends during the holidays. After a pause to draw out the suspense, he turned back to the cabinet and unlocked the second door, this time removing an origami swan. A collective *ooh* rang out from the kids, and Liddie stood on tiptoes to get a better view.

"Who takes credit for this treasure?" Reverend Tom held the tiny paper swan up in the palm of his hand so everyone was afforded a view. "It's lovely," he prompted when no explanation was forthcoming. "It's made with great care…"

After another pause, there came a small cough from somewhere behind Reverend Tom, and a shy teenager who seemed to be trying to hide behind unkempt bangs and her father's oversized sweater crept diffidently to Reverend Tom's side.

"I don't know…" she started, her cheeks crimson, but Reverend Tom put a hand on her shoulder and she seemed to draw strength from that. "I thought perhaps the swan would remind us of the Ugly Duckling and that sometimes a great thing starts out small."

"Excellent, Carrie," Reverend Tom's voice boomed, and he repeated what she had said for the benefit of the whole group standing around. "The promise contained in even the humblest situations—such as a babe born in a manger. Clever. Insightful. And perfect for the lessons of this season. Did you make the swan yourself?"

Carrie McAllister nodded, and, noticing all eyes turned to her, she instinctively shrunk back. Reverend Tom let her go and invited the group to join him in singing "Away in a Manger."

Next to the Advent cabinet was an open crate filled with toys and winter clothing and school supplies for needy families— another church tradition. As she sang with the others, Anne read the hand-lettered sign that explained the needs of the anonymous families who would receive the gifts, and she made a mental note to pick up a few of the items listed when she was out shopping for Ben and Liddie.

Following the carol, the crowd was ready to disperse, but Reverend Tom held up his hand. "One more bit of business, friends, please," he announced, adding with a twinkle, "It's a busy time of year, you know. Helen?"

Briskly, Helen Smith stepped forward once again. "Many of you have already heard, but when we went to get out the Christmas decorations this year, well, we had a bit of a surprise." There was general laughter at this. Helen went on to explain that a family of mice had nested in one of the boxes and reduced the contents to a glittery mess. "Specifically," Helen continued, "this was the box of ornaments for our tree in the sanctuary."

This news seemed to sober the crowd. "We'd like to ask your help in rectifying the situation." Helen paused and scanned the crowd. "If each member or family could contribute one tree ornament by next Sunday, we'd be back in business." Helen's gaze stopped on Anne briefly before she glanced away. "We're hoping that rather than buying something new, you will consider donating something from your own collection. This would personalize the tree in a way that I think would be very appropriate to the season." This suggestion was met by approving murmurs, and the crowd soon returned to its coffee-hour conversations.

While Helen was speaking, Anne had been casting an occasional glance at the Advent cabinet. The thing was fascinating and she wanted to get a better look at it. As the social hour resumed, she stepped up to examine it.

It wasn't exactly fine cabinetry—no fancy inlays or anything like that. But it was a solid piece of construction and seemed to have been built with care. Each of the twenty-four small doors featured a seasonal image that appeared to have been cut from a magazine and applied with shellac. She examined scenes of ice-skating parties, Christmas tree harvesting, and holiday feasting, among others. But it was the tiny locks and keys in each door that particularly fascinated her, and she leaned forward to peer more closely.

"It was built about a dozen years ago by a man named Anderson," said Reverend Tom, appearing suddenly beside her. "He donated it to the church, and we've been making good use of it ever since." He smiled and patted the cabinet fondly as he spoke, and for Anne the name stirred a vague childhood memory of a Mr. Anderson from church, a quiet and gentle man who even then seemed elderly. Noticing her interest in the keys, Reverend Tom added, "Go ahead and look at one," and then he pulled one from a lock and handed it to her.

The key was delicate—long, thin, and wiry. It seemed to Anne to be Victorian in style. It flared out at one end for the metal to wrap around a white enamel disk on which a number was painted. Seeing her take note of this, Reverend Tom said, "Each one is unique. The keys are not interchangeable. Remarkable, aren't they? I speculate sometimes that they are what gave Mr. Anderson the idea. He had this set of little locks and keys lying around, and the Advent cabinet kind of grew from there."

"They're exquisite," Anne said, shaking her head. She reached to return the key to its cubby and then hesitated. There seemed to be two locks without keys. She had to check the number on the key she held, and then looked questioningly at Reverend Tom as she restored it to its lock.

"Ah, yes, well. Things do go missing over time," he said with a smile. "It's the way of the world, I'm afraid. Somehow it went missing last year. Number seven must now remain the locked cubby."

Anne, who hated to see a set of books lacking a volume, frowned in concern. "Wouldn't it be possible to have a replacement made?" she asked.

Tom waved his hand in a dismissive gesture. "Where can you look to find someone who would do work like this nowadays?" He turned slightly as if to step away.

"Surely we could at least get the cubby open?" Anne said. "Call a locksmith? Or a cabinetmaker? If we could remove the lock, wouldn't it be possible to make a new key to fit it?"

Tom paused and blinked slowly at Anne, frowning slightly. "Sometimes we just have to work with what we have," he said somewhat distractedly, and then his genial smile returned as he looked past her shoulder and said, "Ah, Helen. Here's Anne. I think you wanted to talk with her?"

Anne turned to find Helen Smith smiling at her. "I did, Anne, if you don't mind?" Reverend Tom was already stepping away as Anne smiled acquiescence. Helen drew her to the edge of the room. "I had two things to speak with you about, actually. You heard about our little…misadventure with the mice."

Anne nodded, though it had been more a statement than a question.

"Well, I wanted to ask…that is, I was particularly hoping that you would be willing to donate some ornament of Edie's for the church tree. This is our first Christmas without her, of course, and she was such a beloved figure in the church, I just thought it would be especially appropriate if we could have something on the tree in memory of her. Would you…" she faltered, "would you be willing?"

"Of course," Anne said quickly, touched yet again by the affection and respect that the community retained for her late great-aunt. Then, since Helen seemed self-conscious about making such a request, Anne added, "Would you like to come by the library to help pick out something appropriate? I was planning to bring the boxes out of storage tomorrow."

"Oh well, I wouldn't want to intrude," Helen said, but Anne could see that she was pleased by the idea so she pressed the invitation until Helen said, "Thank you, dear, I would love to."

After a moment, Anne asked, "And what was the second thing?"

"Oh yes," Helen said, more businesslike now. "The second thing is the Nativity play. It's an annual tradition—for the children, you know. It's cosponsored by the children's program and the church board. We were hoping that Ben and Liddie would participate. Most of the children do."

"That sounds wonderful!" Anne exclaimed. She looked around for her offspring, but they had drifted back over to the refreshment table.

Anne had been giving a lot of thought to how her family could build new holiday traditions in their new home, and the Nativity play sounded like an excellent outlet for her kids' excess energy and excitement in this season. "They've never participated in one before, though," she added.

"Not to worry, dear." Helen patted her arm and began to lead her across the room. "Suzanne has done them many times, and with many children." Suzanne Brady was the children's program director, and Helen was now leading Anne in Suzanne's direction.

As they approached, Anne saw that Suzanne was deep in conversation with Brad Trowbridge, a seminary student who was currently doing an internship with Blue Hill Community Church. He was a tall, stocky lad with wavy brown hair and dimples when he smiled, which he seldom did, and he spoke with a very slight stutter. Though they considered him earnest and well-meaning, many in the church, Anne knew, found Brad a bit too distant and intellectual in his approach to the ministry. Then again, she reflected, given the congregation's deep love for Reverend Tom, in their eyes even a paragon would come up short by comparison. Anne suspected, though, that the young seminarian was scared to death and that eventually he would come to have the same facility with a congregation that Reverend Tom had with Blue Hill Community Church.

"Anne says yes," Helen announced gaily as they approached Suzanne.

Suzanne shifted her attention away from Brad to Helen and Anne. She looked pleased and relieved. "Yes *and* yes?" she inquired, cryptically.

"Well, only one yes, so far," Helen replied. She turned back to Anne. "I'm afraid the Nativity play is a two-part request…" When Anne raised her eyebrows, Helen continued, "We're also in need of a few adult volunteers to help supervise during rehearsals."

Anne hesitated, foreseeing a significant time commitment, but she remembered her own participation in church and school events. She had always grown nervous when she got near a stage, even in rehearsals, but when her parents were involved it had a calming effect on her. She would make time.

"You see," Suzanne added, "we have an extra-large children's Sunday school department right now. The McAllisters will be formally joining the church in January, and we'd like to have their three older children participate in the Nativity play as well."

Anne nodded. The McAllister family was already quite established at the library. Jason and his father shared an enthusiasm for spy novels and had requested various classic, if now obscure, authors from interlibrary loan. And their daughter Carrie had formed a rapport with Sherri Deveraeux, one of the library's growing number of volunteers, over their shared love of poetry.

Suzanne tipped her head toward Brad Trowbridge and continued, "And with the participation of the older kids who can handle speaking into the microphones, Brad has incorporated more speaking parts and extra elements into the play."

"We'll be bringing forward more of the historical context this year," Brad explained, tucking his chin as he lectured. "The hardship of Mary and Joseph as they traveled to Bethlehem to participate in the census, their daily life in an occupied country..." Behind Brad, Suzanne rolled her eyes and glanced away. "The kids and the audience will empathize with Mary and Joseph, and the miracle of the birth of the Savior will be that much more intense."

"So you see?" Helen said. "We'll need extra help with the play this year." She gave Anne a meaningful look, and Anne realized what was behind Helen's request. Brad was young, and Helen was afraid that pushback from Suzanne or the other parents when the play wasn't done "the way we've always done it" would dampen his enthusiasm for the ministry. "In fact," continued Helen, "we're in need of more volunteers yet, so if you think of anyone you think would be suitable...?"

Anne nodded. "I'll keep an eye out." But inwardly, the new task of recruiting more volunteers became yet another item on a very long to-do list.

Anne didn't think her sigh was audible when Helen and Suzanne turned away, but a calm voice behind her said, "It just *seems* overwhelming. By the end of the season you'll be surprised at all you've accomplished." Anne turned to find Mildred Farley, Aunt Edie's dear friend for many years, standing next to her. The older woman was elegantly attired today in a lavender sweater set and pearls.

Anne smiled wanly. "I know. It's just, Christmas was always so hectic in New York, and I thought in a small town things would be different. And now there's this play. And I just agreed Friday to have the Dickens Night celebration finish up at the library..."

Mildred nodded. "Yes, I heard. Which is why I'd like to offer to bake cookies for it."

Anne shook her head. "I couldn't ask you to do that!"

"It's no trouble," Mildred insisted. "I've already started my Christmas baking and have three different kinds of cookie dough in the freezer. You just tell me how many you need." She cocked an eyebrow at Anne.

"Er, maybe eight dozen?" Anne guessed hesitantly.

"Better have twice that." Mildred gave her a knowing look.

"Mildred, I don't know how to thank you." Anne could hear the tinge of relief in her voice.

Mildred patted her on the arm. "You know I love a challenge. And I know Edie would be pleased as punch to see the library take off the way it has."

* * *

The Blue Hill Library was a new and growing endeavor. Upon her passing, Edie Summers had left Anne and the people of Blue Hill, Pennsylvania, her rambling Victorian home, along with a sufficiently large endowment to transform it into a thriving library. To Anne's delight, her great-aunt had also stipulated that Anne herself take the position of librarian. For Anne, it was perfect. As the mother of two who had been widowed just a few years before, and more importantly, as a librarian who had just been laid off in one of the world's most expensive cities, Anne was thankful to return to her hometown and take on the intriguing task of turning her beloved aunt's familiar home into something altogether different.

It had been quite a journey. The building required extensive renovation, of course, to make it suitable for its new role. And she'd had to build all the book collections from scratch, a daunting but infinitely satisfying task. But now the work was done and the library was open to the public, and she was challenged to find ways to firmly embed this new institution in the life of the community.

And then, of course, there were other challenges. As a college-bound young woman, Anne had left Blue Hill for more urban environments, and there were times she still missed her vibrant Brooklyn neighborhood and the energy and endless variety of New York. But even more, she worried about her children's adjustment to this new life, since they had never known anything but New York.

Both Ben and Liddie were proving themselves to be resilient, however, and Anne was proud of the way they had adapted. Still, she couldn't help but think that the first Christmas in a new place might be particularly difficult, and so she was determined to create an experience for them that would combine familiar elements of their old life with new traditions.

So when they arrived in Blue Hill, Anne carefully stored in the attic the Christmas decorations they had used in Brooklyn. This morning, she brought these out, along with boxes of decorations her aunt Edie had accumulated in her travels over the years, and hauled them to the elevator on the third floor and transported them to their private living room at the back of the second floor. Once Anne had arranged the boxes so that she could access their contents, they took up half the living room. Fortunately, before she could begin to feel overwhelmed, Helen Smith arrived.

Soon Anne was kneeling on the floor with her arms up to their elbows inside a large box, while Helen sat in a nearby chair and sipped tea, looking on. "I think these must be the tree ornaments," Anne said, adding a grateful *finally* in her mind. They had already looked into several boxes that held Edie's decorations for the rest of the house, but so far, nothing for the tree. But now, at last…"Here we go." Anne pulled out a smaller box, stuffed with individually wrapped ornaments, clearly intended for the tree.

They were a mix of store-bought and handcrafted ornaments. There were delicate glass birds, some finely crocheted snowflakes, shiny red-and-silver candy canes, and a collection of musical instruments tied with gold ribbons.

Anne laughed when she came to a crude papier-mâché Santa, and she held it up for Helen to see. "I think I was six when I made this one. It was my gift to Aunt Edie that year."

Another box held four mismatched, hand-blown glass balls.

"How about this one?" Anne said, holding up one hand-blown orb. It was a heavy, clear bulb with blue-and-white swirls encircling it like clouds over the earth, and a closer look revealed small flecks of red, gold, and green in the clear glass.

Anne registered a fraction-of-a-second delay before Helen said, "Oh no, Anne, that's much too nice. You should keep that one for your own tree." But Anne could tell from the gleam in Helen's eyes that she had already picked just the place for the ornament on the church's tree.

"Nonsense," Anne said, rolling back onto her haunches. "The church tree ornaments can't just be a bunch of cast-offs. Besides, you said you wanted something in memory of Aunt Edie. I happen to know that she had this one for many years, because it's one I remember from my childhood. In fact, if I remember correctly, there was a set of these, but this one" — she leaned over the box of ornaments and peered in — "appears to be the last of its kind. So there you are," she smiled triumphantly at Helen, "I think this would make a fine tribute to Aunt Edie."

"Well, all right, Anne," Helen replied with no great reluctance, "if you're sure." She took the ornament and held it up to admire it.

Meanwhile, Anne dived back into the box. "We seem to have hit a trove of particularly fragile items," she observed. "Everything is so carefully wrapped." She continued to rummage through wads of tissue paper, until she noticed a piece of slender wire. "*Hmm*, well, except this."

But when she grasped the thin piece of metal and drew it out, it proved to be not wire, but a long, thin, wiry key that flared out at one end to encircle a small white porcelain disk, on which was painted the number seven.

She held it up, incredulous, to show Helen, who exclaimed, "It's the missing Advent key!"

A Note from the Editors

We hope you enjoy Secrets of the Blue Hill Library, created by the Books and Inspirational Media Division of Guideposts, a nonprofit organization that touches millions of lives every day through products and services that inspire, encourage, help you grow in your faith, and celebrate God's love in every aspect of your daily life.

Thank you for making a difference with your purchase of this book, which helps fund our many outreach programs to military personnel, prisons, hospitals, nursing homes, and educational institutions. To learn more, visit GuidepostsFoundation.org.

We also maintain many useful and uplifting online resources. Visit Guideposts.org to read true stories of hope and inspiration, access OurPrayer network, sign up for free newsletters, download free e-books, join our Facebook community, and follow our stimulating blogs.

To learn about other Guideposts publications, including the best-selling devotional *Daily Guideposts*, go to ShopGuideposts.org, call (800) 932-2145, or write to Guideposts, PO Box 5815, Harlan, Iowa 51593.